Passionate Addiction

RECKLESS BEAT BOOK TWO

EDEN SUMMERS

Passionate Addiction
Copyright © 2013 by Eden Summers

Editing by Rachel Firasek
Cover Art by LM Creations
Formatting by Champagne Formats

This book is a work of fiction. The names, characters, places, and incidents are products of the writer's imagination or have been used fictitiously and are not to be construed as real. Any resemblance to persons, living or dead, actual events, locales or organizations is entirely coincidental.

All rights reserved. With the exception of quotes used in reviews, this book may not be reproduced or used in whole or in part by any means existing without written permission from the author.

The author acknowledges the trademarked status and trademark owners of various products referenced in this work of fiction, which have been used without permission. The publication/use of these trademarks is not authorized, associated with, or sponsored by the trademark owners.

ISBN-10: 149351055X
ISBN-13:978-1493510559

Dedication

I have a lot to be thankful for.

Family—my children, my supportive parents and even my awesome cousins—Boo, especially.

My gorgeous editor—Rachel Firasek. You make my babies shine.

I'm thankful that my 80+ grandmother couldn't get past the first 45 pages of Blind Attraction. I love being innocent in your eyes, Babcia. I really did dodge a bullet with that one.

My "Pimp Squad"—Although it's more of a group to share sexy pictures of men and talk about dirty things, I love you, ladies. Your support, kindness and friendship mean the world to me.

To friends, readers and bloggers, who go out of their way to support me by writing reviews, sharing updates and helping promote my work. With special mention to Kristen McQuiston and Megan Root who put up with my OCD and are always willing to drop everything to help me.

My proofreaders—If there are any typos please blame Lori Whitwam, Tina Reiter, Kaylyn Davis, Megan Root and Sheryl Wheeler. Joking! Thank you all for helping me and for being so excited to read Blake's story. Any mistakes in Passionate Addiction are mine alone.

And finally, to my husband—the man who showed me that love at first sight really does exist. The one that gave me my very own happily ever after…The one who still hasn't finished reading Blind Attraction and keeps telling me he'll wait for the movie to come out. Love you, honey.

Prologue

Lost: *Is anyone there? I need help.*

Blake Kennedy typed with shaky hands, hoping one of the four people in the online chat room would respond. There hadn't been any talk amongst them since he signed on five minutes ago, and he'd begun to worry they wouldn't reply.

This was his last option. His *only* option. He didn't know what else to do. He had no one to turn to. No one to trust. And if he didn't pull his shit together soon, his life wouldn't be worth living.

Modaroo: *I'm here. How can I help?*

He rested his fingers against the keypad. The tattoo marking his right-hand knuckles mocked him in thick black, broken text—*Reckless*. No shit. He should get "moronic" splayed across the other hand.

Lost: *I need a distraction. I can't go back again. I just want someone to keep me company until the burn wears off.*

The demons were overtaking him, clawing, enticing—almost succeeding at dragging him back to the dark side. He huffed out a breath and wiped the sweat of exhaustion from his forehead.

The anonymity of the internet was his only solace. Support meetings weren't an option, neither was rehab. If the paparazzi or anyone in the public found out about his problem, he would be booted from Reckless Beat and disgraced in front of a worldwide crowd.

Modaroo: *I can do that. I'm quite adept at chatting about inconsequen-*

tial things until I put people to sleep. It's a female thing.

He gave a half-hearted laugh, and the noise came out stuttered, maniacal. This was good, though. It was a start. The pounding agitation in his chest even wavered, igniting a spark of hope.

Lost: So you're a female and enjoy staying up late chatting in drug addiction support groups? Are you a moderator or an abuser?

Modaroo: Yes, I'm female. One of, if not the most stunningly brilliant females you will ever encounter. But no, I'm not a late night person. I love my sleep. I assume I'm on the other side of the world to you. I live down under ;) And yes, I'm a moderator.

Blake's cell phone vibrated on the couch cushion beside him with an incoming call. He rushed to grab it, to smother the miniscule noise. The laptop teetered on his thighs, threatening to fall.

"Shit." Clutching the phone in one hand and the laptop in the other, he closed his eyes, breathed deep, and waited for the buzzing to stop. Each passing second tempted him, pulled at him, demanding he answer. His demons knew who was calling. He didn't need to glimpse the screen to verify.

Seconds later, sweet relief rushed through his veins. He passed the first test. If he could ignore the calls, maybe he could overcome everything else. First thing in the morning, he would change his phone number. For now, though, he would turn the damn thing off.

He glanced across the hotel suite toward Mitchell Davies' open bedroom door. The lead guitarist must have sensed Blake's restlessness after tonight's performance and had started asking questions. Questions Blake didn't want to answer, or couldn't answer, if he wanted to keep his position in the band. He'd only been part of the team for eight months and already he'd fucked up. Big time.

Lost: Yeah, I'm in the States. It's three a.m. here, and I'm so fucking tired. I just want to sleep, but the crazy-ass nightmares won't quit.

So tell me about Australia. What's it like down under?

He needed to stop thinking about it. To stop turning every thought process into something that related to the white powder destroying his life.

Modaroo: Withdrawal can be nasty on your mind and body. Just remember, it's all temporary, and it WILL get better. Do you have someone locally you can depend on?

And what's it like down under? Pretty darn awesome. At the moment, the weather is hot, the air con is cold, and the beach is looking mighty fine.

Blake ignored her question. He had no one. Not a single soul, and he refused to tell her why.

Lost: You surf?

Modaroo: A little. I can stay on a board for about as long as I can hold my breath.

He let out another laugh. This time it came easier, more natural, less hysterical.

Lost: Lol. So in other words, you kinda suck.

Modaroo: Now, now. No need to point out my failings. I prefer to think of it as a balance imperfection.

Blake snickered and ran a lazy hand through the tangled spikes at the front of his hair. A total stranger, on the other side of the world, had made him laugh for the first time in months.

She was his savior.

Lost: Your failings are nothing in comparison to mine, honey. I'm going to lose the best thing that ever happened to me if I don't control my cravings for cocaine.

Modaroo: Sorry, Lost, but please don't use specific drug names in the open chat rooms. The reminder can be harmful to others.

Shit. The last thing he wanted to do was make things harder for another addict.

Lost: Sorry.

Modaroo: Not a problem. So is it a woman?

Lost: A woman?

He rotated his shoulders, cracked his neck, and stretched his arms above his head. The state of relaxation was miles away. However, each second chatting with this woman brought him closer.

Modaroo: The "best thing" you will lose.

He clenched his fists. Disgust and self-loathing were his companions, and he was too weak to do anything about it. All of this pain, suffering, and craziness because of one simple little thing—beauty.

Oh, and lust.

Lost: No. A woman is what got me into this mess in the first place.

Chapter One

GABRIELLE SMITH GLANCED at the text message from her colleague, Tammy. *Getting old, Gab. I hope those fragile bones are prepared for a big night out.*

She smiled and tossed the phone onto her bed. Tammy needn't worry. Now twenty-nine years of age, Gabi had a lot of experience with alcohol. She could even drink her father under the table on a good night. Tonight, she'd be putting those skills to use. It was a case of drink to celebrate or stay sober and drown in her sorrows. She chose the former. She always did on her birthday.

Her phone trilled, this time with an incoming email. Instead of jumping to the bed like her excitement demanded, she continued to towel dry her hair and lazily stretched over the mattress to pick it up. At her age, she should've outgrown this overexcitement at the possibility of male communication. Must be her biological clock and all that other hormonal crap.

Oh, who was she kidding? She'd been experiencing the same thrill for the last four years. All because of one man.

When Blake's name came up on the display screen, her heart clawed its way into her throat.

Hey angel, if u r free, turn on Skype.

She scoffed. As if denying him was even an option. She could be in the arms of another man and still find the time to pull away and chat with Blake.

With a click, she turned the application on…and watched…and waited. After ten life-long seconds, a voice call came through from his account. Blood rushed through her veins, the same way it always did when he called, even after all this time. She pressed the button to connect, placed the phone to her ear, and tried to contain her smile.

"If I remember correctly, I think it's a special someone's birthday today," he purred.

God, he had such a smooth, seductive voice. And that accent. She closed her eyes and let the sound sink under her skin. American guys seemed to have sexy, cockiness down pat. Or maybe it was just world famous rock stars.

"Hey, Blake."

"Hey, angel. Have you had a great day?"

She thought it over—easy day at work, great weather, presents, coffee, upcoming ladies night, and a phone call from the man she adored. "It's been awesome."

"You think everything is awesome."

She laughed. "True. I'm just lucky I guess."

"So, are you having a party?"

She shook her head, even though he wouldn't see. For the last five years, she'd felt guilty at the thought of making big plans on her birthday. It didn't seem right to formally celebrate the night her brother had been placed on life support. God knew her parents wouldn't show up for any kind of celebration.

"I'm going out with the girls." She padded to her wardrobe and picked out a pair of comfortable skinny jeans. Going to a club and keeping herself occupied is what she did every year. The drinking helped to numb the pain and guilt.

Blake cleared his throat. "Where's my invitation? Hmm?"

She held the phone to her ear with her shoulder and removed the pink silk halter-top from a coat hanger. "Umm, I'm sorry. I didn't even think, seeing as though you're on the other side of the world and all… You also have a penis. You did hear me say 'ladies night,' right?"

He chuckled, and her chest tightened. Fate was cruel. She'd always been picky with men, yet with a click of her fingers, she falls in love with a guy on the other side of the world. A celebrity, no less.

"Yes, last time I checked, I did have that appendage. It's fully functional, too. So I guess that means I don't get an invite."

Ouch. The reminder of his revolving door woman policy wasn't appreciated. Jealousy turned her stomach, and the more she tried to ignore it, the more persistent it became.

"Thanks for the visual, but just in case you were wondering, I do occasionally read the tabloids, and the reminder of how well *that* part of your anatomy works is always pointed out in black and white." Maybe "occasionally" was an understatement. She had his hashtags saved on Twitter, Google alerts of his name subscribed to her email, and a daily habit of checking the gossip on the Reckless Beat website. Stalking wasn't a term Gabi liked to ponder. Blake just lived on the other side of the world, and the internet was a great tool for her to keep up to date with his life.

Walking back to the bed, she threw down her clothes. Her mood had changed, now hovering far from the previous "let's go dance and have fun" frame of mind. The green-eyed monster demanded she sex it up. Stuff the comfy shoes more appropriate for dancing. She needed shiny, black, three inch heels, with straps that wove around her ankles and tied in a bow at the front. Not that Blake would ever see their awesomeness. She would have to take her frustrations and heartache out on another unsuspecting bachelor.

"So, is that a 'no' on the invitation?"

"What?" She frowned. "Why do you keep bringing that up?"

"Aren't we besties? How come I didn't get an invite?"

She shook her head in frustration and growled into the phone. If only he knew what she would sacrifice to see him tonight. Maybe then he wouldn't taunt her with his crazy-ass questions.

"Oh, you know I love when you make that noise," he cooed.

Damn it. She was laughing again. "Fine, Blake. I would love if you came along to my ladies night tonight." She rolled her eyes and moved to her hands and knees to retrieve the sexy shoes from underneath her bed.

"OK, I'll see you soon."

She paused, her hands embedded in the carpet, her eyes on the shoebox. "What do you mean?"

Silence.

"Blake?"

She sat back on her haunches, retrieved the phone from her shoulder, and stared at the screen. He hung up. What the hell?

Gabi pressed his name on the Skype application and selected a voice call.

No answer. The bastard changed his status to "offline."

Climbing to her feet, Gabi sat on the edge of her bed and started typing an email.

What's going on? Why would you say that?

After the years of emails, internet chats, and voice calls, they'd never met. She was pretty sure Blake didn't even know what she looked like. It had been a stipulation she made months after their communications had turned from occasional chat sessions into a natural part of their everyday life. The same day he entrusted her with the knowledge that he was the world-famous bass guitarist for Reckless Beat.

She had a decent amount of confidence, and still her ego had crumpled under the thought of his scrutiny. It had been bad enough when he was a nameless, recovering addict who effortlessly brightened her day and made her smile with every written sentence. Add to that the sexy bad-boy appearance, those talented fingers, and an enviable lifestyle... Yeah, she'd decided to hide behind the internet for a little longer.

Gabi stared at the phone screen, her heart a wild bird under her ribs. She wouldn't be ready when Tammy came to pick her up, and for once, being late didn't faze her. She was preoccupied with an insane idea that her brain knew would never happen, but pulled at her emotions none the less.

Why would he tease her like that? It didn't make sense. He was meant to be finishing up the UK leg of Reckless Beat's worldwide tour.

Damn him for making her contemplate the possibility. And on her birthday! He knew his friendship meant everything to her.

Her phone vibrated and trilled with the arrival of an email.

Sorry. Bad service. Hope you have a great night. ;)

Her heart slid south, lodging itself in the pit of her stomach. She was stupid. Stupid. Stupid. Stupid. Of course he wasn't in Australia. Reckless Beat weren't scheduled to play in Melbourne until Friday—six days away. And even then, Blake already told her he wouldn't have time to catch up. Between tour performances and promo obligations, he would barely get a lick of sleep. *"We're better off meeting for the first time when things won't be so insane for me. I want to see you when I'm not delusional from lack of sleep and running on caffeine."*

With a huff of frustration, she threw the phone back on the bed and continued getting ready. Bye, bye, laid back, comfy jeans. Her grumpiness demanded one-hundred-percent femme fatale. She stormed to her closet and pulled out her skin-tight, black lace, thigh-high dress. She may need to wear her best underwear and be cautious of giving unintentional glimpses to strangers, but she didn't care. If Blake's attention was unobtainable, she would get it from somewhere else.

She could close her eyes and pretend as good as any woman.

Blake strode down Cavill Avenue, Surfers Paradise, trying to find the night club Gabi's friend had emailed him about. The night was clear, the air warm and thick around him. Jetlag weighed down his mind, making his head heavy, and his body reeled from the abrupt change from the brutally cold weather of London, to the heat and humidity of Queensland, Australia.

Things wouldn't be as bad if he'd caught the private jet across the globe, but he'd wanted to see Gabi, which meant he had to leave earlier than the rest of the band and slum it on a commercial airline. Not that first class was lacking, he just couldn't sleep when people were staring at him. And there had been many people staring, all of them curious and eager for the opportunity to speak to him.

He could deal, though. He could deal with anything right about now. For years, he'd held a flame for a woman he'd never seen. Almost fifteen-hundred days in which he'd fallen head over heels for someone who may likely be a five-hundred pound yeti.

Four fucking years.

When Blake finally sucked up the guts to tell her who he was, not just a weak, drug addicted asshole from the US, but all of the above plus the bass guitarist for a world famous band, Gabi had taken a step back, openly telling him she wanted to remain anonymous.

For the most part she had.

It took over a year to learn her full name. Then another to determine what part of Australia she lived in. He still didn't know what she looked like, and her reluctance to share a photo of herself spoke louder than words. Only he wasn't listening.

Gabi was his best friend. His savior. His angel.

Yeti or not, he would always love her. Although, his interest may change from the sexually charged emotions that kept him hard at night to a brotherly affection, if she resembled an NFL linebacker. He just needed to see her once and for all. To stop his imagination from running wild every time they spoke. Or emailed. Or chatted online.

She had the sweetest, most playful voice he'd ever heard. And her laugh. It drove him senseless.

He shook his head and continued down the street, ignoring the curious glances from people who strode by. If he stopped, even paused, they'd be on him like groupies on gig night. For once in his life, lady luck shined down on him and nobody paid him more than an inquisitive stare. That would all change if he slowed his pace. The people he passed would have more chance to scrutinize his appearance and figure out who the hell he was. So he kept walking, pounding out the pavement, his heart thrumming in anticipation.

Vibrations from dance music surrounded him, and up ahead, he read the name of a familiar club. He paused in front of the glass windows, double checked the business name in his cell, and then glanced back at the blue neon sign on the front of the building—Pink Ox.

This was the place.

He'd been anxious for the last month, knowing what the end of the UK part of the tour would bring. Women had never fazed him before. Yeah, he loved to enjoy them as much as the next guy, to talk to the ones with half a brain and get between the thighs of the attractive ones who were less fortunate. He didn't *do* the whole nervous thing. Yet, right now, standing a few feet away from the bouncer of the Pink Ox night club, his hands tingled with something akin to terror.

No backing out now.

He stepped up to the guy who had a chest the size of a fridge and jerked his head in greeting. "Hey."

The man raised a brow and looked Blake over. The reaction wasn't new. With Blake's preference for dark clothes, the black spiked hair, leather wrist cuffs, and all visible skin on his arms inked, he was trouble personified. The fuck-you expression he currently sported wouldn't help.

"You got I.D.?"

Blake suppressed a scoff. He didn't look a day under his thirty years. Obviously the guy wasn't a Reckless fan.

"No problem." He reached into the back pocket of his charcoal stone-washed jeans, contemplated pulling out a middle finger salute, and showed the bouncer his identification.

The man grunted and Blake stepped past, assuming the caveman reaction meant he was allowed entry. Inside, the noise grew. The main bass beat came from upstairs, vibrating through the walls and muffling the lyrics. Couples sat in booths and along the bar. None of them paid him any attention, all of them engrossed in their conversations. He took his time scrutinizing every female, his heart in his throat, and so far he couldn't find the cluster of partying women he was looking for.

He headed for the stairs, taking them two at a time. The music became louder with every step, pulsing through his chest, as if he needed it to pound harder. When he reached the top, he paused and surveyed the room.

The bar glowed in dark purple light, bathing the rest of the club in shadow. A mass of people danced in the far corner, strobe lights and lasers slicing over the crowd. More booths lined the floor to ceiling windows facing a balcony. A man approached him, ramming Blake's shoulder in an effort to drunkenly get down the stairs. He ignored it, too caught up in finding Gabi to give a shit about some jerk who couldn't figure out the basic fundamentals of walking.

His gaze raked every seated group of people, every person sitting on a stool by the bar. When he reached the middle booth, with its table of laughing women, he paused. Swallowed. They were well into their night of drinking—at the easy-to-get-their-panties-off stage. Empty glasses covered the table, along with more half full. He scanned each face, waiting for a buzz, a connection, some sign of familiarity.

Nothing came.

One lady caught his eye and her gaze brightened. Oh, fuck, was that his angel? He stopped breathing. She was tall, big enough to make him feel like a midget, with broad swimmer shoulders and a healthy tan.

Gabi swam. She loved to surf. This could easily be her.

She slid from the booth, stumbled a little, then righted herself, her expression now alight with a goofy grin. His heart beat harder as she approached. He tried to convince himself it came from nervousness, but he couldn't lie to himself. There was no spark, none of the fairytale love at first sight bullshit he'd hoped for. Instead of moping, he concentrated on being the best friend he was supposed to be and plastered a smile on his face.

"Gabi?" he called over the music.

The woman raised her eyebrows and tilted her head back with a snort. At least he thought that's what that animalistic sound was.

"No, I'm Tammy." She placed a hand on her chest, over a huge amount of exposed cleavage.

Ahh, Gabi's friend. Thank fuck for that.

"Gabi's out there." She pointed to the corner behind him.

He sucked in a breath, let it out, and slowly turned toward the dance floor. The group of people bounced to an unfamiliar song. Most were men, all vying for the few pieces of ass to grind against.

"She's requesting a song," Tammy's voice yelled over his shoulder.

His attention shot to the D.J. and the woman bent over the speakers. Her toned legs were lit up from the surrounding lights—on full display—the lace material at the bottom of her dress riding up her thighs as she leaned in to speak to the guy.

Blake gravitated forward, stopping at a stomach-high table close to the edge of the dance floor. He rested his elbows on the cool wood and stared.

"I'll leave you to it," Tammy yelled.

He should've replied, at least thanked Gabi's friend for all her help in setting up tonight, only he couldn't function. His mind had drowned in awe and deprived him of speech. He stood fascinated, his greedy gaze eating up the woman his heart had claimed as his own.

She was blonde, just like he imagined, with short, wavy hair cut above her shoulders. Her body, from the back view, showed off mouthwatering curves. The black dress she wore hugged her ass and tightened over a lean waist and delicate shoulders.

She was flawless. It didn't take much for a guy with a healthy sexual appetite to imagine those delicious legs wrapped around his hips—or face for that matter.

He shook his head, dislodging the depravity. She had to have a coyote-ugly face. He believed in karma and knew he didn't deserve the front side of her body to match the spank bank material of the back.

She nodded at the D.J. The fucker flashed his teeth in a heated smile like he was getting his pole smoked by a supermodel. Jealousy reared its ugly head, and Blake fought hard to contain it. He gripped the side of the table, and for the first time in a damn long time, he wished he had a stiff drink in his hands. A little something to take away his nerves, his jealousy, his obsession.

She turned.

"Fuck. Me." The words whispered from his lips. He snapped his mouth shut and kept his fingers busy by wiping the sweat from his palms onto his T-shirt.

His angel was gorgeous. A mix of sweet beauty and confident sexuality. Her blonde hair framed a face he itched to see close up and her lips were tilted in a man-eater grin as she maneuvered into the center of the dancing crowd, her arms above her head, swaying to the beat.

The song finished and another began. One he knew by heart. It was her song—*Angel of Mine*. The one he wrote with Mason Lynch, the lead singer of Reckless Beat, and Sidney Higgins, a world famous songwriter with a knack for brutally raw and heartbreaking lyrics.

It spoke of Blake's savior. His angel. The woman who pulled him from the cliff's edge and gave him strength to live. The one and only song he had contributed to lyrically meant more to him than any other career achievement. During his dark days, when Gabi was on the other side of the world, fast asleep, this song gave him the will to carry on. It reminded him of where he'd been and how he'd survived. Only he hadn't told his band mates that the lyrics were his reality. He'd lied, again, telling them that his emotions came from the experiences of an old friend.

You saved my soul. Gave me new meaning.

Fought against my demons, while I lay sleeping.

Did she know this was her song? He'd never mentioned it. Couldn't. The cryptic lyrics held too much significance. They laid out his soul for the world to see, and although Gabi knew she was important to him, she wouldn't have a clue how much he cherished her. He'd hidden that behind a computer screen and a cocky persona for the duration of their friendship.

He smiled, watching her dance, trying not to blink. Every second that passed made him want to be out there with her, beside her, against her soft body. If only he could move. His legs were glued to the spot, and he doubted his brain would work to string together a coherent sentence, let alone the monumental words he should've prepared for the first time they met.

He admired her as men brushed against her, devouring her body with their gaze. Not once did she pay them attention. She thrust her arms about to the hard beat, shook her hips in time and became one with the music. It was like he was in a dream. His angel dancing to the music of his soul.

My savior with a heart of gold.

The song ended and she squeezed her way through the crowd, smiling at men who grinned at her and apologizing to others she bumped into. When she reached the edge of the dance floor, her gaze skimmed past him, toward the bar. She faltered, then paused, stiffening her posture as her attention snapped back to where he stood. Her mouth slowly opened and time stood still.

He was done for. Completely and utterly lost in her eyes. His mind yelled at him to move closer to determine the color. And he would've if he knew how to walk. The club was too dark, the techno lights flashing too quickly to give him the confirmation he craved.

A man bumped into her from behind, and she stumbled on her sexy black heels. Blake jerked to attention, ready to run to her. Unaided, she righted herself and moved forward, her attention never leaving him. With each step, her facial features gained more clarity—the curve of her petite nose, the soft lips, the tanned skin. Each characteristic held beauty, and together they made his mouth dry.

She walked up to him, stopping a foot away. The smoothness of her forehead wrinkled in a frown as her gaze scanned his face.

Blue. Her irises were a light shade of sky-blue, cool and calm and completely intoxicating.

His nervousness faded under her confusion. Gabi was made for him. There was no question. No doubt. Fate had pushed them together, and now, he only needed to prove that he deserved to keep the gift.

He grinned at her, trying to show all the heated emotion he'd kept bottled inside for years. "Hello, angel."

Chapter Two

GABI STARED AT the man who haunted her fantasies and tried to control her shaking knees. She'd only been drinking for the last two hours, right? Surely she couldn't be drunk enough to hallucinate.

"Blake?" Her voice wavered, barely registering over the loud thrum of music.

The man's smile tilted up a notch. "Happy birthday, gorgeous." He stepped to the side of the table, moving closer, giving her a complete view of his deliciousness.

Her body went into meltdown, overwhelmed and unsure whether to heat up in arousal or panic under his scrutiny. Bloody hell. Nobody should be that sinful. A rich, talented, bad boy all rolled up into a package of I-don't-give-a-shit, I-know-how-good-I-look.

What was he doing here? How did he get here? And how did he find her? The questions kept coming, assailing her, making it harder to concentrate.

She sucked in a ragged breath, blinking back the moisture in her vision, and covered her gaping mouth with a numb hand. He was a dream. An illusion. He had to be. Maybe someone slipped something into her drink and her heart's desire had miraculously come to life.

He was menacing and downright dangerous—in appearance and to her heart. A leather cuff hugged his right wrist, with colorful tattoos on either side, running all the way up his toned arms and underneath a T-shirt that strained against muscled pecs. She'd memorized the ink that adorned his body, had fallen under their spell and knew the way they contorted when he played his guitar. His short raven hair was spiked and his sinful irises blended with the color of his pupils in the dim light.

So. Damn. Hot.

She swallowed. Hard. Then took a breath and did it again.

He laughed and the flawless smile he shot her way brightened his devilish features. "Do I get a hug from the birthday girl?"

A noise escaped her lips, something between a whimper and a moan. Thank goodness for the loud music.

She stepped forward, her heart beating wildly, and flung herself into his waiting arms. His chest was rock hard, and she fought to wipe the fantasy of her best friend's naked body from her mind. Wrapping her arms around his waist, she snuggled into him, gripping him tight, never wanting to let go. The alluring scent of his aftershave infiltrated her lungs, increasing the slight intoxicated buzz whizzing through her veins. When he pulled back to look down at her, she bit her lip and tried not to drown in his darker-than-chocolate eyes.

It didn't help that the cheeky bastard couldn't wipe the smirk off his face.

"Can I get the birthday girl a drink?" he raised his voice to speak over the thrum of music.

She glanced at the bar, at all the liquor bottles lining the wall behind it and smiled through her sudden panic. Blake shouldn't be here, in a bar, surrounded by alcohol.

"I'll get it." With reluctance, she released her arms from around his waist and immediately missed the sudden loss of his warmth. "What drink do you want?"

A slight frown marred his brow. "I can get it, Gabi."

She shook her head and reached up on the tips of her toes, leaning into his ear so she didn't have to yell. Well, all right, it was because she wanted to touch him again, but the proximity *would* help him hear. "The least I can do is buy you a drink after you came so far to surprise me. Did you want lemonade?"

His frown deepened, then slowly he nodded.

With a nod of her own, she maneuvered around him and headed for the bar. She tapped her foot, drummed her fingers along the polished wood, and nibbled on her lip while waiting to be served. Once she had their drinks, she strode back to him, unable to bear missing a single moment in his presence. When she rested his drink on the table in front of him, his attention remained on the dance floor, his expression blank.

"Here ya go."

He grabbed the glass and turned to her. She felt his gaze caress her skin causing her spine to tingle with awareness. Instead of licking her lips like instinct commanded, she sipped her water.

"You're not drinking?"

She struggled to hear his raised voice over the loud bass. "No." Well, not anymore. For starters, she didn't want to drink in front of him, and she needed to sober up so she could remember every second they spent together. "Do you want to go out onto the balcony?" she motioned to her ears, "I can't hear a thing."

He nodded. It was a simple movement, just a tilt of his head, but damn, he owned it. It was like he was the god of smooth. And yes, she was entirely aware that her obsession with a mere nod didn't bode well. It wouldn't be long before she made a fool of herself and announced with her actions that her feelings for him went beyond friendship.

Breaking eye contact, she walked to the balcony and opened the sliding glass door to the warm night air. Blake followed behind her, his proximity keeping her nerves on high alert. A group of people were banked up outside, waiting to get back in. People she recognized and had no intention of speaking to.

Apprehension turned her stomach. She couldn't flee. Blake was stuck to her back like a second skin—a delicious, toe curling second skin—not allowing an escape route. She lowered her gaze and continued forward. There was enough room for both parties to easily pass, yet someone rammed into her shoulder and the cool chill of liquid splashed down her spine.

"Shit. Sorry, Gabi." Blake's hand rested on her shoulder. "Fuckin' asshole," he added, louder.

His hand yanked from her shoulder and she turned to find him standing chest to chest with a man she wished she didn't know. Both their shoulders were straight, chins raised as they glared at each other.

"Blake, no!" She swiped the droplets of fluid off her and pushed between them, facing the other man. "Back off, John."

"You know this asshole?" Blake growled from behind her.

She ignored the question and implored John with her gaze. He ignored her, his scowl drifting over her shoulder to Blake. Placing her hands on his chest, she slowly pushed him back. "John, please."

"What are you doing with this piece of shit, Gab?" John's pupils were unnaturally dilated from drug use. "You need to steer clear of guys like him."

"Guys like me," Blake repeated, his tone calm with the faintest hint of menace. "Move out of the way, gorgeous. Let me and Gumby have a chat."

Fear tightened her throat. She turned, knowing John was past the point of listening and swallowed at the hatred in Blake's eyes.

"Blake, he's one of my brother's old friends. He's high." She cupped Blake's cheeks and drew his attention to her face. "Please. Just drop it and walk away. He's not worth it."

"He deliberately shouldered you. Your dress is ruined."

She smiled up at him, touched by his chivalry. "It'll be fine. I promise."

He stared at her, his jaw working as she dropped her hands to her sides. Heaving a breath, he nodded and turned his back, taking the few steps to the balcony door.

"Pussy," John yelled.

Gabi turned to him. She didn't have the anger to glare. All she could do is look at him with pity. "He's a good man, John."

He scoffed. "He's just another tattooed up junkie like the rest of us. You're better than that, Gab, and you owe it to your brother to stay away from drop-kicks like him."

"That's enough." There went her inability to glare. Now she was clenching her free hand to the point of pain while the other tightly squeezed her drink. "You know nothing about him. And he's not a user. Just because he's got a few tats doesn't mean he's weak." She stepped closer and got in John's face. "Like you."

He laughed long and loud, showing his delirium. "There's the high and mighty Gabster that I remember." He cupped her shoulder in a friendly gesture, yet she could see the threatening gleam in his eyes. "I was only trying to look out for you."

He stepped back and turned to walk away. After he gained some distance, he glanced over his shoulder, piercing her with an evil sneer. "At least I'm not as weak as your brother."

The taunt hit her with the force of a truck, exactly how he wanted it to, and she refused to react. In high school, her brother Greg, John, and herself were close friends. Then John and Greg started experimenting with drugs and everything changed.

Gabi raised her chin and didn't flinch until he continued walking. Once he was out of sight, she let out a pained moan and hunched her shoulders to steady her ragged breathing. For a moment, she closed her eyes, seeing the image of her brother gazing back at her in sorrow.

God, she hated drugs. Most of all she hated that they took Greg away from her. He'd been innocent, charming, buzzing with life and potential.

With a deep breath, she glanced toward the balcony and found Blake leaning against the railing, staring at her. His expression held sympathy, and all she wanted to do was fall into his arms, to sink into him and let the rest of the world drift away.

"What's going on?" Tammy's voice called from beside her.

"Same birthday, different year." Gabi shrugged and rolled her eyes at her friend. "John's an ass."

Tammy handed over the handbag Gabi had left at the table.

"And what about your smokin' hot rock star?"

The thought of Blake brought a smile to her lips. Oh, he was damn fine. Nothing wrong with that perfect male specimen. Nope. Only now, there would be an awkwardness she didn't want to deal with. "He's good. I have no idea how he found me, though."

Tammy's eyes gleamed. "I may have had a little something to do with that."

"You?" Gabi narrowed her gaze.

"I emailed him a few months ago when you mentioned they were coming to Australia on tour. I told him that if he wanted to surprise you with a visit, I could help."

Gabi's mouth gaped. "How the hell did you keep *that* quiet?" Tammy held secrets worse than she held her liquor.

Tammy's chest expanded with a deep breath, which she then let out dramatically. "It was so fucking hard. And totally worth it. I'll be living vicariously through you for the rest of my life."

Gabi laughed and glanced over her shoulder at Blake. He was staring, his gaze eating her up one slow inch at a time. "I better go entertain my guest. I think I'll be heading home soon. I have lemonade down my back and now that it's starting to dry, I'm all sticky."

Tammy chuckled loud enough for her to hear over the heavy bass. "Yeah… Right. Whatever excuse you need. Have fun."

Gabi's heart hammered as Tammy walked away. It took another few seconds for her courage to build before she began to make her way back to Blake. With each approaching step, the *thump, thump, thump* in her chest grew more demanding, tightening her throat. She moved onto the balcony, this time shutting out the loud music from the club when she closed the glass door, leaving them alone together.

"I'm sorry." His voice was barely audible, even with the noise from inside muffled.

"Don't be." She shook her head. "John likes to cause trouble. He thought we were together, and I suppose it was his crazy way of showing he cares."

She leaned against the railing beside him, trying to glance at him in a normal, friendship kind of way, instead of raking her gaze over his pecs like she wanted to lick every inch of skin underneath his shirt.

He nodded and focused on the wooden floor planks. "Do you wanna go back to my hotel?"

Her lips pulled in a grin. She couldn't help it. How many times had men asked her that question with the intention of taking her home for a night of hot-n-sweaty? Blake didn't mean it that way. His tone lacked any hint of innuendo. However, she couldn't help the giddiness that sparked to life at the possibility.

He glanced up from the floor and his eyes widened at her expression. "Oh, shit. That totally sounded like a come on." He held up his free hand in surrender. "I seriously didn't mean it that way, Gabi. I'd never…" He pushed from the railing, straightening his posture, his cool façade disappearing.

Laughter burst from her lips. "Oh, and the insult of me not being good enough to sleep with is even better? You really know how to make a girl's night special."

His mouth fell open and he reached for her, grabbing her around the ribs. His chest rumbled with a growl, and he pulled her against his body. "You know what I meant, Gabrielle." His touch was natural, as if he'd held her this close innumerable times before, yet inside, she was ready to combust with shock…and yes, arousal.

She tilted her head to the side and raised her brows, ignoring the heat overwhelming her from her toes to her cheeks. "It's Gabrielle now? You must be serious."

He shook his head with humor and smiled down at her. "God, I love your accent."

Her laughter died as his penetrating eyes stripped away her defenses. She wanted to tell him he'd love it even more if she whispered her dirty thoughts in his ear, only she didn't have the guts. "Let's get out of here," she whispered and cleared her throat. "I'm all sticky."

His smile turned into a smirk. "Well, that's not usually how the ladies feel when they leave a club with me, but I'll take it."

Gabi pushed away from him, holding her hand to her chest in mock outrage. "Now you're flirting? Gosh, Blake, I'm disgusted."

His eyes narrowed for the briefest moment before he poked her in the ribs. "Stop messin' with me, angel, or I'll be forced to get physical."

She tried to disguise her sharp inhale and failed miserably. His threat held too much erotic intent for her heart to ignore. Damn, even her nipples tingled with need. If she didn't start sculling water and clearing her system of alcohol, she would end up doing something she'd regret. Like smothering herself in chocolate and throwing herself at his feet.

Chapter Three

BLAKE FOCUSED ON putting one foot in front of the other while they strolled side by side down Cavill Avenue. The awkward silence was killing him. *"Do you wanna go back to my place?"* What a fucking idiot. And she'd laughed in his face. Even better.

"Damn," Gabi huffed and hopped on one foot. "I've got a stone stuck under my heel. Can you wait a tick?"

"Sure." He paused, remaining close to the walkway, while she limped over to the nearest building and leaned against the darkened shop window. His gaze was glued to her perfectly smooth thighs and the way her dress rode up as she lifted her leg behind her to inspect her shoe.

"Fuck me. Seriously?" he whispered to himself. Another inch and he'd be able to see the Promised Land. His restraint wasn't something he was proud of, even on his best day. Now he had to drag his focus away from his best friend's path to heaven. "Temptation can kiss my ass," he muttered, glancing sightlessly at the buildings surrounding them.

"What was that?" Gabi called.

"Nothing," he spoke louder so she could hear him, then mumbled, "Just trying to keep my gaze away from my fuckin' best friend's panties, that's all." He stepped forward, discretely readjusting the bulge that formed at the crotch of his pants. "Great. Just what I need."

"Hey, mate." A ragged voice called from behind him. "Can I bum a fag?"

Blake paused and ran the words over in his head. "What the fuck did you say?" He turned to glare at the approaching guy. The man's skin was dirty, his clothes tattered, his face unshaven and unkempt. The man was taken aback and frowned at Blake.

Gabi sputtered in the distance. He swore he heard her laughing.

"I just wanted to bum a fag." The douche shrugged.

That was exactly what Blake thought he'd said, and he sure as shit wouldn't stand for that type of slander. He had gay friends. Even if he didn't, he wouldn't let that crap fly. If this type of open sexual slur happened back home, the guy would've been shanked by now.

Blake stepped forward. The man straightened, taking a step back. Blake didn't plan on hitting the old-timer—his life revolved around the use of his fingers. He just wanted to get in the guy's face and teach him a lesson on manners.

"Blake," Gabi called, her heels clicking as she approached. She was still laughing.

He turned to face her. "What the he—"

The sentence died on his lips. Her breasts bounced with every step, the movement far too alluring to drag his focus away.

"How the hell is this funny?" He was pissed off, yet he couldn't help grinning back at her.

She stopped a foot in front of him and raised a hand to her mouth, trying to smother her laughter.

"Stupid Yank," the man grumbled.

Blake shot a glare over his shoulder, but the guy had already turned and walked away.

Gabi lowered her hand, her lips pulled tight in the brightest smile he'd ever seen. "He was asking you for a cigarette."

Blake jerked back, wide-eyed. "How do you figure that? The asshole was propositioning me."

She released another bark of laughter and cut it off with both hands. He stepped toward her, bridging the distance. "Mind filling me in on why this is so funny?"

The humor wavered in her expression, and she dropped her hands to her sides, sliding backward. "He was asking you for a smoke. He wanted to 'bum,' meaning borrow and 'fag' is a very old-school, Aussie term for cigarette."

He continued to move toward her. "I'm not sure I believe you."

She took a bigger step back. "Google it… On your phone… Now."

She was trying to dissuade his approach. He couldn't get close enough. The more distance he ate up, the quicker she retreated. The glint of anticipation in her light blue irises boiled his blood.

Her lips lifted in a playful smile. "As appealing as you seem to think you are, he wasn't propositioning you."

He quirked a brow, their position now a few feet from the darkened shop window. "I'm glad you enjoyed laughing at my expense. It's not like you could've yelled out and warned me."

She bumped into the building and rested against it, gazing up at him. "It was the funniest damn thing I've seen in years."

He tilted his head in acknowledgement, feigning a calm he didn't feel, and leaned into her so his pelvis rested against hers. The heat of her body soaked into every inch of his skin. The way her breath hitched turned his cock to stone. He'd moved close to wipe the smile from her pretty little mouth, and it worked. Now, he couldn't tear himself away from her sweet vanilla smell, her delectable curves, or the temptation of her lips. He was entirely pussy whipped in world record time.

He studied her eyes, the mesmerizing blue turning to a stormy grey. She remained still, unmoving, except for the heavy beat of her pulse at the bottom of her throat and the tiny flick of her tongue against her lower lip.

She was temptation, and again, he was too weak to refrain.

Without thought, he cupped the back of her neck and brushed his mouth against hers, his lips tingling at the connection. He inhaled her gasp and gripped her hip, unable to keep his hand idle by his side. She was soft—her hair, her waist, her thighs—malleable with the scent of heaven and the taste of sweet alcohol. He wanted to grind into her, to feel the friction of her body against the length of his cock.

She whimpered, her hands coming to rest on his chest, clinging to his shirt. The sound startled him, pushing his libido from the control seat and allowing his mind to regain rational thinking. What the fuck was he doing? Forcing himself onto his best friend without warning, when she'd been drinking? He hadn't spared a thought to the consequences. She wasn't a groupie, willing and ready to fall to her knees. This was Gabi. His angel.

Someone he couldn't live without.

He pulled back, severing the connection. His hand drifted from her neck and he watched, holding his breath as her eyes slowly fluttered open, her pupils now huge and penetrating.

"I'm sorry." He dropped his hand from her waist and stepped back. "Just my way of making tonight a little more awkward."

A ragged breath escaped her lips. "It's…fine." A frown darkened her features, and she pushed from the wall, maneuvering around him to continue walking down the sidewalk.

Great, fucking great. Now he had to fix this shit. He couldn't lose her. Not over something stupid like adolescent hormones and a trigger happy cock. If she didn't want to take their relationship further, he could deal. What he couldn't handle was not having her in his life. Why the hell hadn't he waited longer than two seconds before ramming his tongue down her throat? They may have been friends for years, it didn't change the fact that they'd only met moments earlier. Just because he felt at home with her didn't mean she experienced the same immediate connection.

He jogged the few steps to catch up and kept his mouth shut. It was safer that way. He'd done enough to ruin her birthday already. Hopefully, if he remained quiet, he wouldn't compound his idiocy.

They walked the remaining blocks to his hotel in silence. Each step making his chest weigh heavier with regret. When he unlocked his penthouse suite door, he turned to face her and prayed for the right words to fix the situation.

Nothing came.

He watched her raise an impatient brow before striding past, keeping as far away as possible.

Gabi stood before the floor to ceiling window and peered down at the streets below. She crossed her arms over her pounding chest and ignored the way her lips burned from Blake's kiss. And, oh boy, what a kiss. The confident brush of his mouth had seared every nerve in her body, bringing her fantasies to life, and she didn't know how the hell to move on from here.

This wasn't how she envisioned meeting her best friend for the first time. She'd always hoped they would hit it off. That their online flirty banter would somehow transfer into real life. But she never expected uncomfortable awkwardness. She never would've thought she'd be cringing over sticky, now-dried lemonade covering her back, either.

Blake's reflection gleamed back at her from the glass. The strong and confident way he strode toward her made her want to roll her eyes and groan. He was too masculine. Too strong and virile. A five-star dream brought to life, and she didn't know how to stop the tiny shudders that wracked her body whenever she glanced his way.

When they arrived at his suite, he'd disappeared into his bedroom. She'd watched discreetly from the living room while he scrounged through his suitcase. All the while she pretended to be immersed in the lavish penthouse suite. Truth was, she hadn't noticed a damn thing about the room. Her brain, eyes, and heart had all been focused on figuring out what he was doing and when he would come back for her to ogle.

"I'm sorry, Gabi." He stopped behind her, making eye contact through the glass. "I didn't mean for our first meeting to be like this." His hands came to rest on her shoulders, and he turned her to face him. "Forgive me?"

She couldn't help it, couldn't stop her focus from falling to his full bottom lip as her tongue swiped out to moisten her own. His nostrils flared and she glanced away, not wanting to complicate the situation further. "There's nothing to be sorry for." She shook her head and pasted on a smile. "I'm blown away that you're actually here." She stepped around him, needing to sever the potent connection.

He grasped her hand, denying her retreat, and pulled her back toward him. "I've got something for you."

Her nerves tingled at his touch, and her gaze snapped to his smiling eyes, then to the rectangular jeweler's box in his other hand. "You didn't have to—"

"It's your birthday."

Gabi rolled her eyes. "You flew across the *world* to see me. You didn't have to buy—"

He opened the case and the words died on her lips. Lying atop navy velvet was a shiny turtle pendant with tribal markings covering its shell. It was attached to a thick belcher link necklace, and rested beside a silver guitar pick charm on one side and a guitar charm on the other.

"It's…" Her mouth worked. Nothing came out. No words could express how beautiful and fitting the piece was.

"I know you love turtles, so I thought you might like it. The pick and guitar are entirely for my own ego. I don't want you to forget me once I leave."

Her chest swelled to the point of pain, and she knew if she glanced up to his face, she'd blubber uncontrollably. Instead, she reached for the necklace, letting the heaviness of the piece sink into her palm.

"You wear white gold, right? I didn't screw that part up, did I?"

White. Gold. Her lips mimed the words. Holy smokes, it must've cost him a fortune. She yanked her hand back and shook her head. "I can't accept this. It's too much."

She met his gaze and felt her heart stutter. He peered down at her, his face aglow with what she hoped was pride. "You saved my life, *and* you're my best friend. Nothing is too much for you."

She blinked rapidly, batting away the forming moisture. "If you make me cry, Blake Kennedy, I *will* hurt you."

He chuckled and broke eye contact to focus on releasing the necklace from the clasp holding it in place. "Turn around," he whispered.

She did as requested, her throat drying, her flesh breaking out in goose bumps while she lifted her hair for him to place the necklace around her neck. His fingers grazed her shoulders, the slightest brush making her nipples tighten. When the heavy weight of gold rested against her skin, she turned and reached for the charms now lying against her sternum.

"How does it look?" She fingered the guitar pick, feeling the smooth gold.

"Beautiful." His voice was husky, completely seductive, and entirely not fair.

His attention was on the necklace, and she swallowed, hoping he couldn't see her hardened nipples through her tight dress and thin lace bra.

They were so close, almost toe to toe, and all she wanted to do was kiss him. Slowly. Brushing her lips over his in a delicate caress. She wanted to show him how much she loved him. To pour her heart out in the intimate connection.

To hell with it. It was her birthday!

Reaching on tiptoes, she slid her hand over his muscled chest to his shoulders. She peered into his eyes, waiting for him to react or retreat. He didn't, so she inched closer, his heated breath brushing her face, and pressed her mouth against his.

It wasn't a scorching kiss, merely a soft joining of lips, and still her blood ignited, every inch of her skin burning for his touch.

His hands came to rest on her hips, lightly grasping. She yearned to moan, to voice the need building inside her, yet she remained quiet, hoping she could use the excuse of a friendly thank you kiss if he pulled away again, but his tongue stroked the seam of her lips, and she was done for.

She whimpered, clutched tighter to his shoulders, and brushed her body against him. The skin at the small of her back pulled from the dry stickiness of lemonade and she ignored it. There was nothing else in the world except the two of them. She matched the stroke of his tongue with her own, sparring, teasing, devouring. No man had ever kissed her so thoroughly, touching her from the inside out, right down to the tips of her toes.

They joined at the hips, her pelvis grinding into him, rubbing the hardness of his erection against the low of her belly. He growled, sinking his tongue deeper into her mouth. Strong hands moved to her ass, up over her waist, and paused at the side of her aching breasts. God, she wanted him to go further, to mold his hands around her flesh and tweak her nipples through the material.

Then everything stopped.

Déjà vu.

He pulled back and peered down at her. Her throat tightened while they panted heavily into each other.

Say something.

She swallowed and rested back on the soles of her feet.

Please don't apologize and act as though nothing happened. Again.

"Gab, I don't think I can do this and not lose my heart to you."

His words hit her like a thousand tiny sparks of delight. She bit her lip to contain her excitement. Nothing would be more wonderful than holding the most precious part of him. "You've held my heart for so long, Blake, that it feels strange to have it so close."

"Really?" His eyes searched hers.

"Really."

He brushed the hair back from her face, trailing his thumb along her jaw. "What did I do to deserve you?"

She stepped into him, leaving no space between their bodies. "You deserve the world. I just hope I can give it to you."

He trailed his hand down her waist and rested them at the small of her back. She cringed, her sticky skin now clinging to her dress.

"What's wrong?"

"I need to wash off the lemonade. Do you mind if I take a shower?"

"No, of course not." He jerked his head toward what she assumed was the master bedroom. "There's a bag of your clothes on the bed in there."

She stiffened, causing her skin to pull. "Ah, how did you get my clothes?" *Holy shit.* If he'd broken into her apartment, she would be mortified. Not only at the breach of privacy, but there were pictures of him performing posted all over her spare bedroom.

"Not a fan of me going through your drawers?" He chuckled and raised a brow. "Tammy organized the clothes. She said she had a spare key and could sneak into your apartment while you were at school."

The negative side of working and living in the same beachside holiday apartments with your close friend.

"Tonight was meant to be about celebrating your birthday. Meeting you for the first time, the penthouse suite, room service."

She grinned up at him. "You planned on—"

"I had, and still have, every intention of sleeping on the sofa." He narrowed his gaze. "So wipe that sly smile off your face." He leaned in and gave her a peck on the lips. "I didn't plan to be unable to keep my hands off you. Strength against temptation has never been my best attribute."

She hated when he got like this. He'd never acknowledged the determination it took to overcome his drug addiction. It didn't matter that he wasn't a heavy user or took the initial steps to handle his problem as soon as he realized cocaine had a hold on him. Addiction was addiction. Yet Blake always thought himself weak.

"You're the strongest man I know." She cupped his cheek and tried to convey her sincerity with the gentle touch. He gave a derisive laugh, and she ignored it. "And I thank you for everything you've done for me. I couldn't ask for a better..." *Friend* seemed inappropriate seeing as though they'd been groping each other for the last fifteen minutes.

He smirked. "The whole feverish lust and raging erection kinda puts a new spin on our friendship, doesn't it?"

"Yeah, it kinda does." Happiness overwhelmed her, making her giddy.

He moved into her, the barest hint of his stubble rubbing against her cheek, his breath brushing her ear. "You wanna see where it takes us?"

She pressed her lips together and closed her eyes. That was exactly what she wanted. To break free and finally share her feelings, the bottled up desire, admiration and love. "Yes." The word came out on a gasp.

His teeth grazed her earlobe, sending a shot of pleasure through her nipples, then straight down to pool in her sex. "Well then, go have a shower. Patience isn't one of my virtues."

Chapter Four

BLAKE PACED THE kitchen as the echo from the shower taunted him. He was such a weak prick. Any form of temptation and his brain closed up shop, his actions entirely ruled by his base desires. He needed to be in there with her, washing her smooth skin, learning her curves. To show her the things he'd been fantasizing about doing to her body for over a thousand days.

He rubbed the back of his neck and stepped toward the door. She was humming, the barely audible noise giving him an excuse to move closer. Over the rush of water, he listened to her, the tune unfamiliar. The feminine sound called to him, every note demanding his approach, and at this moment, any excuse would do. When he reached the bathroom door, he rested his forehead against the cold wood and held back from banging against it.

"Bright idea this was," he mumbled to himself. "Go see Gabi. Find out if she's hot. That won't complicate things at all." He was such a jackass. He couldn't even blame the influence of drugs for this fuck up.

The devil on his shoulder insisted he walk in there and take what she rightly offered. On the other shoulder sat a poor excuse for an angel who shrugged and said, *"Why the hell not?"*

"Exactly." He straightened. "Why the hell not?"

He vaguely remembered having great reasons against going in there only a few moments earlier. Now, for the life of him, he couldn't think over the image of her wet body in his mind.

Grasping the door handle, he turned the lever and pushed forward. Warm steam hit him like a physical blow. It was nothing in comparison to what the sight before him did to his body. His knees weakened and his thighs tightened. Even his gut did a freaky little flip that had him swallowing hard as he stumbled into the room and moved back to rest against the door.

Gabi stood with her tanned back to him, the rush of water running over her shoulders and down her spine. Steam fogged the glass, restricting the view to her lower half, but he could still make out the roundness of her ass and the outline of the gorgeous legs he soon hoped to have wrapped around him. Her body defied logic—a mix of heavenly temptation and delicious sin—not a flaw to be seen.

With natural seduction, she glanced over her shoulder, scorched him with her wanton perusal, then turned back to face the taps. "Are you going to stare, or are you getting in?"

Green light. Go, go, go, buddy.

Normally, he would've had his clothes off faster than you could say "instant erection," but this was his angel. There was no room for error. If tonight's test of their relationship proved to be too much, he needed to make sure what they shared was perfect. Unforgettable. Not rushed and riddled with regrets.

"You sure this is what you want?" he asked and had no idea why. If she changed her mind, it would bring him to his knees. "There's no going back from this."

She chuckled, the feminine sound penetrating his heart. "I think it's a little late for that." She shot him another glance over her shoulder. "And besides, you've seen me naked now. I won't be letting you outta here until we're equal on that tally."

He raised a brow, and she turned away with a grin.

Far be it for him to let a woman down, especially one so important. The only thing that made him pause with his hands at the hem of his shirt, was the knowledge of what his nakedness would reveal…a lot more than just his mighty Johnson. He had tattoos. Lots of them. And all held special meaning. Gabi knew about most of them, hell, the entire world knew about most of them, but there was one she definitely wouldn't be aware of. One he didn't flaunt. One that kept his hands poised at the bottom of his shirt, contemplating if this really was the right thing to do.

To hell with it. He was finally here with his angel and he wouldn't pussy-foot it now. *Grow a set, Kennedy.*

In seconds, his shirt was on the floor and kicked to the corner, followed by his boots, socks, boxers, and jeans. His cock stood proud, hard as stone and eager as all hell to reach nirvana. He walked to the shower unfazed by his nudity, yet his insides churned with vulnerability. His body had never been a weakness. It was everything else—his mind, his heart, his soul. It all seemed tainted from the stupid choices of his past. And he'd made many.

The one thing that gave him strength to carry on was knowing Gabi knew all his mistakes and continued to be his friend regardless. He would never lie to her. Not even about his feelings. If she asked him what he wanted out of this encounter, he would tell her—no doubt freaking her out in the process. Settling down with a woman didn't scare him. In fact, it was the opposite. He may not deserve love, but it didn't stop him from craving it. From her.

When the fuck did he turn into a chick?

He swallowed his nervousness, clenched his fists a few times, and then opened the screen to paradise. The shower was large, roughly the size of the one in his apartment back home, with shiny black tiles and two showerheads at either end. He had no interest in standing under a spray by himself, though. His place was beside Gabi.

She kept her back to him, not noticing or maybe not caring that he now stood behind her with waning restraint. He paused inside the screen door, staring at the trail of water cascading down her spine, over the indentations at the small of her back, covering the lush ass he itched to palm. He shook his head and convinced himself that tonight wouldn't end well. Anyone who knew the secrets of his life would know he hadn't worked up enough brownie points to earn the pleasure of having this woman in his life on an intimate level. He didn't deserve her.

It was probably why Michelle kept calling him. The viper of a woman was a constant reminder of his lapses in judgment. The coked up heiress-wannabe-celebrity resembled more of the type of woman he would end up with.

But until his past caught up with him, he would take and cherish every piece of heaven he could get his hands on. Pushing the haunting memories to the back of his mind, he stepped forward, leaving an inch between them—one his dick eagerly jerked to fulfill. That's when she turned and stopped his heart completely.

He had a glimpse of her full breasts, the rosy red nipples straining toward him before he dragged his gaze to her face. She peered up at him through flickering lashes, her blue eyes now darker as she grinned.

"Do you know how many times I've imagined you naked?" He couldn't help the smile that tilted his lips when her eyes widened.

"Liar."

He raked his gaze down her body, trying hard not to focus on the petite patch of curls between her thighs. Then he closed the distance between them, the hardness of his erection resting against the low of her belly. Her skin was so soft, so smooth. "It's true. Even though I had no clue what you looked like, I fantasized about you all the time."

She narrowed her gaze, her hands coming to rest on his biceps.

"Still don't believe me?" he asked.

She raised her brows and shook her head. "Not in the slightest. I've had the image of you taunting me for years. *I'm* the one who's been going through hell wanting to see you up close…and completely naked," she finished with a cheeky grin.

He leaned in to nuzzle her neck, hiding his shock. The warmth from her body sunk under his skin and warmed his frigid soul. He was the drug abusing rock star from a deadbeat family. He didn't deserve her friendship, let alone her interest.

Her hands found his hips and trailed up the muscled groove running from his groin to his abdomen. Light fingers ran up the middle of his stomach, fanning out, her fingertips searching his skin, finding the tiny discolored battle scar on his side.

"Gunshot wound," he murmured and loved the way she chuckled in reply. She knew all his stories, all the challenges and achievements that made him who he was today.

When she reached his left pectoral muscle, she paused. A sharp inhale of breath sounded over the running water and he tensed, knowing exactly why she'd done it. Words escaped him while she studied the plane of skin.

His chest pounded as he waited for her to pull away, to flee. She didn't. She stood before him, her eyes focused on the tribal angel design with Gabrielle's name inscribed along the top of one outstretched wing.

Her gaze snapped to his, her eyes wide, her mouth slightly ajar. Fearing the worst, he swallowed, his Adam's apple convulsing uncomfortably. All his tattoos had a meaning, and none of them were more monumental than the one over his heart. "You're my angel, Gabi."

Her mouth closed and her nose scrunched as she began blinking, faster and faster.

"Hey, don't cry." He cupped her chin, tilting it up to place a soft kiss on her lips. When he leaned back, he was smiling. If she hadn't fled by now, with all the awkward insanity and intense emotion, then he was confident she never would. It didn't get much crazier than inking your skin with the name of someone you'd never met.

"You saved my life. I never want to forget that. Even when I'm old and senile. Even if we drift apart. No matter what happens, I will always hold you close to my heart."

Gabi stared at the swirled lines that made up the angel adorning Blake's chest. Each second that passed made her eyes burn hotter and her heart pound harder. A scream tightened her lungs, one of pure happiness and excitement, and she fought not to let it out.

They'd been through so much together. She'd helped him battle his addiction, fight the demons that kept trying to tear him down, and in return, he was her rock. He comforted her through the grief of losing her brother, listened to her pain, and not once had he turned his back.

"Say something," he asked, his voice rough.

"I love you." The words burst free without thought. She'd loved him for so long, as a friend and much, much more. It wasn't the first time she'd made the admission. The words had been shared between them for years in a friendly manner.

This was different. This was a declaration from the very heart of her, and it was a relief to let it out.

She lifted her gaze to his dark, smoldering eyes and felt the undiluted passion coming off him in waves. He growled low, and on instinct, they leaned into each other, their mouths meeting in the middle. His tongue swept her bottom lip, smooth and fluid, making her knees weak and her heart stutter.

He was so strong, so commanding, and she needed to be closer. She undulated against him, making her desire known. He gripped her ass in response, causing tiny whimpers to escape her throat. Their kiss became faster, harder, until she was too delirious from passion to make a sound.

He broke the connection, leaving her reeling and clutching his chest for support. "I want to make love to you," he said between breathless nips to her lips. "I want to spend all night inside you. Touching you. Tasting you." His arms circled her back, hugging her close. "I'm never going to want to stop."

She nodded, running her hands around his neck, stroking the short hair at his nape. Damn, she loved this man, with his black as night eyes and his heart of gold. He had the exterior of a hellion and the soul of the divine—a tangled combination that she had never been able to resist.

He squeezed her tight and spun her around in the snug space. She squealed and gripped him as he reached around her waist to open the shower door. Dripping and naked, he walked them from the bathroom, into the adjoining bedroom. They kissed with each step. The soft pecks curled her toes. The deep thrusts of tongue clenched her womb. Their hands ran over each other in a voracious need, brushing and gliding, skin against skin.

Her calves hit the mattress and Blake spun them again. He lowered to the bed and sat, pulling her with him so she straddled his lap. The hardness of his erection ran along her entrance, teasing her with the implication.

He gazed into her eyes, a playful grin tugging at his lips. "I've died and gone to heaven, haven't I? Or Mitch drugged me and I'm dreaming." He nuzzled her cheek and placed kisses along her jaw. "I've never done anything to deserve this… You."

The warmth of his breath swept over her wet skin, giving her tingles, driving her to madness. Her fingers ran into his hair, scratching, tugging, allowing her something to cling to as his tongue found the sensitive spot below her ear. Her hardened nipples ached for the tenderness of his mouth and she arched into him, giving the tightened buds the friction they craved against the light dusting of hair covering his torso.

"You're so fucking beautiful," he murmured into her neck. One arm held her around the waist, while his other moved to her breast. "I'm gonna make you feel so good, Gabi. You'll never regret what we share tonight."

She leaned back to make eye contact. They were bathed in shadow, only the soft glow from the living room lamp giving them light. It turned his irises an intense black, darker and deeper than the ink running down both arms and over his left pec. "I'll never regret you, Blake. Ever."

For long moments they stared, loving each other with teasing strokes of fingers and slight gyrations of their hips, never breaking eye contact. The moment was surreal. Him being here was surreal. She couldn't get over it, couldn't understand it, but she'd be damned if she would question what was happening between them. This was what she'd always wanted.

As she loved him with her gaze, her skin began to cool from the water dripping from her hair and she shivered.

"Cold, angel?" he murmured low.

She smiled, loving the nickname more than words could express. "A little. Maybe you could warm me up." She pushed her knees against the mattress, moving herself higher, hovering the heat of her sex above his cock. "Do you think you can do that?"

He chuckled and grabbed her forearms, yanking her body around so she lay on the bed and at his mercy. The lower part of her legs hung over the mattress and he towered over her, piercing her in place with his self-assured smile. "I can sure try."

His left palm trailed over her skin, from her shoulder, around the curve of her breast, along her stomach. She held her breath, luxuriating in the way he worshipped her body. Every nerve ending was raw, every heart beat stuttered, anticipating his next move.

He slid over her, bringing his head down to her chest. She gripped the quilt and drifted in bliss as he licked away stray droplets of water from her sternum, her ribs, and finally her tight breasts. His mouth hovered over her nipple, and he peered up at her under thick, black lashes. "Still cold?"

She swallowed, on the verge of begging him to continue. "Mmm-hmm." She nodded and bit her lip, fighting back a smile when he grinned.

"Now's not the time to point out that it's probably your cold heart causing the probl—"

She gripped the short strands of his hair and lightly pulled until his face came up to hers. He chuckled and settled between her thighs, his erection poking her entrance. "I have a cold heart, do I?"

He shrugged, his grin unwavering. "Just my medical diagnosis."

The comfortable familiarity between them was unnerving, and entirely exhilarating at the same time. She'd had boyfriends before, some lasting longer than others, however, it took weeks, sometimes months to lose the awkwardness of insecurities between the sheets.

Not with Blake. His gaze alone empowered her, made her feel special. Adored.

He backed away, reaching for his wallet on the bedside table and retrieved a condom. With efficient strokes he placed the protection over his length, and moved back over her.

Staring into her eyes, he ground into her sex, the head of his cock prodding her entrance. "Are you sure about this, angel?" The playfulness left his eyes, replaced with concern. "I want you so bad, Gabi, but if I lost you…" He closed his eyes and shook his head.

She cupped his face with her palms and pulled him closer. "You'll never lose me. I promise."

He leaned in, dancing his lips against hers in delicate strokes, coaxing every piece of her heart and soul into his hands. She could feel her love for him overtaking her, changing from something she could control and ignore, to something much more potent and demanding.

Inch by slow inch he thrust into her, causing her core to clamp down and convulse with tiny bursts of pleasure.

"God, Gabi, I never expected this."

He thrust again, this time harder, deeper. His lips found her neck while he leaned on one forearm and stroked the side of her breast with his free hand. "You feel perfect," he murmured in her ear. "So hot and tight. Christ, you're heaven."

She moaned and released the covers, placing a hand on the small of his back. His muscles were taut beneath her fingers, flexing with every pulse of his hips. Her other hand gripped his ass, digging her nails in, demanding more. "Make love to me, Blake."

He growled in her ear, the vibration of his chest echoing through her own. She met each tender thrust of his hips and raised her legs to wrap around his thighs, deepening the penetration. They fit together perfectly—

physically and spiritually.

Whimpers escaped her parched lips as he trailed kisses, licks, and bites from her neck to her chest, then sucked her nipple into his mouth. She arched, the spike of pleasure shooting from her breasts, straight between her thighs. His rhythm increased, his thrusts still an intimate slide and retreat, now with more potency.

Gabi gripped his hair, held him to her breast and ground harder into him, squeezing him tighter with her thighs.

"Damn it, Gab. I'm so close."

The friction of his skin rubbed against her clit every time their bodies joined. She whimpered, on the precipice. His mouth trailed up her chest, leaving a burning kiss each time he moved deep inside her. When his stubbled chin brushed against the sensitive spot at the base of her neck, she shuddered, her walls clamping down on his cock.

"I love you, Gabi," he whispered.

His declaration was her undoing. She cried out her climax, tightening her thighs around his sinful body. Her core pulsed, her back arched. The pleasure he bathed her in overtook her entirely. His mouth sucked tight on her neck and his pace increased, matching her eagerness, mimicking her need. Then with a final heart shattering plunge, Blake let out a guttural cry and came inside her.

His movements slowed, as she descended from her climax, sated and dazed. He rolled to the side, taking her with him, their legs tangled, his softening cock still inside her body. They panted into the silence, and Gabi couldn't tear her gaze from him, in disbelief that he was actually here.

"You know it doesn't count, right?" She laid her head on the mattress and traced the lines of his angel tattoo with her finger.

His arm came around her waist, pulling her closer. "What doesn't count?"

"Telling me you love me." She made eye contact and watched him quirk a brow. "It doesn't. If you say it during sex, or in an attempt to *get* sex, it doesn't count." She shrugged. "It's common knowledge."

His lips twitched. "Really? What if I said it now?" He leaned into her, brushing his mouth against hers. "I love you, Gabrielle Smith."

She closed her eyes, memorizing the words before shaking her head. "Still doesn't count if you're floating on an orgasm high."

His lips brushed hers again and again, each press more intimate and delicate than the last. "Oh," he whispered. "Well, I guess I'll have to prove it to you tomorrow."

The sound of a guitar riff broke the moment. Blake released his grip on her body and slid from the bed. "Sorry. It's my phone."

She murmured in protest, already missing his warmth. He disposed of the condom and strode across the room, completely naked, completely stunning.

"I'm waiting on a call from the guys."

She nodded and rested her eyes for a moment. The tug of sleep pulled at her with each passing second, and she wouldn't allow it to take over. She didn't want to miss a second of Blake. Moments later, she startled awake at the sound of his rough voice. Before she could sit up to brush off the tiredness, she drifted off again, her body humming in bliss.

Blake snatched his phone off the kitchen counter, unable to wipe the smile from his face. Telling Gabi he loved her had come naturally. It flowed off his tongue easier than he would've imagined. He'd never felt like this before. He'd thought he'd been in love, had contemplated saying it once or twice, and now he knew he'd been wrong. Totally wrong.

He raised his cell to his ear and kept his voice low. "Hello." Gabi had been seconds from falling asleep when he left the room, and he fully expected her to be dreaming when he returned.

"Blake?"

The feminine voice froze the blood in his veins. Why the fuck hadn't he checked the caller ID?

"This isn't a good time, Michelle. I've gotta go."

"Wait! Don't hang up."

He paused—dick move. With the blunt way he ended their relationship, he still hadn't experienced any closure. Curiosity often ate at him, wanting to know why she kept calling after all these years. Even though he'd walked away without a backward glance, he held hope that one day she would apologize for dragging him to hell with her.

"I need you." Her voice no longer held the hypnotic purr he once remembered. The words were slurred, her speech no doubt affected by drugs.

He edged around the kitchen, striding down the short hall to the front door of the penthouse suite and hopefully out of listening range. It felt wrong to be on the phone to his ex when he'd been balls deep in Gabi only moments earlier. It didn't help that he was buck ass naked with her sweet scent perfuming his body. "I'm sorry. I've moved on with my life. You need to do the same."

He'd been the one to break free of her, and still he harbored guilt for not trying to save her in the process. He hadn't been strong enough to resist her back then. Every time she cooed for him to "come have a little fun," he'd run to her. The decision to turn his life around had involved shutting her out completely.

Best fucking decision of his life.

"Blake, please. My father's cut me off. I've got no money."

He suppressed a derisive laugh. Poor little rich girl. Rumors had circulated in the tabloids that her father, a multi-millionaire building tycoon, had grown tired of his eldest daughter's partying ways. Blake couldn't blame him. If only her old man knew the half of it.

"I'm sorry, Michelle. Please don't call me again."

He hung up, ran a rough hand through his hair, and shuffled back to the kitchen to place his cell on the counter. Gripping the edge of the cold marble, he hunched over and took long steadying breaths. He wasn't an angry guy. It wasn't in his nature. It was only when Michelle snuck her way back into his life or he was reminded of his past that the cloying tightness in his chest took hold. "Fuckin' idiot."

It had been over twelve months since he last spoke to her. He'd learned to screen his calls, to delete her messages as soon as he heard her voice, but every now and then he slipped up.

His phone rang again, and he quickly silenced the guitar riff. She must be flying high to think he'd answer her call after he'd hung up on her. When a voice message alert sounded, he ground his teeth together.

He'd been with Reckless Beat for two months when she sashayed backstage at one of his first live performances and blew him away with her interest...and that talented mouth of hers. He'd been a nobody, the newest member of the band who the fans hadn't warmed to.

She'd smiled at him, batted her long fake lashes, and he was thrust back into the hormones of an adolescent with the brain capacity to match.

Coming from a shitty childhood, he'd never had a woman like her glance his way. She came from a well known family, had loads of cash, and was a stunner in her designer labels.

He hadn't stood a chance.

Drinks backstage turned into a limo ride to his hotel. Then before he knew it, she was pulling out a small baggie of white powder from her purse. Drugs hadn't interested him before, apart from the occasional joint in high school, yet stupidity had him jumping at the chance to try coke for the first time, all in the effort to impress her. That was when his life took a nose-dive and didn't pull up before he hit the pavement.

Scrubbing a hand down his face, he clicked on the message and listened to the voice prompts. He started to play Michelle's recording, "Blake, I'm sorry to do this—"

Before he wasted any more time pitying her, he pressed delete and turned off his phone. If Mason rang, Blake would call him back in the morning. He wouldn't risk another interruption from Michelle tonight.

He planned to spend the next eight hours sleeping and making love to Gabi. The rest of the world be damned.

Chapter Five

GABI COMBED HER hair behind her ears and focused harder on the breakfast menu. Blake's heated stare was distracting. She could feel it on her skin, across her breasts, between her thighs. Bloody hell, she'd had breakfast at this place more times than she could recall, yet for the life of her, she couldn't remember what they served.

Lifting her gaze, she found his eyes focused on her cleavage—her necklace, but it still made her skin ignite. She cleared her throat. No response.

"Blake?"

"Hmm?" Slowly his focus lifted.

She grinned at him, and he hit her head-on with an arrogant smirk. Damn her, she loved that smirk. It matched the bad boy persona he hid behind so well.

"Do you want a drink?" Getting up to place their drink order would stop her from mentally stripping him of his black tank top and taupe cargo pants.

He'd made love to her in the early hours of the morning. Again in the shower when they awoke. Parts of her body were tender from overuse and still she craved more.

He shook his head. "I'll get the drinks. You stay here."

"No." She pushed from her chair and stepped to the side of the table. "It's fine. I'll get them."

There were a heap of cafes in the area, so she'd cringed when Blake insisted on coming to the one pub that served breakfast. He'd said he remembered her stories about their huge hangover cure meals and needed to see what the fuss was about. She'd wanted to go somewhere quiet, more intimate—a place where alcohol didn't line the walls behind the bar.

Blake frowned, glancing over his shoulder. She followed the path of his gaze to the spirit bottles. When he turned back to study her, she scrounged around in her handbag, busying herself.

He grabbed her hand, stilling her movements. "Gabi, you know I don't have a problem with alcohol, right?"

The raw emotion in his tone made her throat dry. Slowly, she dragged her attention back to his face and pressed her lips together at the shame in his eyes.

"Angel, my problem was with coke. Only coke. I stopped drinking because my drug use tended to revolve around being drunk and I don't like the reminder."

She nodded. "I know. I just…" She shrugged and readjusted the shoulder strap of her lemon sundress—apparently Tammy's idea of appropriate clothing involved anything with easy access to Gabi's underwear. "I don't want you to feel uncomfortable. As much as we've talked about it online, I've never been around you to see the effect it has." Her voice was faint, each word grating over raw memories. She couldn't help recalling the experiences with her brother when he was at the height of his addiction. Blake deserved more respect than that. He wasn't like Greg, nowhere near it. "My brother's eyes would glaze over at the slightest reminder of drugs or alcohol. I don't want to put you in that position."

Blake pushed his chair out and tugged her down to sit on his lap. "You're gorgeous, you know that?" He kissed her lips and placed his hand at the low of her spine. "I'm not your brother, and you don't have to worry about my issues anymore, OK? They're over. They have been for a long time."

She closed her eyes and leaned into his body, resting her head against his shoulder. "I know. I'm just edgy, I guess. I always get like this around my birthday."

He kissed her forehead and wrapped his other arm around her waist. "I hate that you worry about me. I'll never go back there."

They sat in silence while her insecurities ate away at her. It wasn't that she didn't trust Blake. It was the distrust her brother had earned that rubbed off on her. Greg promised too many times that he was fine, that he could fight temptation. And yet five years ago, on her birthday, he'd overdosed and ended up on life support, dying four days later.

"Do you speak to her often?" The question came from nowhere. She hadn't even felt the words brush her lips. After all this time, the memory of Blake's ex still hovered at the back of her mind. When they first started communicating online, he'd told her about the temptation associated not only with drugs, but with Michelle Clarkson herself. Back then, the woman had been alluring in every way imaginable—beautiful features, great body, wealth, and popularity. Gabi didn't blame him for falling for the actress. If Gabi was that way inclined, she probably would've given the woman a crack, too.

He stiffened at her question, and she straightened to look him in the eye.

"Not willingly," he murmured.

She frowned, endeavoring to suppress the mix of jealousy and distaste toward the woman who dragged Blake into the world of drugs. "What does that mean?"

He squeezed her tighter, and she noticed the way his skin paled at her question. "She calls sometimes, whenever the band's in the spotlight, usually. I've learned to screen my calls and delete her messages without listening to them."

Gabi snuggled back against his chest, not wanting to announce her insecurity. Michelle would always be a part of his life—a big part of his past, anyway. And although Gabi no longer saw the beauty in the heiress's features, she wasn't certain if Blake did.

"When was the last time?" She kept her voice low, masking the way her body vibrated with dread. Each passing second compounded her anxiety, until it was a tight ball in her stomach. She concentrated on the way his heart pounded through his chest and closed her eyes, willing him to respond.

"Last night," his voice was a whisper.

Her heart stopped. "What? When?" She sat up straight to look at him. "Before you came to the club?"

He winced and shook his head. "No. After we were together."

Bile rose in her throat, and she grabbed at the charms on her necklace, working them back and forth to occupy herself and ease the jealousy taking hold. She had nothing to worry about. Blake loved her. He'd said so last night. After all they'd been through, all the trust he'd given her, all the skeletons he'd revealed, the least she could do was trust him.

"She was the one that called before I fell asleep?"

He paused with his arm still snaked around her waist. "Yeah."

And he'd answered. She'd heard him say hello before she drifted off.

Gabi gave a shaky nod and pushed from his lap. Plastering a smile on her face, she turned to face him. "So, how about that drink? What would you like?"

She would appreciate a shot of vodka right about now. Even scotch would do. The burn would take her mind away from Michelle. She wouldn't beg for a play-by-play recount. If he didn't want to talk about it, that was fine. She could deal. No problem.

He grabbed her hand and entwined their fingers as he brought it to his lips. He peered up at her, his pain clearly evident in the dark depths of his eyes. "You have nothing to worry about, angel. I don't want anything to do with her."

She would probably believe that if she didn't know every intimate detail of his relationship with his ex. He'd been in love. His first love, and that wasn't something you easily forgot.

Gabi nodded, this time with more enthusiasm. She needed to step away, to take a breath and put things into perspective. He was here with her. She had to remember that.

"I know." Her voice was upbeat, and still, he winced. He was too perceptive for his own good. "So did you want orange juice with breakfast? I'll place the order for our meals while I'm at the bar."

The guilt at withholding information on Michelle burned Blake's throat. He could see Gabi's anguish, could sense her anxiety. Damn it, her hands were even shaking. Cutting the conversation short seemed like the only way to stop the carnage. He'd kept that part of his life from her for years. Not that it was a secret; he just didn't see the point in worrying her unnecessarily. Michelle's calls were a nuisance, nothing more, and for once, he wanted to fix his own problems, without dumping it on Gabi.

"Juice, thanks," he answered.

Trust him to fuck up every moment they spent together. It came naturally. His karma cycle struggled to cope with too much of a good thing and liked to throw life bombs at him wherever possible.

"OK, I'll be back in a minute."

He dropped her hand and swiveled in his chair to watch her leave. Christ, he loved her, from those cute little sandals, all the way up her smooth, toned legs and beyond. Inside and out, every inch was made for him.

"Hey, Gabi," he called when she reached the bar.

She turned to face him, along with the female bar attendant and numerous people on surrounding tables. Her smile was sweet and sparkled in her eyes this time, instead of the fake tilt of her lips she'd sported for the last five minutes.

He grinned at her. "I love you."

He blocked out the murmurs from strangers and focused exclusively on Gabi. Her eyes widened, glinting in the fluorescent light. Her cheeks lifted, darkening those beautiful, kissable lips. Before she could reply, he winked and pivoted in his chair to face the table, giving her his back. He wasn't looking for a response. His work here was done.

By his estimation, he'd hit her punk-ass love declaration rules out of the ballpark. *Just try and tell me that one didn't count, little miss.*

Two minutes later she returned with their drinks, slid into her chair, and rewarded him with her dazed expression.

"So, did that pass the rules and regulations?" He raised a brow and reached for his drink.

Her eyes were glowing, glazed with what he hoped was happiness. "Ah…yeah." She nodded in quick jerks and fumbled with her straw before taking a large draw of O.J. "That one definitely counts."

The heavy lump of heat in his chest felt better than anything he'd ever experienced before. He loved the physical release of sex, had experienced the consuming bliss that came from a drug high, yet nothing could compare to the clear-headed, emotional paradise currently flowing into every inch of his being.

He reached for her hand, needing to show her by touch what he couldn't explain with words. Before their fingers met, his phone vibrated in his pocket. A second later, the familiar guitar riff ringtone filled the silence.

Gabi's face fell, the happiness vanishing from her features as she looked away and cleared her throat.

"It's probably Mason." He retrieved the cell from his pants pocket and felt a giddy sense of relief when the band front-man's name stared back at him from the screen. "Do you mind if I take this?"

She shook her head. "No. Not at all."

Liar. Fragility had settled into her voice. He couldn't believe Michelle still had the ability to mess with his life. Hadn't he paid enough for those sins? Obviously not.

Christ, Michelle hadn't even been a blip on his radar in the last few years. Her phone call had been bad timing, one of those random connections that she liked to throw his way on a whim…or more accurately—while high. All he could do was look on the bright side. They'd discussed his ex, and he'd learned it'd be a topic to keep to himself in the future. He would never lie to Gabi, however, not mentioning things that he knew would upset her was different.

He pressed connect and raised the cell to his ear. "Hey, pretty boy."

"Hey yourself, asshole," Mason replied. "How's the heat down under?"

He glanced at Gabi, her gaze still downcast. "Not too bad," he lied, knowing Mason wasn't talking about the weather.

"Not too bad? That sounds like a fucking let down. What's wrong with her? She doesn't like the emo look?"

Emo. The jokes never end.

"I'm not fucking emo," Blake bit back, then let go of his annoyance once he noticed Gabi grinning.

"Yeah, OK, whatever. So, when do we get to meet her?"

He raised a brow. The Reckless Beat guys—not only the band, but the roadies and their manager, Leah—were his family. The only family worth meeting, anyway. Introducing the gang to Gabi would be a big step. One he couldn't wait to take. "Hopefully soon. We haven't discussed it yet."

"Well, get your shit into gear. We're already in the air."

"And you're talking on your cell?"

"Yeah, the *naughty* flight attendant gave me the all clear if I was quick,"

Mason's tone turned slutty, something Blake didn't appreciate while he was on the other end of the line.

"That'd be a first. Usually the ladies are pissed at how fast you are."

"Oh, ha ha ha, very funny pin dick. But no, this *lovely* lady is very generous."

"She's standing right beside you, isn't she?"

"Totally… Anyway, Mitch and I have something planned in Melbourne tomorrow and we need you there."

Blake frowned. "What've you planned? Mitch didn't mention anything to me."

The lead guitarist was the closest thing Blake had to a brother. They usually paired up on tour and spent most of their time sharing suites and sometimes women. That all changed when Mitch's girlfriend, Alana, entered the picture. Now Blake had the duty of making himself scarce or ramming plugs into his ear canal to stop himself from overhearing all their panted cries to the heavenly father.

"It's secret squirrel stuff. And you've gotta be there." The phone connection crackled. "Bring yo—girl."

"You're cutting out. Can you get Leah to email me the details of our hotel? I'll try and get a flight to Melbourne tonight."

Gabi's head snapped up and the slight crease in her brow deepened. He smiled at her, trying to wordlessly explain that everything would be all right.

"Will do. Catch ya soon."

Blake ended the call and placed his cell on the table. "How do you feel about a trip to Melbourne?"

"I'd love to…but I have to work tomorrow."

"You sure about that?" He grinned at her narrowed gaze. "I asked Tammy to arrange for you to get time off work. I never heard back from her though, so you'll need to check."

Gabi reached into her handbag. "You thought of everything, didn't you?"

Not even close. He only hoped Tammy had been successful in organizing something with Gabi's shifts. He wasn't ready to leave her. He doubted he ever would be.

Chapter Six

"I ORGANIZED FOR Janice to take your shifts on Monday and Tuesday. And the boss arranged for someone else to be on call for those nights," Tammy answered over the phone.

Wow. That came from left field. Gabi usually had her finger on the pulse, especially when it came to work. She part-time managed the apartment building she lived in, and handling the allocation of shifts was one of her duties. She also spent most evenings and weekends on call for tenant emergencies, which made up for the hours she needed to study and attend class for her degree. How had she not realized Tammy was Blake's undercover agent?

"And the boss didn't care?" Gabi asked. "Are you sure I'm going to have a job when I get back?"

"Don't fret. It'll be fine and you already have Wednesday off on annual leave…"

The uncomfortable silence that followed crawled under Gabi's skin. Every year she made sure she didn't have to work on the fourth day after her birthday. The anniversary of her brother's death was always spent with her parents.

"Great." She forced a chipper tone. "Thank you for organizing everything. You're a champ."

"So, are you going to give me details?"

Gabi laughed. She'd expected the question sooner. "Nope."

"That bad, huh?"

She lowered her voice. Even though she stood outside while Blake had gone to pay for their meals, she didn't want to be overheard gossiping. "Far from it."

"Well then, spill, woman! You're killing me."

"I don't want to make you jealous," Gabi whispered over a bubble of contained laughter.

"Jealous of what?" Blake asked.

She gasped at his whispered voice so close to her ear and melted into his chest when he wrapped his arms around her waist from behind.

"I've gotta go, Tam. We'll catch up later in the week."

Blake kissed the curve of her neck and ran his hand under the front of her shirt, teasing the low of her belly with his fingers.

"You can't leave me hangin' like that! Come on. At least give me a few juicy details," Tammy begged.

Gabi withheld a moan while Blake's touch slid over her skin. They were in broad daylight, in the middle of a busy thoroughfare, and all she could think of were his hands moving higher to cup her breasts, to tweak her nipples.

"Can't... Gotta go... Sorry." She disconnected the call, threw her phone into her handbag, and turned within Blake's arms. The sight of him—his heavy lidded eyes and lips mere inches from her own—stole her breath.

"Who were you making jealous?" He leaned in and nuzzled her cheek.

Her head fell to the side, giving him better access to work his magic. "None of your business," she moaned.

"How can I make it my business?" he murmured.

Something sparked to life inside her, something heated and fluttery and overwhelming. She wanted nothing more than her whole life to be his business. For them to share everything. However, the distance between their lives made it seem unobtainable.

"Blake." She straightened, needing his attention to be able to read his eyes.

He didn't pull his lips away from her neck. "Hmm?" He kissed her again, delicate and light. "What will it take, angel?" His hands slid around her waist to grip her ass. "For me to be your everything?"

She closed her eyes and shuddered. Pleasure overtook her—at his words, his touch, his emotion. He brought her to life, but she knew that would fade once they were no longer together. The thought was too much to bear.

"What's going to happen to us once I come back from Melbourne?" she asked.

He stopped kissing her. "You're coming to Melbourne?" He straightened and slid his hands to her waist.

She nodded up at him. "Yes."

His eyes flashed. "Is it too much to ask you to come home with me?"

Her heart squeezed at the vulnerability in his tone. She wished it was as easy as listening to her heart and saying, "yes."

Gabi couldn't leave. Not so soon, anyway. Her Bachelor of Hospitality Management was mere months from completion. And she needed to graduate. She *had* to graduate. Six years of part-time education, including six months of overseas study and one deferred year to recover from Greg's death, and she was ready for this stage of her life to be over.

"Blake, I'd love to, but you know I can't. Not yet." It wasn't like she hadn't dreamed of running away with him for years. She would give up her world to be with him, if only he would wait a little longer.

"I know." He shot her a sad smile. "I didn't expect you to. It was more of a wish, I suppose."

You're killin' me.

He was so strong, so loyal to his friends, and still he didn't believe his own worth. If only he knew she'd been mentally planning their wedding and picking out baby names since they first started voice Skyping. Moving to America wasn't an issue.

Placing her hands around his neck, she peered up at him, staring into those dark eyes until she had his full attention. "I *would* move to be with you."

Hope flickered in his irises and he bit his lip, waiting.

"I just can't do it right now. I need to finish my degree. But after that…"

He cupped her face, searching her expression, reaching into her soul to take another tiny piece of her. "You'd move for me?"

There went her heart again, aching at his vulnerability. "I'd do anything for you."

A kaleidoscope of emotions flickered in his features—disbelief, awe, happiness, and then his cocky persona settled back into place, and a wide grin tilted his lips. "I might have to test that theory."

She raised her chin, ignoring the way he hid behind a thin veil of arrogance, and pulled the strap of her handbag higher on her shoulder. "Test away."

"Teach me to surf."

It sounded like a good test at the time—he was in Queensland, Australia, the place of the mighty surf and scorching sun. Now, he'd gone well past second guessing the profound stupidity of his suggestion. What had he been thinking? Well, he'd been thinking exactly what any guy would've been thinking. *Gabi in a bathing suit? Rock on!*

What Blake hadn't anticipated was the unrestrained erection tenting his swim trunks or the mass of people staring at him. Women, children, even men.

"Just lie on the board and pretend you're paddling." Gabi bent over above him, her feet at the head of the board, her delicious rack tempting the unyielding shit out of him. "Then what I want you to do is, jump up—"

"Gabi, this isn't gonna work," he muttered.

Not even the discomfort of sand scratching his stomach could lessen the eagerness of his cock. He doubted an electric sander against his balls would. There was no way he could "jump up" in his current state without scandalizing the locals.

"It's easy. All you have to do—" She bent lower, her breasts hovering above his head.

Yeah, get Gabi in a public place, dressed in a teeny, tiny, black string bikini. Fucking brilliant idea.

"Gabi," he growled and leaned on his elbows to look up at her. "If you don't get the twins outta my face, I'm going to fuck you where you stand. You got me?"

She stared at him wide-eyed, her tongue sliding out to moisten her curving lips. The sight alone had him squeezing his eyes closed.

"I'm not sure about US law, but that's totally illegal here," she whispered with a chuckle.

"I. Don't. Fucking. Care."

Her laughter increased, and when he opened his eyes again, her taunting mounds of flesh were jiggling up and down, her nipples hard and beading against the thin material of her bathing suit.

"You were warned." He pushed off the board, moving to stand in a rush, and swept her off her feet.

She squealed and swung her delicate arms around his neck. As he ran into the waves, her hold tightened, her squeal turning into demands to put her down. He ignored her until his third leg was out of view, doused by the warm Australian water.

He concentrated on the waves. The sound of the ocean distracted him, and the hot midday sun made the tainted darkness inside him a little brighter. He'd never felt so at home. Even in a foreign country, with a woman he'd seen for the first time last night, his heart felt full.

He'd never truly belonged. Anywhere. In high school, he'd been the poor kid with the dead-beat parents. Other students teased him about his secondhand clothes and barely wearable shoes. Close friends had been hard to come by, and even those tended to stab him in the back when he needed them the most.

His only solace had been music, and more specifically, the music teacher who tried to steer Blake away from the wrong crowd by occupying him on lunch breaks with guitar lessons. From the first moment he held the cold wood of a bass in his hands, he'd known what he wanted to do with his life. And it took a lot of unpaid gigs and determination to get there.

Then came Reckless Beat. The guys didn't judge him on anything other than his ability to rock the strings. Even his position as bass guitarist didn't seem secure, though. He held too many secrets and made too many mistakes to ever feel like his place within the group would last forever. One day his skeletons would fall from the closet, and he'd be kicked to the curb without a second glance.

Now, here with Gabi, he knew he had someone to belong to. A person he yearned to make a permanent fixture in his life, even if he didn't deserve it.

"You're a tease," he whispered into her ear, jumping over the first waist high wave. He needed to keep moving, to drown himself under the salt water until blood flow went back into his brain, instead of his cock.

She chuckled and kissed his jaw. "Maybe."

Maybe? He looked down at her and took another hit of water. "That was deliberate?"

Her grin widened.

"The tits in my face? The rubbing up against me? The smallest fucking bikini known to man? You did all that on purpose?"

Her cheeks lifted, her smile growing to show dazzling white teeth as she shrugged.

Minx. "You'll pay, my gorgeous angel." He leaned into her, the water now lapping at his chest, and took her lips with his own. There was nothing delicate about his kiss. It was hard, unyielding and unremorseful, just like the thickness growing between his legs.

Gabi clung to him, hitching her thighs around his waist, sparking his arousal to new heights. The lust and love he held for this woman beat so hard through his veins that he wanted to kneel at her feet and beg her to be his. Not for a weekend. Not for a month. Forever.

She broke the connection with a gasp and glanced behind him. "Wave!" she shouted, then pushed off his chest, diving into the deep blue.

He had a second to peer over his shoulder and follow her under before the water crashed, pounding at his kicking ankles. When he came up for air, Gabi was in front of him, her shoulder length hair now slicked back in light curls.

"Come out further. There won't be as many waves." She grabbed his hand, entwining their fingers while they walked to deeper water.

When another swell formed, she released her hold and dived under the approaching rush—so fluid and lithe. This time when he dived after her, he opened his eyes, ignoring the sting of salt water, and grasped her around the waist. She didn't flinch, didn't even falter as he pulled her into his arms and brought them up for air.

He gave her a second to catch her breath before he plastered his mouth against hers, his tongue delving between her lips. His chest rumbled, voicing the fierce demand his body made for this woman. He didn't care if he drowned in the process of kissing her. Breath seemed like a far second to passion in his current state.

She wrapped her legs around him again, grinding her heat against his length. His body jolted with the pleasure, demanding him to pull her bikini to the side and take her. Right here. Right now. Surrounded by surfers and swimmers and parents and children.

Fuck the world. They didn't matter. Nothing did. Except Gabi. Her sweet body milking him, taking him to a place he'd never been before.

He deepened the kiss, gripping the back of her head with his hand, while the other grasped her ass. The pull of the ocean tugged against his thighs and he broke their connected mouths to find a massive wave forming.

"We'll make it over." Gabi released her grip on his body and swam ahead, rushing to get over the wave before it broke.

He took off after her, trying damn hard to ignore the erection-made rudder that slowed his progress. They both reached the top of the wave as it began to break and sailed down the back end, a yard apart, staring at each other with feverish need.

When the water leveled, he dived under again, resurfacing against her body. He didn't have time to kiss her or grasp her hips, before she was on him, her tongue in his mouth, her hands on his chest. Her touch slid lower, over his waist, to grab his cock, causing him to jerk.

"Holy hell." He was close, so hyped on touch and taste and lust that it wouldn't take long for him to blow. "Careful, angel." He treaded water, the ocean lapping at his chin. Taking Gabi's hand, he swam a few feet back to shore where he could feel the sand between his toes. Once he had his footing, he grasped her hips and pulled her into his waist. "I wanna make you come."

She pressed her lips together and smiled. "What's stopping you?" Her gaze turned seductive, peering up at him under wet lashes, her hair dripping around her face.

He growled and smashed his lips against hers, breaching her mouth with his tongue while his hand slid from her hip to the crotch of her bikini bottoms. She sucked in a breath. *Christ.* They were both a bundle of hypersensitive nerves. He held her around the waist with his free hand and swiped her pussy lips with the hand already nestled against her heat. Her body shuddered against him, her eyelids fluttering while her back arched into his chest.

The ocean surged around them, dragging them off the ground and closer to the shore before receding. His fingers teased her entrance while his mouth devoured hers. The pleasure of her body made him burn, made him hunger to drag her to the shore and take her in front of a beach full of strangers. But he couldn't. He couldn't even take her in the depths of the water where their actions would be hidden under the deep blue waves. He didn't have protection and hadn't had an STD check in six months. When he played, he played safe, and he would never risk Gabi's health for his gratification. Knowing he would have to wait until they were back at her place only made the ache throb harder.

"You want me to make you come?" he growled into her ear.

She mewled and nodded into his neck.

He smiled, loving how he could make such a beautiful woman needy and dazed with passion.

"You sure?" he teased, stroking his fingers back and forth down the centre of her core.

"Oh, Blake, please." She dug her nails into his skin and rubbed her erect nipples against his chest. "It won't take much… I'm… Just stop teasing me, please."

With a soft slide, he drove his fingers into her. She moaned, the walls of her core immediately clamping down on his digits.

"You're so damn beautiful," he whispered in her ear.

Her lips were parted, her eyes closed, her cheeks warm and pink. Water rushed around them as they glided over a forming wave. He ignored it, tuning out the world around them. He wanted to give Gabi something to remember him by, something to think of every time she looked at the ocean. And pleasure was one thing he excelled at.

Working his fingers in and out of her body, he found a rhythm. He pulled her tighter against him and worked his thigh between her legs, adding pressure. His balls pulsed, his cock throbbed, yet he focused solely on her. Everything was for her.

"Does it feel good, angel, to be out here in front of hundreds of people with my fingers in your pussy? I never would've picked you to be a naughty girl."

She whimpered into his neck, sinking her teeth into his skin. "It… feels…so…good."

He moved his fingers faster, stretching the material of her bikini to rest his thumb against her clit.

"Oh…shit," she panted and bucked against his hand. She raised her leg, wrapping it around his thigh, giving him better access to her tight heat. "More, please." Her mouth sucked at his skin and her touched travelled down his body, underneath the waistband of his trunks. "Please, Blake." She gripped his erection and began to stroke.

He clenched his jaw, swallowed hard, and thought about basslines, airport delays, anything to drag his focus away from the rhythmic stroke of her silken grip. They'd been making love all night, and he couldn't get enough.

He had no immunity to this woman.

"Oh, Blake." She kissed his neck, tiny teasing nips that made his thighs tense.

"Are you going to scream for me, gorgeous?" He moved his lips to her ear and scraped his teeth against her lobe. "I want to hear you call my name. I want everyone to hear, so they know you're mine and will never doubt who you belong to."

He thrust into her grip, so close to the edge, not wanting to go over without her. Placing more pressure on her clit, he sunk a third finger into her pussy and felt his balls tighten at her moan.

"I'm… Ah…"

Her voice drove him crazy. Then her core began to pulse around him. Blood rushed in his ears, deafening, and her hand on his cock tightened into a strong hold. He stood still, continuing the thrust of his fingers as she arched her back and gasped in pleasure.

From the corner of his eye, white foam caught his attention and he snapped his head around to see a wave looming above them.

There was no time to think.

"Gabi!" He slid his hands from her sheath and grabbed her arm.

Her eyes fluttered open, not registering the danger as he took a deep breath and went under. He tried to drag her with him, but the force of the wave against his back tore her arm from his grip. The torrent pulled at his legs, twisting his body, squeezing the breath from his lungs. Then just as quickly as it hit, it was gone.

He kicked to the surface, breaking the water with a gasp and turned in a quick circle to search for her. Where was she? Gabi always made it up before he did. She was the water baby, the one who loved to swim, yet he couldn't see her anywhere.

His heart pounded and fear tightened his throat. He was about to put his hand up to call for a lifeguard, when her head came up from under the water over ten feet away. She was closer to shore, now stuck in the main area where the waves were breaking.

"Gabi." He pushed off the sandy ground and swam to her. She didn't smile, didn't wipe the mass of tangled hair from her forehead. She simply stood there, the water now lapping at her breasts as she blinked in a daze.

He kicked harder and felt another wave pulling at his heels. "Gabi!"

Her chin lifted, searching for him.

"Gabi, get under." His whole body stiffened, his erection now lost to torment.

She sighted the wave behind him and he waited for her to dive under before he did the same. He searched for her under the tumbling rush and came up holding her around the waist.

"Are you OK?"

She leaned into him and winced. "Worst…orgasm…ever."

He squeezed her tighter and gave a half-hearted chuckle. "Yeah?" Something wasn't right. She was swaying on her feet, staring into the distance as if disoriented. He needed to get her out of the water. "I thought it would've rated highly seeing as though you still look stunned."

She gave a perfunctory laugh which amped his concern. There was nothing perfunctory about Gabi. She was enthusiastic, jovial, passionate. Always. Not the person who stood before him, glancing straight through him.

"I need to get you some help."

She shook her head, then grimaced. "No, I'm fine." She placed her fingers at her temples. "I just need to sit down. That's the first time I've been dunked in years."

He led her from the water, holding her close to make sure she didn't fall with the continued pounding from the waves. When he reached the shore, a lifeguard came at them, running into the ankle high water in his bright red shorts and a yellow T-shirt.

"Gabi?" The guy went to her other side and placed his hand around her waist.

The familiarity between them blindsided Blake. He wasn't the jealous type, but having this pretty boy wrap his arm around Gabi had the same result as waving a red flag at a bull. Nobody touched his woman. *She isn't really your woman.*

"I'm fine, Troy. You're both being melodramatic."

Troy—her surfing instructor. Blake remembered Gabi speaking about him more than once.

They led her up the beach, helping her to sit on the soft sand near their towels.

"Seriously," she shaded her eyes from the sun and peered up at them, "I'm fine. You can both drop the protective act. I just need to catch my breath."

"She was dunked and stayed under for a while," Blake gritted through clenched teeth. He had no medical training and if the blond, buff lifeguard was the only one he could rely on to check her, then so be it.

The douche gave Blake a dismissive glance, then turned his attention back to Gabi. "What the hell were you doing to get smashed so hard? You're usually one with the ocean."

Insecurity had Blake kneeling down to remain close to Gabi. Fuck irrationality, he didn't care. He suddenly felt overwhelmed with the need to stake a claim. "This time she was 'one' with me." A smirk pulled at his lips. Yeah, he was an arrogant prick, but he wanted the guy to know the score.

Gabi snorted and raised a brow as she turned her gaze to him. "Yes. It was entirely your fault." She grinned.

"Ahh... Right," the guy murmured, taking a step back.

Gabi's grin deepened. "Blake, this is Troy. Troy, this is Blake, the bass guitarist for Reckless Beat."

Blake still sported the I'm-sleeping-with-her-so-kiss-my-ass smirk when he turned on his haunches to Troy. The guy wasn't impressed. He looked down his nose, his gaze roaming over Blake's tattoos with disgust.

"G'day," Troy muttered and thrust out a hand for Blake to shake.

"Hey." Blake jerked his head in acknowledgement and shook the guy's hand. They gripped for longer than necessary, staring each other down, neither one willing to break eye contact.

Gabi cleared her throat and pushed to her feet, and still the asshole didn't loosen his grip. With a roll of his eyes, Blake dropped his hand and stood, ignoring the way Troy continued to size him up. Fuck the lifeguard and the little rubber duckies he floated in on. It wouldn't be the last time Blake had to deal with someone's disapproval where Gabi was concerned.

"Let's go home," Gabi said, dusting sand off her ass.

The way she said "home" made him swallow. It conjured images of a family and feelings of long-term togetherness. It was sweet relief against the anxiety that wracked him at the thought of being without her again. God, how he wanted that. He wanted to deserve that.

Troy stepped forward. "I need to check you over first."

Gabi paused and pierced Troy with an incredulous stare. "Are you serious? It's just a little headache. You've seen me take hits like this before."

She wiped the wet sand off her tanned belly, jiggling her luscious breasts. Blake was pissed that he wasn't the only one following the movements.

"I'm on shift, Gab. If you end up in hospital after I've let you walk away from here, I'll be in the shit for not checking you properly."

Gabi placed a hand on her hip and glared at Troy. Blake had no clue what a "proper check" involved and already hated the thought, however, he would step back and let the pretty boy handle the full force of her wrath.

Sadly, they looked good together. The surfer chick with the lifeguard. Both tanned, toned, and by societies aesthetic standards—perfect.

"Fine," Gabi growled. "Check me." She swung her arms out in annoyance.

Troy stepped into her. Their bodies close, intimate. When his hand gently gripped her chin so he could peer down into her eyes, Blake nearly lost his shit. All this time, he'd listened to Gabi share the details of who she dated, and although he'd wished to be in their place, he hadn't dwelled on it. It had been out of his control. Now this asshole's fingers were in her hair, roaming her scalp and Blake had the urge to castrate the fucker, just to take away any threat in the future.

"I don't have a head injury, Troy." Gabi looked back at him with annoyance.

"Like I said, I've gotta check."

"Sure you do," Blake mumbled and turned away. The thing that hurt the most was knowing Troy would be hanging around once Blake went back to the US. His relationship with Gabi wouldn't be a case of living a few miles apart with visits on weekends. They had to deal with being in different countries, across the world from each other.

When Blake pivoted in the sand to glance back at her, she was staring at him, her brow furrowed in apology. Her lips moved, mouthing the words, "I love you," and his heart lurched. She truly was an angel, and maybe he was kidding himself for thinking things between them would work.

He had no problem being faithful. That wasn't an issue. However, living his life without her, no matter how temporary, would kill him. It'd been hard enough for the past four years. Going home now, knowing Gabi was so far away, knowing what they'd shared and how right it felt would be unforgiving torture.

"I love you, too." He mouthed back.

She smiled, happiness twinkling in her bright blue eyes.

"Did you lose consciousness?" Troy asked, dropping his hands to his side.

"I dunno, maybe for a second." Gabi shrugged. "It was more the shock of being blindsided that had me in a daze. I wasn't expecting it."

Troy stepped back. "And what about fatigue? Are you feeling tired?"

"Oh, come on, Troy. You know I'm fine." Gabi moved toward Blake and reached for his hand. She entwined their fingers, placing a kiss on the *Reckless* tattoo that adorned his knuckles.

Troy's gaze followed her actions, his jaw ticking. "It's a simple question, Gabi."

She scoffed and shook her head. "Yes, Troy, I'm tired. And do you want to know why?" She raised her brows, cocking her head on an angle to give him a full dose of attitude. "Cause I was riding Blake *all night long*."

If Blake would've had a mouth full of water, it would've sprayed all over Troy's shocked face. Neither one of them saw that coming.

"Yeah, you heard right. And don't think I didn't notice the distain in your gaze when you looked at him." Gabi let go of Blake's hand and bent over to pick up their towels. "I introduced you to my best friend, Troy," she spoke over her shoulder, "and all you did was glare. So thank you for your concern, but I'm sure if I need anything, Blake will be able to provide it."

Bam. Prissy boy just got served.

Blake felt sorry for the dude. From the way Troy's mouth gaped and his shoulders slumped, it was obvious the guy felt like his balls had been shredded. Blake contemplated sticking up for the douche… Fuck that.

Muscle man would have time to suck up to her once Blake was gone. He believed in helping a brother out, but not when it came to Gabi.

She walked away, heading for the road, and he tried not to smirk when he followed.

Blake had always been a guy's-guy. Bros before hos and all that crap. But as he caught up to her and they walked hand in hand to her apartment, he couldn't stop thinking that no other brother—Mitchell or the other band members included—would ever mean more to him than Gabi.

Chapter Seven

"How are you feelin'?" Blake murmured into her neck from the seat beside her in business class.

He'd asked her the same question more times than she could count, his concern making her smile. Since the tumble at the beach, he'd acted like a complete gentleman—bathing her with soft kisses, gently washing her hair in the shower, and picking out a floral sundress for her to wear. The design was prim and proper, making her feel like a Stepford wife, especially when standing next to Blake, but she wore it anyway because of the way his gaze devoured her with it on.

He'd sat on the edge of her bed, watching her unpack the clothes from last night and re-pack warmer ones for the cooler, late-spring Melbourne weather. Not once did he act on the lust glazing his eyes. And she was thankful. Although her need for him hadn't faded, she was still shaken from the hit she'd taken at the beach. Her legs had been pummeled by the ocean, her head hitting the ground hard, leaving her dazed and confused and possibly suffering from a minor concussion.

"Good." She grabbed Blake's hand on the arm rest and gave it a squeeze. Apart from a killer headache, she was fine. Once her feet were back on solid ground, she'd down a couple of aspirin and be right as rain.

"You look pale."

That could have something to do with the stabbing pain that sliced through her head whenever the plane jolted from turbulence. "I'll be fine once we land." And if aspirin didn't work, she planned to test the theory that sex cured headaches.

Taking a deep breath, she focused on the leather cuff around Blake's wrist. Damn sexy. Damn naughty. It was strange that one piece of jewelry could melt her insides like butter. Then there were the tattoos that wove up his arm. With her index finger she followed the patterns, tracing over familiar song lyrics, tribal swirls, and musical notes, enjoying the way his gaze tracked her movements over the collage of images.

The plane jolted with another burst of turbulence and she squeezed her eyes shut, digging her nails into Blake's skin at the sudden slash of blinding pain.

"Holy…shit." Blake choked and grabbed her hand. "Retract the claws, kittycat."

She opened one eye a crack and winced before closing it again. "Sorry."

"Why don't you get up and stretch your legs? It might make you feel better."

The throb between her temples receded while the plane coasted forward smoothly. "Maybe later." Right now her only comfort came from him, and she didn't want to lose that.

He brought her hand to his lips, and she rested back against the headrest to look at him. His eyes were the darkest shade of brown. The hue bordered on black and spoke of bedroom sins and heated lust. She had no resistance to this man. He had the ability to seduce her with a single glance. Even when she struggled under the threat of a migraine, he made her body ignite.

"Do you need me to distract you?"

She loved that tone of his—the one that fell from his lips with such tempting masculinity.

He placed his mouth around the tip of her index finger and bit down lightly on the nail. Her nipples tingled in response, and she discreetly shuffled in the chair, trying to dislodge the ache that formed between her thighs.

"You know, maybe taking a walk is a great idea," she rushed out, already falling under his spell. "I'm going to go to the bathroom and freshen up." He'd already proved that her moral compass didn't work while in his presence. Christ. They'd been molesting each other at the beach this morning for god's sake. In between the red and yellow flags and surrounded by a mass of people. Classy. If she wasn't careful she could find herself straddling him in front of business class.

Unclicking her belt, she ignored his smirk and maneuvered into the aisle. "I'll be back in a minute."

She walked through the cabin on shaky legs, gripping at stray headrests every time the plane dipped. When she reached the bathroom door, a firm hand landed on her hip, startling her. She turned fast and grimaced through the throb in her head to find Blake hovering over her, his lips tilted in a wicked grin.

He leaned into her, placing his mouth at her ear. "Whatchya doin'?"

His warm breath sent a thrill through her traitorous body, dousing her discomfort with something warm and tingly. "Blake," she warned. "I came up here to get away from you and your sticky fingers."

"Mmm," he growled into her neck. "My fingers aren't sticky yet, but we can change that."

The air left her lungs, and she stepped back to save herself. Her mother would be horrified if she knew the lascivious thoughts currently rushing through her daughter's mind.

"Honey, you don't look well." He raised his voice, loud enough for nearby passengers to overhear. The smirk left his features and the sudden change from horndog to concerned lover made her feel self-conscious. Surely she didn't look *that* bad.

"You are weird, my friend," she whispered and unlatched the toilet door.

"Is everything all right here, Mr. Kennedy?" A feminine voice asked.

Gabi rolled her eyes and turned to find one of the flight attendants batting her long lashes at Blake. There seemed to be a pattern of them rushing to his side whenever he coughed, or sneezed, or breathed. And this one liked to show her concern with added cleavage.

"I'm really worried about her," Blake told the stacked brunette. "Gabi took a knock to the head this morning, and I'm pretty sure she's suffering from a concussion. I don't want to leave her alone."

The woman spared Gabi a fleeting glance before focusing back on Blake. "I understand your concern, however, company policy doesn't allow for more than one passenger to be in the bathroom at a time."

"Yeah, I know. I just don't want to leave her alone," Blake continued. "Especially when she says she's nauseous and lightheaded."

Gabi ignored them and stepped into the tiny bathroom. Before she could close the door on their conversation, he placed his foot between the frame.

"I don't want you closing the door, *Sugar*." He ended with an exaggerated southern twang. "What happens if you pass out?"

Gabi rolled her eyes. There was no risk of her passing out. She had a headache, and the only reason she was the slightest bit nauseous was because the pilots didn't know how to fly the damn plane in a straight line.

"Blake." She frowned at him, placing her hands on her hips.

When his smile increased and he winked, her stomach did a little flip. *Riiiiight*. Maybe her concussion was more serious than she thought. This was a mile high thing, not a worried about concussion thing. She had totally missed his implication.

She narrowed her gaze and tried to think while her heart thumped like elephant feet against her ribs. Did she really want to skirt the skanky line and join the mile high club with a sexy rock star who she loved without remorse? Ahh, yep… She definitely had a concussion if she had to contemplate that question.

Letting out a defeated sigh, she attempted an Academy Award performance. "Well, I don't want to yuck my guts up in front of passengers, do I? So either get in or get out." She kept the annoyance plastered on her face while she fought hard against the burst of laughter demanding to break free.

The flight attendant jerked back at Gabi's snarky tone. "Umm, if she's truly ill, I'll leave you to look after her, Mr. Kennedy. If her condition worsens, please come get me immediately."

"No problem," Blake answered while his gaze raked down Gabi's body one slow inch at a time. He stepped forward, dominant and maybe a little arrogant, as she retreated into the far wall of the compact bathroom. When he closed the door, shutting them into the tiny space, she swallowed down her excitement.

"It took a while for you to catch on, angel. Maybe you're not as naughty as I thought you were."

She raised a brow. Her steady stream of past lovers made her far from pure. However, she wasn't even close to being a mile high ticket holder. Or an ocean pass holder. Before today, anyway.

"Or was it the bump to your head?" He grabbed her hand and tugged her into his chest.

"Maybe I was trying to get away from you, after the way you almost drowned me with the last orgasm."

He chuckled and leaned in to kiss her jaw. "I'll make it up to you."

She closed her eyes and began drowning again, this time from the consuming burst of pleasure that pulsed through her at the touch of his lips.

With a gentle nudge of his hips, he turned her to face the tiny basin, her back to his chest. He never stopped kissing her, caressing her, his hands roaming her body in a mad rush. She gripped the counter and ground into his erection, loving the feel of hard flesh against her ass.

"We shouldn't be doing this." Her conscience spoke aloud. "There are hundreds of people on the other side of that door." *Just like at the beach…* The thought had her eyes bursting open. "Do you enjoy this type of thing?"

He paused, and their gazes connected in the mirror, his long dark lashes framing fierce eyes.

She cleared her throat. "I mean, are you an exhibitionist? Do you like having sex around lots of people?"

He tilted his head on an angle and studied her. "I'm a musician, Gabi. I love a crowd."

She stopped breathing. Although this morning at the beach had been a rush, she didn't think she could do that all the time. She'd never been the kinky type.

He leaned in and sucked hard on her neck, jiggling the necklace she couldn't bear to take off. "But not when it comes to sex," he spoke in her ear. "I'd die before I let another man see you naked. I'm too jealous for that." His hands trailed along her waist, bunching her sundress so the knee high hem drew to the top of her thighs. "I want you all to myself."

Both hands went underneath the waistband of her panties, his fingers teasing her clit with light strokes. Her core convulsed with the promise in his touch, and she rested against his body, raising one arm behind her to cup the back of his neck while the other gripped the counter for support.

"I don't want to share you either." Her admission stunned her. She didn't want to share him, never had even in friendship, only they lived so far apart. He was a terrifyingly gorgeous man, and his life was surrounded with free and eager women. Would he put that on hold, temporarily or permanently, for her?

"What are you thinking about?" He asked into her hair.

She snapped out of her thoughts and pasted a smile on her face. She needed to enjoy every minute she had left with him, not dwell on what would happen once the fairytale was over.

"Nothing." She shook her head and turned to kiss his jaw.

"Angels shouldn't lie," he purred and pulled his fingers from her underwear.

He placed a hand on her shoulder, adding pressure, turning her back into his embrace. They were inches apart, his hands now resting on the counter on either side of her hips as she looked up at him.

"Tell me." His gaze raked her face, a faint glimmer of concern surfacing in the deep irises.

She gripped his belt and began yanking it undone. This wasn't the time or place for this conversation. *This* time, *this* place, was reserved for one thing—the mile high club, and she was suddenly in a hurry to be a fully fledged member. "We can talk about it later."

"Tell me, Gabi."

She tugged at his buckle and undid the clasp of his jeans. "Not now." She ignored the way he puffed out his chest in defiance, and lowered his zipper. "I want you." More than anything, she wanted him to take away her doubt and for even a few fleeting moments, make her feel like there was nothing to fear in the future.

Placing her hand on the hard length of his erection through his boxers, she stroked. He leaned into her, resting his forehead against hers.

"You *will* tell me," he groaned.

She continued to stroke, longer, harder, and couldn't help the wicked grin that pulled at her lips when his eyes closed in pleasure.

"Maybe…not right…now," he continued and finished with a soft moan. "But you will…tell me, Gabi."

Gripping the waist of his jeans and boxers, she yanked at the material until they rested mid thigh. His thick cock fell forward and she palmed it in her hand, rubbing her thumb over the sensitive head.

"Jesus," he hissed and opened his eyes. "Do that again."

She complied, rubbing the pad of her thumb over the fluid beading his slit.

"Damn, angel. Your fingers have a direct line to heaven."

His lips smashed hard against hers and she gasped into his mouth. He ground into her, pushing his erection against her pubic bone. She continued to play with him, stroking over his head and down his shaft. Their tongues tangled and teeth collided while he lifted her onto the counter.

"Shit, wait." He placed her back on her feet and yanked his shirt over his head. "Here, sit on this." He laid his shirt on the counter and picked her up to sit on it. Damn, he was so dreamy. How could a man, tattooed and rife with emotional scars be so... perfect for her? His tenderness knew no bounds.

She stared up at him, her ass hovering on the edge of the counter with barely enough room to rest her weight. Did it matter? Hell no. He gripped her hip with one hand and held her tight with his other arm around her waist.

"Can you reach my pocket?" he panted into her mouth, nipping her lips.

She inched back, confused.

"Front left." He kissed her ear, her jaw, her neck. "Condom."

Oh. She searched for his pocket, eager and impatient. Her blood was rushing through her veins, her pussy now uncomfortably soaked and waiting to be filled. The foil packet crinkled against her fingertips and she pulled it out in a rush.

He continued to lavish her in kisses, his hand moving from her ass, over her waist, to pull down the front of her sundress and the cups of her bra. The first tweak of her nipple caused her to suck in a breath, and the condom almost fell from her fingers. Pleasure skittered from her chest, pinging through every limb, coalescing with the deep throb of lust in her core.

"I want you to put it on me," he whispered. "Hurry, Gabi. I want inside you so fucking bad."

She stifled a whimper and ripped the condom packet apart. Her fingers shook as she threw the wrapper to the floor and worked the protection over his length. His erection jerked in her hold, pulsing with each stroke of her hand. As soon as she reached the bottom of his shaft, he had her dress lifted up to her waist and her panties pulled down to her ankles.

"Oh, fuck me. You seriously have the most gorgeous pussy I've ever seen."

"Shhhhh." Gabi slapped a hand over his mouth. It would be hard enough walking back to their seats if they had silent sex, but when Blake made no effort to be quiet, she was going to die of humiliation.

"What?" he whispered. "It's true." He grasped his shaft in his hand and worked the head of his cock up and down her slit. "Mmm, so damn good."

He raised her thigh, holding her open, and then in one swift thrust he plunged inside her, filling her to the hilt. She opened her mouth to scream, to whimper, to moan, and he slammed his mouth against hers, numbing the sound, heightening the pleasure with a swipe of his tongue.

She rocked into him with tiny movements of her hips and ran her hands over his chest his. His skin was smooth under her fingertips, his muscles contorting with each slam of his pelvis. A tingle started to vibrate in the low of her belly, growing with each passing second. She could feel the fast approach of climax in her nipples, her stomach, her pussy. Every part of her was alive for him, thrumming and vibrating with the delicious friction of his cock.

He growled into her mouth and increased his tempo. "Gabi?"

"Yes… I'm close."

His hand found her breast, tweaking and rubbing her sensitive nipple. "I'm gonna have to stop."

She shook her head, her hand snaking between them to find her clit. She was so close, her orgasm within reach. Filtering out the rest of the world, she pulled back and focused on the pleasure. Blake's brow was wrinkled with strain, his hand still holding her thigh, keeping her open so she could see where they joined. The condom glistened with her juices, his balls slapping against the low of her ass.

"Oh, god, I'm coming." She bit her lip to hold in her scream, her body convulsing with spasm after spasm of climax.

Blake moaned long and low, following her over. His hips pistoned, pumping harder, becoming wild out of rhythm jerks. The tiny room filled with the noise of flesh slapping against flesh. Slowly, the cloud of pleasure began to waver, and she loosened her tight grip on him. They came down from the high together, their movements stilling as the peak of bliss faded.

"You," he panted into her neck, "rock."

Placing her arms around his back she held him close, not wanting to let go. They were made for each other. Her heart knew it as much as her soul. "You aren't too bad yourself," she replied and felt the heat of his breath against her shoulder as he silently chuckled.

After his heart rate returned to normal, Blake disposed of the condom, straightened his clothing, and gave Gabi a quick kiss on the lips.

"So, you're going to go out there and pretend like I'm still freshening up?"

She was panicking. Her eyes were wide, her throat convulsing with a deep swallow.

"You'll be fine. Just walk out there and pretend like nothing happened."

"Yeah, sure, pretend like nothing happened. And hopefully everyone will miss how my dress is now sporting a thousand wrinkles and my face is flushed."

His lips curved. "Don't forget the hickey on your neck."

Her eyes bugged, and she turned to lean into the mirror. "Are you kidding me?"

He laughed, and she pivoted on her toes to slap a hand over his mouth…again. "Laugh all you want, Blake, but if I get arrested and my parents find out it was because my tattooed, rock star boyf—" She fumbled, breaking eye contact before continuing her rant. "Because I was getting rammed in a commercial airline bathroom, you can deal with my father's wrath all by yourself."

Boyfriend. Fuck that sounded good, even though her eyes were now wide in what he assumed was embarrassment. He'd been in relationships before, and normally, the title made his balls shrivel and kick start his mind into planning an escape route. Not this time. Now he knew he'd found what he'd been looking for and couldn't wait to meet her father.

"He'll castrate you." She diverted her gaze to his shirt and poked him in the chest.

OK, well, that tarnished the thrill of meeting her dad just a little bit.

"You won't get arrested." He pretended to ignore the boyfriend comment, not wanting to increase her anxiety. He tapped her ass, enjoying the way she jolted in shock. "Follow me out in a few minutes and act natural."

"Act natural," she mumbled. "Spoken like a man of experience."

He tapped her ass again, this time harder, in warning. His "experience" meant jack shit when he now felt like a teenage virgin around Gabi. "I'll see you out there."

She sucked in a sharp breath and nodded.

Blake escaped the bathroom, closing the door behind him, and headed for his chair. He puffed out his chest and couldn't wipe the I-just-got-laid expression from his face. Oh yeah, everyone in business class knew. Some glared at him in disgust, most grinned, sharing in the awesomeness. He couldn't shake the pride from his step and didn't bother trying to hide it. Why the hell should he? When it came to Gabi, he was happy to let the world know how much of a love struck fool he was.

Once he took his seat, the flight attendant walked toward him, giving a barely discernible shake of her head, her plump red lips curving.

"Mr. Kennedy." She crouched down in the aisle beside his chair and raised a brow. "I hope your friend is feeling better."

He struggled not to laugh. "Yeah, I'm sure my *girlfriend* will be perfectly fine for the rest of the flight."

He'd never felt the need to clarify a relationship with anyone before. Ever. Yet right now he wanted this woman to know he was taken. He wanted to wipe the flirtatious smile from her face and make her realize that no other woman would ever tempt him.

She inclined her head and reached into her pants pocket. "Would you mind signing this for me?" She handed him a small notepad and pen. "It's against company policy to ask, but seeing as though you're probably overwhelmed with...*relief* from your friend's sudden recovery, I thought you wouldn't mind."

Translation: Sign the notepad or I'll tell the captain you were caught fucking on the plane and have airport security greet you once we land. It wasn't the first time he'd been threatened because of the enjoyment he participated in while thirty-six thousand feet in the air.

"Sure." He grabbed the pad and signed his name, scribbling underneath it

—Totally enjoyed the ride.

When he glanced up to hand her the pad, Gabi was standing behind the flight attendant, her face blank, devoid of emotion. Was she jealous? The green-eyed monster accompanied every relationship he'd been in since he started playing live gigs. Even back in the days of small stints at local clubs, the women he dated never trusted him and hated the attention he received. It was a pain in the fucking ass, but he was used to it. He also couldn't fault Gabi when he'd had the same aggressive feeling earlier in the day because of Troy.

"Hey, gorgeous." He passed the notepad to the attendant and reached for Gabi's hand, pulling her in to sit beside him. "How are you feeling?"

She cleared her throat and sat down. "Umm…" She squirmed in her chair, her gaze going from him to the brunette now standing beside him. "Fine."

The woman leaned in. "I'll leave you alone to enjoy the rest of your flight."

Blake remained focused on Gabi, determined not to give the flight attendant the attention she craved. When the attendant's hand came to rest on his shoulder, squeezing lightly in a silent goodbye, he worked his jaw and hoped like hell that Gabi's blank expression didn't hide the spite he anticipated.

Gabi watched the woman walk away, following her to the front of the cabin before her focus came back to him. "How bloody embarrassing," she hissed through smiling lips. "She totally knew what we were doing in there, and she was still hitting on you."

He waited for her annoyance. For the scorn to replace her cheerful expression. "Yeah. Fans will do crazy things."

Gabi shuddered. "I'm glad it's you and not me."

"It doesn't bother you?"

"What? A crazy woman asking for your autograph? Or was she asking for your number?" She shrugged. "Either way it doesn't matter. You can't help that other people think you're awesome. It kinda makes me feel sorry for her 'cause I know the real you, and it ain't all that flash." Her smile widened.

He ignored the cheekiness, needing to make sure she wasn't placating him. "You aren't jealous?"

She gazed into his eyes, her smile softening in a look he hoped was admiration. "Maybe a little. But I trust you. If I can't do that when you're a few feet away, how will I cope when you're on the other side of the world?"

Damn her perfect logic. He grabbed her hand and brought her knuckles to his mouth for a kiss. "I love you, you know that."

"Doesn't co—"

He plastered his hand over her mouth, paying her back for the times she'd done it to him in the bathroom. "It does count," he leaned in to whisper in her ear. "It counts every damn time I say it. It doesn't matter if I'm fucking you, loving you, or trying to drown you in the Australian ocean. I love you, Gabi, more than life."

He meant every word. Nothing mattered more to him. Reckless was his career. Gabi was his forever. From now on, he'd always put her first. "And while we're discussing us, I want to talk about the whole boyfriend-girlfriend thing."

The tops of her cheeks reddened. "I didn't mean to say that earlier. I was flustered. It just came out."

Her nervousness did funny things to his stomach. "So you didn't mean it?"

She stilled and focused on the back of the chair in front of her. "No… I just… I don't know what this is classified as." She lazily waved her hand between them. "Like I said, I trust you…with my heart, and I know you wouldn't deliberately hurt me. I'm just unsure what this thing between us is and what exactly will happen when we're apart."

Her nervousness may have done funny things to his stomach, however, hearing the vulnerability in her voice made his balls shrivel.

"Look at me," he kept his voice low, not wanting their private conversation to be overheard and somehow included in an upcoming celebrity gossip column.

Slowly she turned to face him, leaning her head back against the chair. "What do you want to happen?"

She broke eye contact to stare down the aisle and he dragged a finger along her jaw, drawing her attention back to him.

"I want whatever I can have, Blake." Her voice was raw and entirely brutal against his heart. "I want everything you'll give me."

Chapter Eight

Blake had been on auto-pilot for the remainder of the flight and the traffic-filled drive to their hotel. Things between them were too effortless, too right. They both wanted the same thing, so why did it feel like he was skirting disaster instead of being happy with the glimpse of a perfect future?

He kept freaking out, wondering if Gabi's feelings would change when she faced the harsher aspects of his life. So far, things had been quiet. Only one security guard had been necessary to escort them in and out of the airports. He'd been asked for one or two photographs, had signed the same amount of autographs and that was it. Barely anyone recognized him.

That would all change once he caught up with the rest of Reckless Beat—the unruly fans, the lack of privacy, the distance it would place between them while on tour. Right now was the easy part. Yet, when they pulled up to the Crown hotel, well past nightfall, and their chauffeured ride was surrounded by a hoard of screaming fans, his initial panic was doused by her glance of admiration. She waited patiently beside him as he chatted to the crowd before making their way into the hotel.

It was surreal. And way too easy.

"You're quiet," Gabi broke the silence as they rode the elevator to the 31st floor. "Are you tired?"

He shook his head. "No, angel, but you look beat." He hadn't allowed her much sleep last night, and the darkness of exhaustion had settled under her eyes.

She let out a derisive chuckle. "Oh, you're so sweet."

Closing the space between them, he cupped her face and rubbed his thumb along her cheekbone. "Don't get sassy with me." He pressed into her, leaving a tender kiss on her lips, again and again and again. "How's your head?"

The elevator pulled to a stop and the doors opened.

"Better than my stomach," she replied, moving around him to walk into the hall. "I'm starving."

How could things between them be so simple? Overnight they'd fallen into a relationship with a foundation more solid than anything he'd ever experienced. Now they only had to figure out how to keep it going.

Monogamy would be a major component, for him anyway. He couldn't be far away from her, knowing that any man could lay claim to her gorgeous body before he finished the Australian tour. Once the remaining concerts were over, he'd be able to spend some time with her, maybe a week or two, before heading back to the US. And by then, it wouldn't be long until she graduated.

It still wasn't enough. He couldn't stand the thought of watching her leave on Tuesday. It made him feel like a pansy-ass to acknowledge it, but being around Gabi made him warm—his chest, his shattered heart, his frigid soul. She brought him back to life, and he wanted to be able to repay her unwavering support.

He waited on the couch for their luggage to be delivered while Gabi freshened up. By the time she came out of the shower, dressed in a mouthwatering pink negligee, his taste buds no longer craved the food that room service had delivered.

"Oh, gosh, that smells good," she groaned and collapsed into the seat across from him at the dining table.

"Looks good, too," he murmured, his sight never leaving the feminine curves of her body.

She swiped her tongue over her lips, bringing his cock to life in one simple action.

"You're insatiable." She chuckled and began cutting her steak.

"Only for you."

He forked food into his mouth. He didn't know and didn't care what it was, he was too focused on the way Gabi briefly closed her eyes with every mouthful and moaned low in her throat. "This is so good. I feel like I haven't eaten in days."

He felt like he hadn't touched her in days.

"You spoil me, Blake Kennedy."

God, he loved how she said his name—part chastising, part seductive. He'd be happy to bathe her in money and take her to fancy hotels every night of the week if she continued to repay him with affection. The way her face lit up at the mere sight of their suite and the view of Melbourne below was priceless. Alluring. Uplifting. Sexy as hell…and damn, he had it bad.

Focus.

He'd come up with another opportunity where they could spend more time together and wanted to broach the subject before his cock took over. Reaching for her over the dark wooden table, he maneuvered around plates and glasses to squeeze her hand. "I want to go back home with you on Tuesday."

Her eyes widened and she cleared her throat.

"We already have access to the concert venue," he continued, "so the guys and I can set up early. I can be with you on Wednesday and catch a late flight back."

She didn't respond with the excitement he anticipated. Her throat convulsed with a swallow, and she moved her gaze to stare at their entwined fingers. "Blake… I don't think that's a good idea. I'll be spending Wednesday with my family, doing the same thing we do every year on the anniversary of Greg's death." Her focus slowly lifted to his, her face now pinched.

"I know, and I want to be there for you. I'd like to meet your parents." Shit. He was putting his heart on the line, and for some reason, he didn't have a good feeling about the outcome.

She slowly shook her head. "It wouldn't be the best time to meet them."

"I know the timing isn't perfect, but I'd still like to be there. For you."

She smiled at him, squeezing his fingers. "You're sweet. But I can't."

He waited for her to explain, to give him a reason other than bad timing. Only silence came.

"Why?" He slid his hand away and leaned back in his chair. For years he'd listened to her cry on the anniversary of her brother's death. Not being able to hold her in his arms and comfort her had torn him apart…and now that he had the opportunity, she was pushing him away.

She focused on his hand as it retreated. "My parents."

"What about 'em?" He picked up his knife and fork and started to brutalize his steak.

"Blake," she pleaded.

The pain in her voice was his undoing, and there was something underneath all that, something she tried to hide from him. He needed to know what it was.

He placed his utensils back down. "What about your parents?"

Gabi winced and looked him straight in the eye. "No matter how I say this, you're going to take it the wrong way, and I don't want that."

Fuck. Now he was beyond worried. His forehead started to break out in a cold sweat. "Tell me."

She stretched across the table in search of his hand, and he reached up to meet her. Something bad was coming. He could feel it in the warmth that dissipated from his chest.

"My parents will judge you."

He fought to contain his annoyance. People always judged him. The concept was far from new when it came to his appearance. So why had it never bothered him until now?

He nodded and shrugged. "Don't worry about it." He patted her hand, then pushed from his chair, no longer hungry. Grabbing his empty glass, he walked to the nearby kitchen and filled it with water, chugging the contents to drown out the hurt.

"Blake." He heard her chair scrape and her soft footfalls as she approached.

"I said don't worry about it, Gabi. I get it."

She moved in behind him and wrapped her hands around his waist, resting her head against his shoulder blade. "They worry about me."

He got that. Really. He did. He was just sick of living with the knowledge that he wasn't good enough for her. For not being the guy she deserved. He never would be. Even before this weekend he'd known. And those were his own thoughts. What would it be like when someone else was there to reiterate how unworthy he was?

"I've told you before that they're judgmental. They've always wanted to see me with an investment banker or lawyer or something equally pompous." She continued to talk against his back. "And that's their problem. I knew sooner or later they'd have to deal with what guy I brought home, because their opinion on what type of man I should be with is far from what I envision. But…" She squeezed him tight and pressed a kiss to his shoulder. "You will remind them of Greg. The tattoos. The clothing. The confidence in who you are. They'll take one look at you and panic."

He tightened his hold on the glass and gripped the counter with the other hand. Every word ripped him apart. Every reminder of his lack of worth. But like a masochist, he couldn't tell her to stop.

"And on any other day, I wouldn't care, Blake. I swear to you, I wouldn't. I just can't do it to them on the anniversary of Greg's death."

He turned, poised to walk away and gain some space. "I understand. And they have every right to draw those conclusions. I *am* everything that Greg was. I'm the drug addict from the wrong side of the tracks." He took a step around her.

She grabbed the front of his shirt, pulling hard. "No, you aren't." She reached up on her toes so they were mouth to mouth, her heated breath drifting over his skin. "You like to think you're the bad guy. But you're not. You're a soft teddy bear hiding behind tattoos, leather wrist bands, and dark clothing." Her fingers found his nape, and he closed his eyes briefly at the sensation. "I love you."

He wanted to push her away, to place distance between them so he could brood in private. Gabi wouldn't let him.

"I can't wait for you to meet my parents," she continued. "For us both to prove them wrong. Together." Her lips pressed against his, soft and sweet, making his uncontrollable body react. When she pulled back and made eye contact, her irises were fathomless in the deepest blue. "But Wednesday isn't the day for that. Let me spend this last anniversary with them, because next year, hopefully, I'll be spending it alone with you."

Gabi had a way of turning things around and making him hopeful.

"Come lay down with me," she continued. "My head hurts and I need to rest for a while."

He stood still, his heart pounding. He would always feel this way. Inferior. It was tearing him apart, and yet, no matter how much it clawed at his chest, he couldn't fathom walking away. He'd fight anything to be with her, even if it meant his own insecurities.

She moved around him and tugged at his hand. "Come on, sexy rock god. If you're lucky, I'll let you make love to me."

And as quick as that, his mood shifted from self-deprecation, to "let's ride."

Gabi woke later that night with a start, the bedside clock now reading twelve forty-seven. They'd gone to bed, made love, and must've fallen into an exhausted sleep. A loud knock sounded on the suite door, startling her again. She lifted from her stomach onto her elbows and squinted into the darkness.

"Blake?" she whispered. "There's someone at the door."

He groaned and rolled onto his back.

"Hey, lover boy, open the fuckin' door." The shout rang through the suite and made Blake's head jerk to attention.

"Damn, Mason," he growled and sat up, brushing a lazy hand over his face. "Go away!" he yelled.

A masculine chuckle echoed in the distance. "No can do, buddy. We've got plans to make and I want to meet the woman with beer flavored nipples."

Gabi's stomach dropped. They wanted to meet her? Well at least she assumed they meant her. Not that she had any body part that was beer flavored.

Blake groaned again. "He's not going to go away." He leaned over and placed a kiss on her shoulder. "Go back to sleep, angel, and I'll see you in the morning."

"Where are you going?" she asked in a rush. Suddenly, she was overwhelmed with the inevitability of meeting a band of famous rock stars. Blake's arrival had been a surprise, and they'd known each other for years. His friends on the other hand were a completely different matter. They were the highly coveted men of Reckless Beat.

"I'll go to Mason's suite so you can sleep. I won't be long."

He grabbed his clothes from the chair in the corner and dressed.

"Do you want me to come with you?" She held the sheet to her naked chest.

"No. Mason sounds like he's in the mood to stir up shit. You don't wanna be around that." He strode to the door, holding the frame as he glanced back at her. "You can meet them in the morning." Without a goodbye, he strode away.

Light entered the bedroom when he opened the suite door and Mason's voice became louder. "Where's the hottie?"

"Sleepin'. So keep your fuckin' voice down."

She heard claps of flesh on flesh and hoped they were hugging and not punching the crap out of each other.

"I bet I could find a pleasurable way to wake her." Mason chuckled.

"She's too much woman for you, Mace. You couldn't keep up."

"Fuck that. I'm willing to try."

"Move outta the way. Let her get back to sleep."

The light began to fade.

"Goodnight, beer-flavored-nipples-lady."

Gabi smothered a laugh with her hand.

"You're a dick," Blake replied. The suite door closed with a click, leaving her in darkness.

Gabi's humor faded as she flopped back onto the bed. Her concerns from earlier seeped back in. Maybe she shouldn't have been honest with Blake about meeting her parents. She could've made an excuse for him not to come home with her instead of telling the brutal truth. But that wasn't her. She didn't lie. She couldn't stand people lying to her, so she gave him the same respect he always paid her. Only, she'd hurt him in the process and fallen asleep before she could make sure he was all right.

"I'm such an idiot." She squeezed her eyes closed.

First thing in the morning she would talk to him—when her head no longer throbbed and she could think straight. Until then, she needed all the beauty sleep she could get if she had to meet the family that was Reckless Beat.

Chapter Nine

Blake strode beside Mason to the elevator and waited for the lead singer of Reckless Beat to hit the button.

"So… Is there a reason why you woke me in the middle of the night?" Blake yawned and blinked his eyes until they stayed open on their own.

Mason jabbed him lightly in the ribs with his fists. "I missed ya, bro."

"Don't give me that shit. It's only been a couple days."

The doors to the elevator opened and Mason stepped in, holding his hotel card to the security panel before pressing the number to the floor above. "Yeah, I never was a good liar."

Blake followed him in for the short ride up to the next floor. "So, what then?"

Mason waggled his brows. "We've got plans to make."

He followed Mason into the hall. "What plans?"

"I'll let Mr. Smitten fill you in."

Mr. Smitten? Mitch, Obviously. Unless someone else had fallen head over dick in the last few days.

Mason opened the door to the only suite on their side of the hallway and led him into a dimly lit dining room. Mitch sat on a coffee colored sofa, his head resting back, his eyes closed. Leah, their band manager, was on the far end reading a magazine.

"Blake." Leah greeted him with a smile and threw the magazine onto the coffee table in front of her.

"At least one of us is getting some sleep," Blake grumbled.

Mitch sat up straight and opened his eyes with a yawn. "Good to see you, too, ass-wipe."

Mason dropped onto the opposite couch and crossed his legs.

"Where is everyone?" Blake strode around Mason and sat on the armrest.

"Sleepin'. Alana and I are downstairs on the same floor as you." Mitch jerked a thumb over his shoulder. "And Sean and Ryan are back there, snorin'. How's your woman?"

"Gabi's fine. She'd be even better if I was sleeping beside her, so get on with it."

Mitch smirked. "Consider it a returned favor. I won't forget the day you dry humped Allie in her sleep."

Blake's lips curved. Although his playing days were over, the memory of that morning with Alana and Mitchell made his blood pump faster. "I can still taste her on my lips."

Mitchell's smirk changed to a glare and his hands clenched into the sofa cushions. "Payback, motherfucker. It's coming." Blake chuckled. Mitch was way too easy to rile. "Yuck it up. You'll get what's comin' to ya. Someday soon, Gabi might wake up with me rubbing against her."

Leah pivoted in her seat and pinned Mitch with her blue-green stare. "Don't you think that's a little inappropriate seeing as though you and Alana are getting engaged?"

Engaged?

Mitch crossed his arms over his chest and glowered. "You know what I mean, Leah. He's gotta pay for being such a cocky prick. I'll get Mason to do it if I have to."

Engaged? A lot had changed in a little over forty-eight hours.

"Don't worry. If she's a hottie, I won't need encouragement." Mason grinned and they all turned to Blake waiting for him to bite. "So, is she a hottie?"

Blake frowned. He'd been away for two days and the whole dynamic changed. "When the hell did you get engaged?"

Mitch smiled and sat forward in his chair. "I'm proposing tomorrow."

Blake ignored the tightening in his throat, not wanting to acknowledge that the sensation sprung from envy. It had nothing to do with Mitchell's gorgeous girlfriend and everything to do with what Blake wished he could have with Gabi.

He wanted to be the one proposing. He wanted to be the one getting down on his knee and peering up into the beautiful face of the woman he loved. Except, he was stuck in the secret boyfriend zone, not even able to meet her parents.

Pasting on a smile, he stood and stepped to the side of the table, holding a hand out for Mitch to shake. "Holy shit, bro. That's awesome." It *was* awesome. Mitch had scored above his pay grade when it came to Alana. She was a special kind of woman. One you didn't let go of, and they both belonged together.

They clasped hands over the corner of the coffee table and knocked each other's shoulders in the only form of acceptable masculine affection.

"Thanks. That's the reason you're here."

Blake stepped back and took his seat on the armrest.

"I need help planning it." Mitch sighed. "I want to make it special for her."

Blake nodded. "Well seeing as though your first attempt was done in a superhero costume with no thought or prior planning, I think you're a step ahead."

Mitch gave him the bird and mumbled, "It was a pirate costume, asshole, and you were the one who dared me to wear it."

The shit talk continued for over an hour until none of them could keep their eyes open.

"I need to get some sleep, guys. Are you all right with the basic layout of the proposal tomorrow?" Leah stood and peered down at Mitch. She didn't seem herself. Hadn't since Blake first walked into the suite. Lines of concern wrinkled her forehead, and her normally constant smile was nowhere in sight.

"Yeah, I guess." Mitch leaned forward and scrubbed his hands down his face. "I'll still fuck it up somehow."

Mason nodded. "True. Fortunately for you, it's always the thought that counts."

"Ha ha, pretty boy. At least from now on, I'll always know the name of the woman I'm sleeping with."

"Pfft." Mason scoffed. "Names are overrated."

"And so is common decency, apparently." Leah turned and started walking to the door. "I'll see you all later."

"Wait up. I'll go with you." Blake stood and saluted the guys in farewell.

Mason leaned over the couch and cupped his mouth with one hand. "Careful, tiger. Leah's been grumpy as hell since London. Make sure your balls are protected at all times."

Blake stared at Leah's retreating back while she continued slowly down the hall to the front door. "How come?"

Mason shrugged. "Methinks the red dragon might be paying her a visit."

For Leah to be this distant, Blake knew it had to be more than female issues causing problems. "Right… Well, I'll see you guys later. I've got a date with heaven."

Mitch scoffed. "Make sure you lock the door. You never know who might end up spying on you from the closet."

"Seriously, man." Mason sat up and stared at Mitch as Blake sniggered and started after Leah. "You can't say that shit anymore. I'm the man whore of the group and even I know that's wrong."

Blake jogged the remaining steps to the front door that Leah held open.

"You know what I fucking mean!" Mitch's yell echoed down the hall, cutting off at the close of the door.

Leah strode ahead and Blake had to lengthen his step to keep up. She didn't do standoffish and unapproachable. Although she became stressed at times, she always had a smile ready and waiting.

"What's going on, Lee-Lee?"

She glanced over her shoulder, piercing him with tired eyes. She wiped a length of blonde hair from her face and sighed. "I'm sorry. I know I've been grumpy tonight."

He placed a hand around her shoulder and pulled her into his side. "Wanna talk about it?"

She shrugged and shook her head. "I can't… I shouldn't."

"Surely, it can't be that bad."

Silence.

"Lee?" Her lack of response made him nervous. Their lifestyle didn't usually have a grey scale. Things were either awesome or a living hell. There was no in between. And if their band manager was acting like this, things couldn't be good.

"It's one of the tabloids back home. They say they have an exclusive and want the other side of the story before it goes to print." She heaved a sigh, her shoulders slumping under his arm. "If what they claim is true…" She shook her head. "No. It has to be bullshit." She straightened and stepped into the elevator as soon as the doors opened. "I just don't know how to approach it. Their claims are going to hurt one of you. Badly."

Blake followed her, his shirt suddenly too tight around his throat. Had they found out about his past? Was that what all this was about? Was Leah trying to protect him?

"Is it me?" He tilted his head to move into her line of sight. "Is the story about me?"

She swallowed and the wrinkles around her eyes deepened. "I shouldn't have said anything." She gave the button to the floor below a whack. "I've become too attached to you guys. I can't stand to see one of you hurt."

His palms started to sweat. His sins had caught up to him, he knew it. Bile began to rise up his throat.

"It's not you," she whispered.

Oh, thank fuck. He breathed deep and let it out slowly, glad he no longer felt the urge to purge his dinner. The elevator doors opened and they stepped into the empty hall.

"Then who?" he asked as Leah began walking in the opposite direction to his suite.

She stopped and pivoted on her toes. Her lips curved in a sad smile. "Forget it for now." She began to turn again.

"Like hell I can. These guys are the only family I have. I can't forget it."

Her shoulders fell and she stood still with her back to him.

He closed the distance between them in three strides. "Tell me."

She sniffed and when she turned her eyes were filled with unshed tears.

"Oh, Lee." He opened his arms and she fell into his chest, grasping him around the waist.

"Please ignore the breakdown. I'm exhausted and contrary to Mason's way of thinking, it *isn't* red dragon week."

He laughed and held her close. There was a glimpse of the normal Leah. "You heard that?"

She scoffed into his shoulder. "That man deliberately says things loud enough for me to hear. He does it because he thinks I won't pay him back. One day soon, I'll prove him wrong."

His chest rumbled with a half hearted laugh. So if she wasn't worried about him or Mason, that left Sean, Ryan and Mitch. *Fuck*. Could it have something to do with Mitch and Alana? If it meant saving them from public humiliation, Blake would gladly throw himself in front of a tabloid grenade for the both of them. They didn't deserve the backlash like he did. None of his band members did.

"Who is it, sweetheart?"

A half sob, half laugh echoed between them. "You don't give up, do you?" She pulled away and his hands fell to his sides as she stepped back. Wiping the tears from her cheeks, she made eye contact. "It's Ryan. They claim to have photos of his wife with another man."

Blake jerked back.

Ryan? He was the good guy, the loyal one who never spoke a negative word about his wife, Julie, even though she deserved it. And Blake had a lot less faith in Julie's fidelity than Leah did. He could see her cheating on Ryan at any given opportunity.

"Have you seen the photos?"

Leah shook her head. "They want to speak to Ryan first."

"That's bullshit. If they had the proof they'd send it through."

She nodded. "Yeah, that's what I'm hoping."

"So what happens from here?"

She pressed her lips together and shrugged. "I let the New York office deal with it. They're currently speaking with the tabloid. They just wanted me informed in case they contacted Ryan directly."

Despair thrummed from her and it stemmed from more than mere exhaustion.

"You care about him."

Her eyes widened. "Of course I do. I care about all of you."

"Yeah, but you care more about him."

She chuckled. "I care more about him in this regard because he doesn't deserve it. If I received a phone call about a PR nightmare, I'd instinctively expect it to be about Mason because he's an arrogant deviant, or Mitchell putting his foot in his mouth, or you and Sean being smart-asses. You guys create drama and thrive on it." Her smile faded. "Ryan doesn't."

True. Well apart from Blake being a smart-ass. He preferred to think of it as quick-witted.

"Well, let me know if you need me for anything. If you want me to talk to him—"

"No! Please don't. I want to keep it quiet in the hopes they're fishing for inside info. I don't want to hurt him unnecessarily. Being away from Julie is hard on him. They don't need the added strain."

Yeah. Ryan was having a hard enough time with celibacy as it was. Having groupies hound him to ditch a cheating wife would only test the poor guy further. "Don't worry. I'll keep my mouth shut. But if *you* need someone to talk to, you know I'm here."

She smiled and this time it reached her gleaming blue-green eyes. "Thank you, Blake. That woman of yours is lucky to have you."

He gave a derisive laugh. "I disagree. Gabi is definitely more than I deserve." He turned on his heels and headed toward his suite. "Night, Leah."

"Night, lurver boy," she giggled. "Make sure you get some sleep, OK?"

Chapter Ten

The late morning sun peeked through the curtains, helping Gabi to memorize every last detail of Blake. He slept peacefully on his back, his right arm resting on his stomach, while the left lay on the pillow above his head.

For a man who tried to appear rough around the edges, all she saw was gentle beauty. His black hair, which he usually spiked, lay loose around his forehead, his sensual lips slightly parted. She wanted to lean in and kiss him. To wake him with passion and love, but she knew he hadn't had a lot of sleep. He hadn't crawled back into bed until after three-thirty. So for now, she'd curb her lust by learning the intricate details of all his tattoos.

Slowly, she ran her fingers millimeters above his skin, following the trail of ink with her shadow. Around his wrists were thick, black tribal bands that held the appearance of manacles. Above the band on his right arm was the tail of a snake. The reptile wound around his forearm, all the way up his bicep. In the space around the snake were smaller images, lots of intricate designs of musical notes, symbols, even a sprig of deep pink cherry blossom—her favorite tree. They all meshed together in a beautiful collage of light and dark, joy and despair.

"I feel a little violated."

Her hand paused as her gaze snapped to meet his. "Good morning." She smiled. His irises, so deep and dark, did things to her that no man should ever have the power to do.

He stretched his arms above his head and groaned. "How long have you been fondling me with your eyes?"

She crawled over him, placing her naked body on top of his and settling between his thighs. "Too long." She ground her pelvis into his hardening cock and relished the vibration of his chest under her palms.

Gabi grinned when their gazes collided. She loved this man, with all her heart. She always had. He was honest, open about his failings, and even though she knew he tried to hide behind a tough shell, she could read the emotion clearly in his features.

"Are we OK?" she whispered. The conversation from the night before sat low in her belly, congealing.

He lowered his hands to her waist. "What do you mean?"

"About me going home…alone?"

His brows narrowed. "I told you it doesn't matter, so don't worry about it anymore."

"I know what you told me," she spoke softly. "But this is me, Blake. Although we haven't spent a lot of time physically together, I still know you. I can read the hurt in your eyes. Please be honest with me."

One corner of his lips curved, and he nudged at her ribs making her squirm. "Turning back into my little Modaroo are you? Trying to counsel me and make things better?"

Her stomach clenched. "Don't do that."

His smile faded.

"Don't turn every conversation into a reminder of what you used to be. I haven't been your drug addiction supporter for a long time. I'm your friend." She swallowed. "Your lover. Your girlfriend. You aren't that man anymore, so stop torturing yourself and let me in."

She didn't know how he'd hidden his struggle from his friends for so long. To her, his pain was blindingly obvious. His scars as visible as the ink on his skin.

"I wish I was good enough for you," he whispered.

Her mouth gaped. "You are *perfect* for me." She broke eye contact, needing to blink away the burn in her eyes and lowered her chin to kiss the smooth skin beside his angel tattoo. "I love you. Not only are you good enough, but you make me whole. I wouldn't be who I am without you."

He shook his head and remained silent.

"When you meet my parents," she continued, lifting her gaze, "we are going to show them just how perfect we are. They'll see how happy you make me and get over their misconceptions." They would. She would make sure of it. Once Wednesday was over she would talk to them.

His stare bore into her. "Sounds good."

Gabi's stomach growled between them and Blake ignored it. He'd never lain like this with a woman before. Ever. To be comfortable, simply staring at one another made his stomach do weird things. Things he'd never felt before.

"Are you still with me?" she asked softly, interrupting his thoughts.

"Yeah, gorgeous. Just thinking." He grinned, but she didn't appear convinced.

She stroked her fingers over his pecs, across the wings of his angel, leaving a trail of goose bumps in her wake. "What about?"

He chuckled to distract her. There'd been too much deep and emotional shit between them already. Once they were separated, he wanted her to remember the fun they shared, not the drama. "About you…" He placed his hands on her ass and ground his erection into her abdomen. His cock had been on a hair trigger since the moment he spotted her across the crowded dance floor. With the friction of her body and the knowledge that her tight heat was only inches away, it now thrummed, demanding action. "And me…" He tilted his neck and took her mouth in a passionate kiss. Their tongues tangled and her nails dug into his skin. "Gettin' busy."

He gave a final swipe of his tongue over her lips and enjoyed the way her light blue irises turned dark and sensual.

"Do you always frown like that when you're thinking about *gettin' busy*?"

Busted. He didn't want to drag her into his thoughts. She'd been through enough. It was time he dealt with his own shit without pulling her into the darkness. Rather than answering her, he kissed her again. Hard. Mashing their lips together and taking the breath from her lungs.

When he came up for air she was panting, her hands gripping his shoulders. He flipped her over, placing her on her back and loomed over her. He nudged her legs apart and sank between them, all the while reaching for the bedside table and blindly rummaging for a condom. When he found a square foil packet, he brought it to his mouth and ripped it open with his teeth. In the space of bare heartbeats, he sat back on his haunches, sheathed himself, and then rested back against her body.

She was warmth and comfort and home. All the things he'd never had. All the things he'd find hard to live without when they were separated.

"Trying to distract me?" she asked, then whimpered as he lowered his mouth to suck on her nipple.

He ran his tongue around the stiffened peak, flicking the hardened flesh.

"When will I get to meet your friends?"

He released her breast with a pop and raised a brow. "You're asking me this now?"

"Yes," she panted, blinking at him in a daze. "I want to know."

Trailing his tongue around her areola, he skimmed a hand up her side. "Once I've marked every inch of you with my hickies and my scent is all over your skin."

Her eyes drifted closed for a second. "And how..." She moaned when his hand cupped her other breast, teasing the tightened peak with light strokes. "And how will you do that? How will you get your scent all over me?"

Damn, she was persistent. He couldn't think past getting inside her, and she was dragging on a longwinded conversation. "I'll blow my load on your belly and smear it all over your skin."

"Eww!" Her eyes snapped open and she stiffened. "That's disgusting." She smacked his chest and began to laugh.

He chuckled along with her, happy to have sucked her out of the nirvana vortex seeing as though she'd done it to him first.

"I love making you laugh." It was the sweetest sound in the world. Along with the feminine noises she released when he made her come. "I love that I can say anything around you and you'll know when I'm joking."

She grinned back at him. "Well, I sure hope you were joking."

"What?" He pushed onto his elbows and frowned down at her. "You don't like the thought of my baby gravy all over your body?"

"Yuck, Blake." She squirmed under him.

He responded by lightly biting the skin of her neck, making her squeal.

"In me?" She nodded. "On me? Maybe. Smeared all over my body like you're icing a cake? Piss off." She pushed at his shoulders, but he didn't budge. "It sounds like fetish porn. So, no. No, thank you."

He tilted his head in contemplation. "I'm kinda impressed that you know about fetish porn."

"Pfft." She rolled her eyes. "My grandma knows about fetish porn."

"I'm really beginning to like Australian women."

"Oh, really?" She seductively trailed a delicate finger under his chin and held his gaze. "Australian women in general, or one in particular?"

He shrugged, and the curve of his lips turned into a smirk. "It'd be mean if I narrowed it down to just one. Imagine all those poor, heartbroken *sheilas*." He used his best Aussie accent on the last word and it was so bad he cringed.

Gabi glared at him, but she couldn't hide the humor in her eyes as she curled her legs around his waist and tried to flip him. He didn't budge. She grunted and lines of exertion formed on her forehead. Still he didn't move or bat an eyelid. When she dug her fingers into his ribs, he threw back his head and laughed.

"OK. OK. I'll stop teasing you." His laughter died down and he rested his hands on her belly, leaning his chin against them to peer up at her.

They remained quiet, both smiling at each other like smitten, love struck fools. Even though the cloud of lust had been broken, his nerves thrummed, eager to be one with her again. And each moment that she stared down at him with admiration made it more palpable.

"Can we go back to the part where your mouth was doing really nice things to my body?" she asked softly.

His eyes narrowed, and he couldn't help playing with her a little longer. "Can you refrain from talking about my friends while I'm trying to maintain an erection?"

She pressed her lips together, smothering her laugh. "I promise."

He raised a brow and moved his head to her breast, licking the tightened nipple. She mewled as he continued lapping with torturing slowness. When her thighs loosened around his waist, he climbed up her body, taking her breath away with his lips. Her hands glided around his neck, holding him in place, sending a shiver down his back all the way to the base of his spine. He was on top of her, the warmth of her body enveloping him, yet he wasn't close enough.

"We'll discuss this…" She broke off in a huff as he nudged inside her, the head of his erection breaching her slick walls. "…later."

He chuckled and sunk further, watching as her back arched off the bed. She was a fist around him, squeezing, tormenting, driving him to the brink with no effort at all. Running a hand down her thigh, he encouraged her legs to circle his waist. She rocked into him, lifting her hips each time he thrust, and still they weren't close enough. He wanted to be deeper, to be inside her heart, her soul. He wanted to be a part of her life that she could never live without. He wanted to be her addiction, like she was his.

Wrapping his arms around her waist, he pulled back, lifting her with him. He folded his legs under him, keeping their bodies connected as he rested on his heels and sat Gabi down in his lap—on his cock. Her arms ran around his neck, her fingers playing with his hair, her nails scratching his scalp.

Now this…this was heaven. He hugged her close and slammed his mouth against hers, loving her as they ground into each other. Their teeth clashed, their tongues danced and with each slam of his cock she moaned into his mouth.

"Harder," she panted, tugging at his hair.

"Yes, ma'am." He moved to his knees and walked them up the bed. Resting her back against the head board, he held her up and slammed home. She cried out and grazed his chest with her nipples. The scent of her arousal hung heavy in the air, intoxicating him.

He worked his hips in slow circles, grinding into her before breaking the rhythm with a hard thrust. Pleasure pooled in his balls and tightened the base of his shaft. He was close. Too close. A touch away from paradise.

He opened his mouth and cleared his throat, unable to speak. "How…close…"

"I'm coming," she panted, and her legs tightened around his hips.

Shit. He followed her over, without thought or feeling, and groaned her name as he came. She convulsed around him, her pussy clamping down, drawing out his pleasure. He closed his eyes as his mind blanked and his heart soared. There would never be anyone else for him. His heart had been claimed.

He rested his forehead against her shoulder, his chest expanding and falling with deep breaths. She kissed his jaw, her fingers loosening in his hair as her body went languid against his.

"I love you," she murmured, nuzzling his cheek.

He turned his face into her neck, nibbled the sensitive spot below her ear, and whispered, "It doesn't count."

Chapter Eleven

"Do I look all right?" Gabi asked for the third time as the elevator jerked to a stop. She was nervous. Beyond nervous. Earlier she'd been on a smexin' high, eager to meet the men of Reckless Beat, but now… What if Blake's friends didn't like her?

Oh, god. She was going to vomit.

"Gabi, you're gorgeous." Blake led her into the hall with an arm around her waist. "And they'll love you. Especially Leah and Alana."

He placed a kiss at her temple, the comforting action doing nothing to calm her nerves.

"But stay away from Mitch and Mason. They're likely to cause trouble."

"T-Trouble?" Her voice broke.

He chuckled, the vibrations of his chest echoing into her ribs. "You'll be fine. Just don't take any shit."

"Shit" she could handle. It was disapproval that worried her. What if they hated her? These people were his family.

"Stop worrying." He led them to a door and knocked loudly. "Be yourself and you'll be fine."

She nodded. No problem. She could do that.

The door opened and Mason Lynch stood before her, his greedy gaze taking her in from her black strappy sandals all the way up her three-quarter length pants, along her peach colored tank top to finally rest on her eyes. "Well, hello, foxy lady."

Her mouth gaped, and she had to concentrate to snap it closed. Mason Lynch. She swallowed hard, resting her hand on her stomach to calm the fluttering butterflies. Was there a correct way to respond to that type of greeting?

"Fuck off, Lynch." Blake chuckled.

Well, OK, apparently Blake knew how. He shoved Mason in the chest and pushed his way into the suite, dragging Gabi along beside him. "That was Mason," he offered. "Mason, this is Gabi."

"Yeah, nice introduction, bro," Mason called from behind them.

She glanced over her shoulder at the world famous singer, poised to apologize for Blake's rudeness, only to find Mason's gaze glued to her ass. The rumors about him were obviously true—he was sexy as sin and obnoxiously arrogant in equal measure.

"That's not my face," she mumbled and turned her attention back to the way they were walking.

"Wasn't interested in your face, honey, but if you wanted to put those sexy lips of yours around my—"

"Zip it, Lynch." Blake didn't slow his pace, he didn't even glare or raise his voice. "She isn't a groupie and doesn't need to be tested."

"Tested?" she squeaked.

Blake peered down at her, his expression blank. "To see if you'd leave me to go suck his—"

"To see if you were worthy," Mason finished, coming up beside her and placing an arm around her shoulders.

Again, Blake didn't flinch. He didn't appear fazed by Mason's nearness at all.

"My man deserves a great woman," Mason added. "Are you that great woman, Gabi?"

"Ahh," her mouth fell open again, her head turning from the gorgeous man to her left, to the gorgeous one on her right.

"She is." Blake squeezed her waist and winked at her.

She could've swooned if Mason didn't ruin the moment.

"I think that was your first PDA, man." His arm fell from around her shoulder. "I don't know if I should be horrified or happy for you."

They stopped and Blake glanced at his friend. "Be happy." He lowered his hand from her waist and entwined their fingers. "And now that I assume the first phase of your fucktardness is over, Mason, I'd like you to properly meet Gabi."

Gabi looked at Mason, a devilish smile still tilting his lips, only now it held humor, not arrogance. He inclined his head and held out his hand.

"Nice to meet you, Gabi." His smile was infectious, playful and entirely adorable.

"You, too."

Mason let go of her hand, the pretence of flirtation vanishing in an instant. "Come meet the others."

She nodded and began following him into the dining room when Blake tugged at her hand, stopping her.

"You OK?" he asked.

She turned into his body, thankful that he enveloped her in the security of his arms. "Yep."

"One down, six more to go," he spoke into her hair.

She suppressed a groan and followed him into the room edged with floor to ceiling windows. A woman in a tailored pant suit stood in the far corner, leaning against the glass, looking down at the Yarra River below. Underneath the white crystal chandelier in the center of the ceiling was a table surrounded by people—famous people—all of them chatting and laughing over plates of food, glasses of orange juice, and mugs of coffee.

"Gabi!" The feminine call was followed by a chair scrapping over the tile floor.

Gabi swallowed the panic drying her throat and tried not to show her surprise at the woman who hurried toward her. Blake dropped her hand as the green-eyed, dark haired beauty, embraced her in a quick hug.

"I'm sorry." The woman pulled back. "I'm Alana. Blake's told me so much about you."

He has?

"He has?" A masculine voice came from the table, followed by another scraping chair. "When the hell have you been talking to my woman?"

Mitchell Davies. Lead guitarist and rock legend strode forward, his hazel glare focused on Blake.

Blake shrugged, "Every time you leave the room, we start making out. It's become a habit."

Mitchell gave Blake the one finger salute, his handsome face contorting in a sneer. Then his gaze turned to Gabi, and she held her breath. His dark brown hair framed eyes that gleamed with contained amusement. Maybe she should be jealous or even a little offended at the way Blake teased Mitchell, but she knew this was their thing. Over the previous months, Blake had enjoyed sharing the stories of how he riled Mitch about his beautiful girlfriend. The way he recapped the stories always made her laugh. Seeing the play-by-play in person hadn't changed that.

"Hi, Gabi." He held out a hand, and she clasped it in her own, letting the gentle touch take away her nervousness.

"G'day."

These people were family. She could see it in the way they conversed with genuine smiles and the underlying communication that was exchanged beyond the words they spoke.

Mitch grinned at her. "If you ever feel compelled to find a better man, you know where to find me."

Gabi's mouth fell open. At the same time Alana's hand slapped Mitch's chest.

A feminine gasp came from the far end of the room. "Mitchell Davies! You need to shut your mouth," the other woman spoke.

Gabi turned to the blonde in the tailored suit as she pushed from the window and came toward them. She was professional and authoritative all in a cover model package. "Ignore him. He has foot in mouth disease. I'm Leah, their manager."

Gabi could only smile in greeting as Alana gave Mitch a death stare.

"What?" Mitch asked in a huff. "Oh, come on!" He threw his arms in the air. "How come Blake can say that shit, but I can't?"

"You do realize I was right beside you," Alana mumbled.

"Yeah, kinda awkward," a man with close cropped hair added from the table.

Sean? Gabi thought she recognized him as the band's drummer.

"Hey," he gave her a lazy wave. "Welcome to the drama."

"Drama, my fuckin' ass," Mitch snapped. "How come Blake can talk dirty to my girlfriend, but I can't say diddly squat to pay him back?"

"It's nice to see you too, Blake." Alana ignored her boyfriend and stepped forward, embracing Blake in a hug. "I missed you."

Gabi stood still, trying to blend into the wall. Her chest was heavy, trying to contain her laughter although she wasn't entirely sure if Mitch was playing along or genuinely offended.

"I bet you did, sweetheart," Blake purred and winked at Mitch over Alana's shoulder.

Mitch shook his head. "Are you fucking kidding me?" He turned to the table and addressed the others. "Why the hell doesn't he get roasted for saying that? Huh? You guys can shove your smart comments up your ass, 'cause I've had enough." He strode from the room in a huff.

Silence fell heavy between them. Then as soon as the front door slammed, Gabi watched everyone break out in hysterics.

"My poor baby," Alana cooed once the laughter died down. "You guys really have to stop picking on him."

"Us?" Another man asked—the only man Gabi hadn't been introduced to. He shook his head, his light brown, wavy hair shaking around his ears. "You're worse than Mason, with your offended woman routine. I honestly don't know how Mitch didn't see through that."

"'Cause he lurves me," Alana smirked and made her way back to her seat.

"That's Ryan." Blake leaned into her and pointed a lazy finger to the man with youthful blue eyes and a full beard of stubble. He seemed so young. Too young to be the only married man of the group.

Ryan jerked his head in greeting and smiled. "Nice to meet you, Gabi."

"You, too," she added.

A hand came to rest at the small of her back, relieving her tension and filling her with comfort.

"Do you want to sit down?" Blake spoke into her neck.

In front of all these people, as nervous as she was, the feel of his breath against her skin still aroused her. She ignored the tingle that started to form in her belly and nodded, nervously playing with her necklace as she followed him to the two vacant chairs beside Alana.

"Oh, that's exquisite. Where did you get it?" Alana focused on the edgy way Gabi played with the jewelry.

"Ah…umm," she stuttered, feeling the weight of more than one person's stare on her cleavage. "Blake gave it to me for my birthday." She dropped her hand and shuffled in her chair.

Alana's eyes flashed. "It's gorgeous."

"Thank you." The necklace had become more than just a gift. It gave her strength, made her feel loved, and once they were apart, it would be a constant reminder of their time spent together.

"Wow, Blake, you did a great job picking that out," Leah added. "What are the charms?"

Gabi held the necklace out from her chest, showing them each of the charms.

"She loves turtles," Blake added.

"And your ego added the guitar charms?" Mason laughed. "Nice way to mark your territory."

"Yeah," Blake shrugged. "A collar with the words 'property of Blake Kennedy' didn't seem appropriate, so I settled for this."

Gabi snorted and elbowed him in the ribs. He was different in front of his friends—more laid back. Happy. Or maybe this was another persona he hid his pain behind.

He chuckled and pulled her close to kiss her forehead. "You know I'm joking," he murmured in her ear, nuzzling the erogenous zone below her neck.

"Yeah, I know."

He inhaled, rubbing his nose along the patch of skin she'd sprayed with perfume. "Christ, Gabi, you smell delicious."

"Shh." She nudged him away. Had someone turned up the thermostat? Suddenly her top was clinging to her and her thighs were damp with sweat.

"Are you coming shopping with us?" Alana asked, pulling Gabi out of the lust haze.

She shot Blake a glance. "Umm, I don't know. Am I?" They didn't have much time together, and the thought of being away from him made her heart clench. These women were nice, welcoming, but they weren't who she was here for.

Please, Blake, tell them we have plans.

Blake clenched his jaw, reading the wordless plea in Gabi's eyes. He hadn't had time to tell her what needed to be done today. Well, that was a lie. He'd had plenty of time. Only whenever he went to tell her about Mitch's proposal, his cock took control and they ended up naked, in a tangle of arms and legs and lips.

She didn't know about dinner tonight or the formal dress code. Going shopping would allow her the time to pick out a cocktail dress while he went with the guys to get fitted for suits.

"Sorry, angel." He leaned in and placed a kiss at her temple. "Me and the guys have some stuff to take care of. We won't be long." The regret he felt echoed in her irises.

She gave him a fake smile and nodded. "No problem."

But it was. He wanted to be with her, all day, every day, without interruption or social interaction. Only he couldn't turn down the offer to help set up Mitch's proposal. The guy could fuck up a love letter let alone something this monumental.

"Where are you going?" She turned her attention back to Leah and Alana.

"I'm not sure," Alana frowned, "I can't remember what the concierge said—Church Street?"

"Chapel Street," Leah corrected, rubbing her hands together with glee. "I thought us ladies could get dressed up for dinner tonight."

"It would be great if you could come." Alana pushed back in her chair. "I better go check on Mitchell and see if he's OK."

Mason sniggered. "Yeah, as if you guys didn't plan that all along." He continued in a high pitched tone, *"I'll pretend to be offended and run back to our room like a little girl, then you can come after me in a few minutes. I'll be waiting in bed, nekkid and covered in baby oil."*

Alana raised a brow and pushed her chair in. "Frankly, I'm disgusted that you would even think such a thing." She turned her attention to Gabi, a smile pulling at the side of her lips. "Nice to meet you, Gabi, and I hope you'll come shopping with us." Inclining her head in farewell, her lips pressed tightly together, she turned on her toes to walk from the room.

"Oh, I'm so proud," Sean stared at the doorway in a whimsical manner. "Our boy's getting lucky. It feels like only yesterday he was spending all his time on his laptop, jerkin' off to porn… oh, wait," he focused on Blake with a smirk, "that was you."

The porn jokes never got old…for them anyway. It didn't matter that they now knew he'd been chatting with Gabi the whole time. To them it was always porn. Would always be porn—even when he was chatting to Gabi online in the future.

"What can I say," Blake shrugged, "your momma looks great on screen."

Gabi chuckled and the sweet noise made him smile. She would fit in perfectly with his friends. He could tell Mason and Mitch already liked her, Ryan would too—he got along with everyone, and Sean…was Sean. He wouldn't voice an opinion either way and always went with the group consensus.

"Help yourself to a late lunch," Leah offered, indicating the food across the table. "I'm going to get ready for the shopping spree." She pulled a business card out of her pocket and slid it across the table to Gabi. "We'll be leaving in an hour or so. Call or text me if you want to come. We'd love it if you joined us."

"Thank you." Gabi reached for the card and fingered the writing. "I'll definitely tag along. I'll need something to wear tonight."

A pang of regret hit Blake in the sternum. He discretely rubbed at the pressure and silently inhaled until his lungs were at full capacity. If this was the way he reacted to the thought of being away from her for an hour, how the hell was he going to feel tomorrow afternoon when she went home?

This wasn't good. He was in deep—bottom of the ocean, with a brick tied round his ankle—deep. And from the panic in Gabi's light blue eyes, he could tell she was right there beside him.

Chapter Twelve

GABI PULLED A black dress off the rack and sighed. It was breathtaking. Spaghetti straps, low neckline, boning through the heavily beaded corset that flowed into a willowy knee length skirt. Both Leah and Alana had already bought what they planned to wear tonight, five stores ago, and she was still fretting over the boutique store prices.

"That's divine," Alana said from over her shoulder. "It would look great on you, too. Even better in a lighter color because you have such beautifully tanned skin."

Gabi flipped over the price tag and winced. The beads must be crystal, the thread made of gold, and stitched together by princesses in the Middle East. "Holy shit."

"Don't look at the price," Leah demanded. "Blake's paying. And before you start arguing, remember that he'll be the one benefitting from seeing you in this. It'll be worth every penny."

Gabi *did* want to argue. He'd already spent too much money on her. First there was the ticket for the commercial flight from London to Australia, when he could've flown on their private jet days later. Her necklace, which she lazily caressed with her finger. Then the business class flights from Queensland to Melbourne. She would never be able to repay him.

"I shouldn't." She didn't want to take his money, no matter how generous he was.

Leah pulled out her phone and snapped a picture. "Give me a sec."

Her fingers typed with super speed.

"You'll regret it if you don't." Alana glanced at the price tag. "And it doesn't cost *that* much."

Gabi raised a brow.

"Well, OK, it might be a little pricey, but I'm sure Blake will get his money's worth."

Leah put her phone back in her pocket. "You know it has nothing to do with style and everything to do with how quick he'll want to get you out of it, right? And he *will* want to get you out of it. Consider it an enjoyable form of torture."

"Go try it on." Alana gently palmed Gabi's shoulder and pushed her in the direction of the fitting rooms. "If it doesn't look absolutely perfect, we won't push the issue. We have another ten blocks worth of stores we can visit."

Gabi groaned and trudged ahead, placing the dress on the changing room hook. There was no way she could buy a dress that cost more than a small African country. What if she spilled something on it?

A phone beeped in the distance as she pulled the curtain across and began undressing.

"Blake says," Leah called out, "If she doesn't buy the dress there will be no smexin' tonight."

Gabi laughed and pulled the dress over her head, straightening it down her thighs. Blake would never live up to that threat.

"I'm joking," Leah chuckled, "He said 'Tell her she deserves the dress, and I can't wait to see her in it.' He then said, 'tell her I love her and to hurry up and get back to the motel.'"

Gabi scoffed and pulled the curtain across. "He did not." Blake was sweet, unbelievably so, however, she couldn't picture him telling his band manager to pass on a love filled message.

Alana gasped and Leah stepped closer.

"You look stunning," Leah said and handed her the phone. "Check if you don't believe me."

She took the phone and read the message on the screen. *Tell her she deserves the dress & I can't wait to c her in it. And tell her I love her…and get her to hurry up and get back to the motel. I've got needs. ;)*

The phone beeped in her hand and another message popped up underneath the last one.

If she still refuses to get the dress, ask the shop assistant to put it behind the counter and I'll pick it up myself. I want that dress, Leah.

Tingles wracked her body from her toes to her nipples. She no longer cared what they did with the dress. She just wanted to get back to the hotel and shower Blake with appreciation. How was she going to live without him when she went back to Queensland? It turned her stomach, clenched at her heart, and made tears well in her eyes.

"Fine. I'll get it, but let me try the cream one on first."

"I'll get it for you." Leah strode away.

"Blake is going to flip when he sees you in this," Alana's eyes gleamed. "You guys are so great together. He's so sweet and funny and passionate."

An unwanted weight of jealousy settled on Gabi's shoulders. The "sweet" and "funny" she could handle, but "passionate" spoke of intimacy. An intimacy Gabi didn't want to know about. Her insecurities must have shown in her expression because Alana stiffened and her throat convulsed with a swallow.

"I'm sorry, that came out wrong." The top of Alana's cheeks darkened.

Gabi didn't want to ask. She shouldn't ask. Her heart couldn't handle her asking. "Have you…two…umm."

Awkward didn't come close to describing the air between them, but she needed to know the answer. No other man had made this uncomfortable nagging sensation crawl under her skin. Or she'd never cared enough for anyone to be affected by it.

Alana glanced away, her gaze searching for Leah.

"You have." The words staggered from Gabi's mouth. The apprehension in her stomach turned to lead, and she sucked air into her lungs to fight off the evilness trying to take over. Alana was beautiful, probably the sweetest person Gabi had ever met…and funny. The perfect package. It didn't matter that her love for Mitch was evident in the way she spoke about him, or that Gabi trusted Blake without question. It was simply unjustified insecurity.

"I'm sorry." Gabi shook her head, needing to dislodge the stupidity. She didn't *do* jealousy. She never had, and it wasn't time to start now. "It's none of my business."

"No, we haven't… I haven't… There was this one time—"

Gabi held up her hands in the universal please-don't-fucking-go-there sign and backed into the fitting room. "Seriously, none of my business." And it wasn't. What Blake did before they hooked up had nothing to do with her.

She pulled the curtain closed on Alana's pained expression and leaned back against the wall. *Get control of your hormones, woman!* She had no right to be upset over this.

Seconds later the curtain yanked open and Leah stood in the doorway, brows downcast. "What's going on?" She placed the cream evening gown on the wall hook and stepped back, her gaze darting between Gabi and Alana.

"Nothing." Gabi shook her head, embarrassment warming her cheeks. This was ridiculous.

Alana stepped forward, her eyes soft with apology. "It was a misunderstanding."

"About?" Leah asked.

Alana looked straight at Gabi. "Blake has been present on one occasion when Mitchell and I…"

Leah cleared her throat, smothering a laugh, and Alana shot her a filthy glance.

"He watched…" Alana continued.

Curiosity had Gabi asking questions when she should've kept her mouth shut. "He watched?" A giggle broke the awkwardness. Her giggle. "I can't imagine Blake just watching."

Alana's throat convulsed. "Well, he kept himself…busy, I suppose you could say."

Leah snorted. "Sorry. Didn't mean to ruin the moment."

"As I was saying, he enjoyed himself, while Mitchell and I…"

"Fucked," Leah blurted. "For god sake, woman, spit it out!"

Alana crossed her arms over her chest and raised her chin. "Fine. We were *fucking* while Blake watched." She turned her attention back to Gabi. "But he's never touched me in a sexual way. Ever. I promise you. Mitchell is too possessive to allow it."

Obviously not possessive enough to stop someone else from watching. "Wow. I didn't see that coming." From her experiences between the sheets with Blake, he didn't seem restrained enough to simply watch. He was sexual and voracious and eager. She couldn't picture him not being in charge.

Leah sniggered. "I bet Alana did."

Gabi laughed without thought, and then winced. She had so much to learn about the rock star lifestyle.

"Don't worry." Leah squeezed her upper arm. "The Reckless guys aren't really into the twenty-four-seven sexathon anymore. I know Sean and Mason share women every now and again, but they're timid in comparison to some of the bands I've represented.

They get a lot of offers and when single, they do enjoy their playboy ways. I'm sure all of them are capable of monogamy, though. Well, maybe not Mason. I'm still undecided on whether that boy can keep his dick in his pants for longer than it takes to play a full set."

Alana stepped forward and leaned against the fitting room wall. "Blake loves you, and he'd never do anything to hurt you."

"I know," Gabi replied, focusing her attention on the evening dress. Trust wasn't the issue. It was plain stupidity. Nothing more. "I was shocked, that's all." She smiled, trying to show her apology. "Sorry for worrying you."

Alana pushed from the wall and embraced Gabi in a hug. "OK. It's all finished and forgotten." She pulled back. "Now all we have to do is convince you to let Blake buy this gorgeous dress."

Blake sat in a sofa chair, staring out the window. He'd spent an hour with the guys, under heavy security guard, organizing tuxedos for them to wear tonight.

An hour.

The women had been gone for three and still they weren't back. Five men fitted and sorted in one hour. Three women who would look flawless no matter what they wore and three hours wasn't enough.

His cell buzzed in his pocket. Again. This time it was short and sharp, announcing a text message. His heart played giddy-up thinking it might be Gabi until he remembered the voice message Michelle left earlier today and dread entered the mix. He only listened to the first frantic words of "Blake I need—" before he deleted the message, but it still made him skittish to check his own fucking phone. He needed to change his number.

He was sick to death of changing his number.

Praying for another picture update from Leah, he unlocked his screen and opened the message. His stomach hollowed and his legs would've buckled if he'd been standing.

This definitely wasn't an update from Leah. Nope. This came from a private number and without reading the text underneath the image, he knew it came from Michelle.

He stared at the picture of himself, his throat tightening with every passing second. The secrets of his past were on the screen before him. He was on his knees before a glass table lined with white powder, shirtless, his pupils dilated and crazy as his hand sat at the corner of his nose about to wipe away the coke lining his nostrils.

"Fuck. Fuck. Fuck. Fuck."

You have two options. Either help me or I will have to sell this image along with many more to the tabloids. I'm sorry, Blake, I really need the money.

His brain packed up and left the building, leaving him in a shaking, panicked mess. Leah would kill him. Mason would boot him from the band—if their record label didn't do it first. Mitch would look at him with disappointment and disapproval, and Gabi... *Oh, fuck.* He was going to lose Gabi during the tabloid manhunt.

What do you want from me? His hands trembled as he typed the message and pressed send. Maybe if he paid her off she would leave him alone.

Christ. He pushed from his chair and began to pace. He wasn't that naive. Michelle must be desperate if she was willing to blackmail him in the early hours of the US morning. He'd bargain, he'd beg, he'd do whatever he had to in the effort to destroy those pictures.

He released a derisive laugh and rubbed the back of his neck, trying to alleviate the ache. Yeah, bargain with a determined drug addict who had every fucking ball in her court. Michelle had nothing to lose. No money, a tattered career, her reputation was in the gutter, and her billionaire father wanted nothing to do with her.

A noise sounded at the front of the suite, sending a thousand volts through his heart. *Fuck.* He wiped the sweat from his forehead and turned his attention to the hall, listening as the door opened. Gabi's heels clicked on the tile, and he breathed like a woman in labor, trying to calm himself until she came into view.

He couldn't tell her. Not now. Not so close to the anniversary of her brother's death.

"Hello, stranger." She beamed at him, dumping her bags on the lounge before sauntering toward him. "Did you miss me?"

He ignored the way his chest throbbed and shoved his cell into his pocket, bridging the distance between them in two steps.

"What's wrong?" She placed her hands on his chest and studied his face.

"I missed you." He kissed her, hard, stopping her from scrutinizing him further. His chest weighed heavy with regret while their tongues tangled and her hands came around his neck. He held her close, battling the guilt that overwhelmed him, knowing he was going to hurt her, worry her, no matter how this ended.

She pulled back and stared into his eyes. "Is everything all right?"

"Sure is. Let me see your dress." He made a grab for the bags on the couch, needing to place distance between them.

"Hey!" She swatted him away. "You aren't allowed to see until tonight." Grabbing the bags, she clutched them to her chest and strode to the bedroom. "What time is dinner so I know when to start getting ready?"

He breathed a silent sigh of relief and glanced at his watch. "We have an hour or so."

"What?" She turned on her heel. "An hour? I thought we were going for dinner. It's only four-thirty."

His phone buzzed in his pocket and he closed his eyes for a brief second to pray that it was a message from Leah or Mitch or even Mason. "Mitch has a surprise planned for Alana tonight."

Gabi gasped and began walking back toward him with a spring in her step. "What is it?" Her eyes were alight with anticipation.

"He's going to propose."

She squealed and bounced on her toes. The reaction was so girlie and cute that for a split second his troubles vanished.

"How's he going to do it? At dinner? Are we all going to be there?"

He shook his head. "No and yes, that's why we need to get ready early. We're taking a scenic helicopter flight down the coast. Then having dinner at a private property overlooking the ocean."

Gabi's eyes widened, and she pulled a teeth-clenching expression of excitement that made him chuckle. "I better get ready." She reached on the pads of her feet to place a smacking kiss on his lips and bounced from the room.

When the shower started, he released the breath tightening his chest, and then remembered the unread message on his phone. He retrieved the cell from his pocket, his stomach turning in dread.

I need money and help to get me out of the slump I'm in. Call me.

She listed a number at the bottom of the message.

At least she was an optimist. He would consider her problems far from a "slump". More like a permanent vacation in the gutter. Her outlook could only work in his favor. If she was delusional, maybe things wouldn't be so bad. He could give her the money and convince her to hand over the photos or sign a legal agreement to have them permanently deleted.

"Fuck!" He clenched his fists. He would never truly know what she'd done with the images, no matter what agreement he made her sign.

He bowed his head. Again he was on his own. No one to turn to. No one to rely on. And this time he was determined to keep Gabi out of it. He wouldn't hurt her with this, and besides, no woman could ever respect a man she had to keep saving. It was time to fix this once and for all—on his own.

Striding into the bedroom, he yanked his suit from the closet and grabbed his shoes. He needed space to think and a quiet place where he could call Michelle without being overheard. With a deep breath, he opened the bathroom door and paused. Gabi stood under the shower spray, her flawless curves glistening from the overhead lights.

She turned with a grin. "Are you joining me again?"

He shook his head when words failed him. It was a sign—having Michelle contact him now. A sign that Gabi was above his worth and didn't need to be dragged into his crap.

"I wish, angel." He smiled, hoping to curb her intuition until he left. "I'm going to get dressed, then step out for a while. I've got a few things I need to organize before tonight." It was the truth. He needed to organize the gigantic mess called—his life.

"Oh." Her brow furrowed. "OK. When will you be back?"

"I shouldn't be too long." He clutched the door handle, hating himself for hiding things from her. "When you're ready, send me a message, and I'll come get you."

"No worries." She nodded slowly. "Are you sure everything's all right?"

He turned to leave the room, needing to shield his face from her gaze. "Yeah. Everything's going to be fine."

A knife sliced through his chest, knowing he just lied to the woman he loved. *Everything* wouldn't be fine. In fact, his mind kept chanting that this was the beginning of the end.

Chapter Thirteen

BLAKE SAT ON a lounge chair in the far corner of the empty VIP room on the third floor of the hotel, staring blankly at Michelle's phone number on his cell screen. He'd been doing the same thing for the last fifteen minutes, unable to connect the call.

At the moment, he could convince himself that things would work out. He could give her whatever money she needed—he'd never had an attachment to the stuff anyway—and in return he would demand to have every image of him she possessed. Easy enough, right?

A middle-aged couple walked into his periphery, taking a seat by the windows. *Shit.* He bowed his head and sunk further into his chair. He was running out of time. The last forty-five minutes hadn't been mentally productive. There'd been a shitload of wallowing in self-loathing while he fought the basic instinct to run and hide. Now he had no choice. He had to do this.

With a deep breath he connected the call and tried to ignore the way his chest tightened with each ring.

"Blake?" Michelle's voice was rough, from sleep or drugs he didn't know and didn't care.

"How much do you want?" He didn't have the stomach for pleasantries.

"It's not just about the money—"

"How much, Michelle?"

"F-forty grand." Her tone held a hint of remorse that he chose to ignore.

"Done." Forty thousand dollars wouldn't hurt his bank account. If that was what it took to rid him of the past, he would hand it over without reluctance. "I want all the photos. Everything you have on me. I don't care what it is, I want it. CD's, clothes, everything. Once I pay you the money, that's it Michelle. I want you out of my life."

She cleared her throat. "The money isn't all I need, Blake."

He clenched his teeth. He'd been on a roll, making demands and growing confident while she remained quiet. "What else?"

"I need…I need to pull my life together. I need you to help me."

"How the fuck do I do that?" He pushed to his feet and ignored the stares from staff and entering guests. He was about to lose his shit. His shoes were too tight, the formal suit and tie weighing him down, choking him, making him yank at the collar.

"I want to get my career back on track so I can look after myself in the future. I need to be in the public eye so producers will be willing to hire me again."

"No." He didn't need to hear anymore. The direction of the conversation was becoming too dangerous.

"That's the deal, Blake—the money as well as your help. You'd only need to pretend we were dating for a little while. A few months max, just until people start taking notice of me again."

No. Hell-to-the-fucking-no. "I can't do it." There was no way.

"Then I have no choice but to sell the photos. The gossip magazines will give me what I need. Both money and a temporary spotlight."

Blake clenched the phone, squeezing so hard his knuckles hurt. "Don't do this to me, Michelle. I've got a good thing going here. My life's on track." *After you helped me fuck it up.* "I can't help you like that. I'll give you more money. Eighty grand, a hundred. I don't care. Just don't blackball me with having to be around you again. I can't do it."

She gave a derisive laugh. "You can't be around me? As if you didn't enjoy yourself when we were? I didn't force you to do anything, Blake. In fact, I seem to remember you being more than eager to please me back then."

"Things change," he grated, raking his fingers through his hair.

"Well things are going to go back to the way they were. For the sake of the public, anyway. You'll take me to social events and help me build a new name for myself. Once I'm back on my feet, you can have your stupid photos."

This was worse than money. Worse than having his bank accounts wiped clean. This would hurt Gabi, and the thought of doing that made a little piece of his soul die. "I can't do it," he whispered to himself.

This couldn't be happening. He'd been so close to heaven. His love for Gabi had cemented itself in his soul. She mentioned moving to the US to be with him, which was more than he deserved, yet he'd been excited. Now all of his hopes for the future were crumpling. His life was nose-diving with no way to pull up.

"Fine. Good luck with the backlash—"

"Wait!" What choice did he have? Maybe, he could make a few calls and get her a job before he finished the Australian tour. Then he wouldn't have to see her at all. Yes. That's what he could do. He'd call in some favors. Make sure she had an acting position, then things would be over and done with. For good.

"I'll help you get a job, Michelle, and I'll give you the money. But you'll have to wait until I get back in the US and speak to an attorney. I won't let you blackmail me again after this."

His phone released a muted beep, announcing an incoming message. Gabi must be looking for him.

"Whatever. Just be aware that I know when your tour finishes, and I expect to see you a few days later. I need that money."

Yeah. He bet she did.

"And I expect you to stop hounding me until then," he snarled. "No more calling or messaging. Leave me the fuck alone until I get back to New York."

"Deal."

His chest hollowed at the word. Caving in under her threats only endeavored to increase his self-loathing. He was so weak it made bile rise in his throat. Without a goodbye, he ended the call and strode from the VIP lounge.

Now he had to figure out how he was going to live with himself once he told another lie to the woman he loved.

Gabi touched up her eye shadow and ran her hands down the cream material of her dress to stop herself from hovering over her phone. Blake had been gone for almost an hour, without a word. He hadn't even replied to her text message.

A knock sounded at the door and her stomach flipped, hoping it was him. She padded across the tile in bare feet, making it half way down the hall before she realized he had his own key and didn't need to knock. Curious, she peered through the peep hole to find Mason, Sean and Ryan.

Where was Blake?

She opened the door and tried not to ogle. They were gorgeous. All immaculately dressed in black suit and tie, their hair done and faces clean shaven. Even Ryan.

"Hawt dayum, woman. You're smokin'." Mason jerked back in shock. "How the hell did you end up with Blake instead of me?"

She smiled and raised her brows. "Because Blake has a subtle way of complimenting a woman that makes her feel beautiful. Whereas your approach leaves a skanky aftertaste."

Mason's eyes gleamed with laughter and Sean sniggered, resting his shoulder against the wall beside the door.

"You look stunning, Gabi." Ryan inclined his head with a soft smile. "Are you guys good to go? The others are downstairs making sure the limo's ready."

"Ah." Gabi swallowed down the anxiety that started to bubble. "I thought Blake would be with you. He left about an hour ago and said he had things to organize."

The men frowned and glanced at one another.

"I sent him a message over five minutes ago, but he hasn't replied to that either," she added.

Sean pushed from the wall and grabbed his cell out of his pants pocket. "I'll call him."

"You might want to get your shoes," Ryan spoke softly. "We're going to be late if we don't find him soon."

She nodded and let Mason hold the door open as she rushed to the bedroom. She grabbed her purse and her cobalt-blue high-heels by the ankle strap and strode back to sit on the couch.

"He's not answering," Sean mumbled. "What are we gonna do?"

The ding of the hotel elevator echoed into the suite. Gabi tilted her head to listen as she reached for her purse and stood.

"Where the fuck have you been?" Mason barked.

"Bangin' your mom," Blake replied.

Gabi let out a relieved breath and walked from the living room toward the front door. She entered the tile hallway, her heels clicking with each step as Blake strode into the suite and came to an abrupt halt.

He took her breath away.

He was transformed, all his bad-assness covered under the formal attire, yet nothing could hide the hungry gleam in his eyes. The suits made the other men look suave and confident. With Blake it was the opposite. He owned the outfit, working it with easy sophistication.

The mere sight dried her mouth. He blinked at her, his gaze roaming from the strappy blue high-heels, over her dress, to her face and all the way back down again.

"Wow." He stepped forward, his eyes wide with admiration. "Just… Wow." He wrapped an arm around her waist and pulled her against his body. "You're stunning."

"You're looking mighty dapper yourself." And his scent was divine, taunting her to lick the hollow at the base of his neck.

He placed a gentle kiss on her lips, then pulled back to run a finger along the top of her bodice, rustling the charms on her necklace. "You're dressed in white."

"Cream," she clarified and narrowed her gaze on his face. He seemed different, and it had nothing to do with what he wore. His skin was pale, his eyes skittish, and his jaw tense.

"You look like…" He glanced down at his suit. "*We* look like…" He shook his head in dismissal.

"We've gotta go, buddy," Ryan spoke from the door.

Blake kept staring at her. "Just give us a minute. We'll meet you in the lobby."

His lips thinned into a tight line, the seriousness in his expression making her heart stutter.

"I know you're quick, Emo," Mason called down the hall, "But we still don't have time for your thirty second marathon. We're gonna be late."

Gabi pressed her lips together, struggling not to smile.

"Fine, pretty-boy, go get the elevator and we'll be there in a sec," Blake muttered.

He pulled her down to the couch so they sat side by side. Their fingers entwined, their thighs touched while the happiness faded from his features.

"What's wrong?"

He peered over his shoulder and waited for the suite door to click shut. "I need you to trust me."

Her chest filled with butterflies, their movements pounding like falcons' wings in her lungs. There was nothing playful about his statement. Something had happened. Something important. "About what?"

He glanced at their hands and his Adam's apple bobbed. Now they were close and the surprise at seeing him had faded, she noticed the fine sheen of sweat on his forehead.

"Something's happened, and I need you to trust me to do the right thing."

She frowned and shook her head in confusion. "I've always trusted you."

"I know. But this time I want to handle things on my own. I can't involve you."

A shiver ran down her spine and spread through her limbs. "Blake, you're scaring me."

"Christ, Gabi, I'm sorry. That wasn't my intention. I just couldn't keep this from you. I also can't drag you into it." He made eye contact, and the dark brown of his eyes pierced her with apology.

"Why? I don't understand. Is it drugs? Is that why you don't want to tell me?" She was rambling, her mouth voicing all the random thoughts that shot into her head.

"No. God, no." He squeezed her hands. "My stance on drugs will never change. You're the only high I need, Gabi. But this is something I want to do for myself, without the help of you or the band."

The front door thundered from someone's fist. "Hurry the hell up."

Blake growled, his eyebrows closing together in a tight frown. "I promise that you have nothing to worry about. I'll sort it out. I just don't want to feel like I'm hiding anything from you."

"Right…because telling me you're withholding secrets is entirely different than hiding things from me," she whispered and turned her attention to her shiny shoes.

"Gabi." Blake's hand came to her chin, dragging her gaze back to him. "I always want to be honest with you." He let out a defeated sigh. "I just… *damn it!* I shouldn't have said anything." He closed his eyes and massaged his forehead.

Gabi was beginning to wish the same thing.

"Blake!" Mason shouted.

Christ. She knew from experience that new relationships were often filled with turmoil, however, this was ridiculous. "We better go." She stood on numb feet, wanting to distance herself from whatever the hell that evasive conversation was about.

Blake followed her to her feet and tugged on her hand, bringing her body into his. "You mean the world to me, angel, you know that don't you?"

She nodded, half-heartedly. She knew it, or had known it until a few moments ago.

"Thank you." His low voice was rough.

"What for?"

"For not pushing."

Gabi moved closer, placing a chaste kiss on his lips. "I never want you to keep things from me, and I hope one day soon you'll tell me what all this is about. But for now, I just want you to know I'm here if you need me."

What else could she say? She could tell he was hurting, had noticed something wasn't right when she came back from shopping. She would never push him to tell his secrets, though. Their lips met, and his hand came to rest at the top of her neck, possessively holding her close. He kissed her with intensity, like the world was crumpling around them, and she clung to him, needing the reassurance of his passion.

"You two better not be fucking!" Mason yelled.

Blake's chest rumbled, and Gabi broke away with a laugh. "Come on. We better hurry." She grabbed her purse off the couch, and they rushed from the suite.

"Nice of you to join us," Mason muttered, striding forward to the elevator that Sean held open.

The suite door shut with a bang as Gabi and Blake walked hand in hand into the elevator. Blake leaned against the side wall, pulling her into his side, while Ryan and Sean rested against the back wall and Mason stood poised at the buttons.

"Everything OK?" Ryan asked.

"Apart from Blake being unable to keep his dick in his pants when we're in a hurry?" Mason growled.

Blake squeezed her fingers gently as he glanced down at her. There was a storm of emotion erupting in the dark brown depths. The hurt emanating from him sank under her skin, gnawing at her from the inside out. She wanted to beg him to let her in, but she wouldn't. He didn't owe her a free pass to all his troubles. He was entitled to his secrets.

"Angel, have I ever told you about the time Mason took a walk on the bi-side?"

"Oh, fuck off." Mason snapped and whacked his hand across the lobby button.

The misery left Blake's eyes. He was hiding again, masking his pain behind a cocky smirk and the arrogant tilt of his head.

"No, sweetheart." She smiled, continuing the pretense that everything was apples. "What do you mean?" It was a flat-out lie. He'd told her the story months ago, but enabling him to make fun of Mason would lighten the mood.

"Well, we were at an after party for the release of our last album, and Mason starts hitting up a hottie in a red, low-cut dress at the bar."

"You're really going to tell that story?" Mason asked, glaring. "After all the shit I have on you?"

Sean sniggered and Blake didn't pause. "The two of them hit it off and end up disappearing. Half an hour later I find pretty-boy here in the bathrooms, slumped over a toilet, puking his guts up."

Gabi smothered a laugh behind her purse-filled hand.

"Turns out the hottie had more than a nice rack. Didn't he, Mace?"

"Suck my dick," Mason snarled.

"You're not my type," Blake bit back. "And besides, I think the moral of the story is that you don't like your pole smoked by a guy."

Ryan shook his head. "It never ends, Gabi. They'll go on like this all night long until Mason concedes defeat or starts sulking."

The elevator jolted to a stop and the doors slid open. She walked into the lobby beside Blake, her heels clicking with each step. She spotted Alana and Mitch hiding in an alcove beside the reception desk, body to body, staring into each other's eyes, oblivious to the attention from guests who strode past.

In a burst of noise, screams erupted from outside, startling her, almost sending her stiletto heels flying out from underneath her. Then the cameras started, flashing in a fury of blinking light.

"Bloody hell," she gasped and huddled into Blake's waiting arms, hiding her face from view. The thought of fans and paparazzi had slipped her mind. Entirely. And no, she wasn't thick, she had anticipated the first class flights, chauffeured cars, expensive suites, and screaming, crazy people. However, being here and experiencing it firsthand was…overwhelming. Especially when Blake's presence had gone unnoticed to most of the Australian public until now.

"Mason and Mitch can't go anywhere without a tail," Blake murmured into her ear. "We've got those guys, though, so don't worry." He pointed to a team of six burly men standing next to the reception desk. Their attention was focused on Leah who stood before them, her chin high and her expression confident as she rocked a skin-tight, mauve dress with sparkling silver shoes. The material hung low on her back, showing a mass of flawless, soft tanned skin, while her stiletto heels emphasized her calf muscles.

"Damn, is it wrong to want to tap that?" Sean asked, and then pierced the air with a wolf whistle.

"Yes," Mason and Blake replied in unison.

Leah peered over her shoulder, fixing Sean with a cheeky glare before turning back to the security detail. Moments later, they disbanded and Leah strode toward them, the hem of her dress sticking to her toned thighs. Mitch and Alana followed, bringing them all together in the middle of the lobby, causing the crowd outside to burst into another mass of screams.

"Let's do this." Leah smiled and discreetly winked at Mitch who gave a jerky nod.

Three security guards led the way, holding open the glass doors to let the delirious noise enter the building. Outside, metal barriers held back the crowd, making a path toward a stretch limo with the back door open and waiting.

"Are you OK?" Blake paused in the middle of the lobby and squeezed her hand.

She nodded, even though nervous tension wracked her body. People were everywhere, waving their arms, bouncing up and down, becoming louder with hysteria. And the flashing, god, the flashing of cameras was driving her nuts.

"You're shaking." Blake raised his voice over the screaming crowd.

"I'm fine." She smiled and held her breath as he led her outside. The noise grew, the mixed chanting of the guys' names echoing all around them. Someone shouted for Blake, and he turned into her body to glance over her shoulder. He smiled, gave a lazy wave, all the while holding her close, protecting her. She followed his line of sight, stopping at a group of women who squealed in excitement.

An uncharacteristic spark of unease siphoned the adrenaline in her veins, replacing it with something cloying and weak. Bloody hell, there was a river of cleavage before her, undoubtedly tempting to even the strongest man.

"Stop thinking whatever you're thinking," Blake spoke against her cheek before placing a fleeting kiss on her lips. "I love you."

Camera flashes bathed them in a bright white glow while gasps and screams and cries answered to the public display of affection. It was a declaration, a statement to his fans and admirers—I'm taken. Reporters with notepads shouted questions at their backs, while they continued to the limo and waited for the others to climb inside.

"After you, milady." Blake waved his hand forward, ignoring the mass of people vying for his attention, and devoured her with his gaze.

For a moment, she stared, transfixed by crazy love and wonder. What a man. What a gorgeous, talented, sweet and funny and caring man. There was no use. She was lost to him. Forever.

Dipping her head, she slid along the back seat to the far wall. *Holy shit.* The interior of the limo was huge. Deceptively so, and once Blake slid along beside her and a security guard closed the door, it was a whole heap quieter too.

Pink, white, and purple lights marked out an aisle on the floor and along the bar running down one side of the vehicle. Mason, Ryan, Sean, and Leah sat along the seats opposite the bar, helping themselves to the liquor, while Alana and Mitchell sat at the far end wall, snuggled against one another.

Leah leaned forward from her position at the closest end of the wall seat and mouthed Gabi's name. "Did Blake fill you in on what's happening?" she whispered.

Gabi glanced at Alana who was currently occupied by Mitch's mouth, before nodding. "Yeah. Do you need me to do anything?"

Leah sat back and shook her head. "It's all under control. Well, until he—" she jerked her head in Mitch's direction, "—screws it up, anyway. It's inevitable."

"You never know, he might surprise you."

"That's what I'm praying for." Leah smiled. "And didn't I say you'd look fabulous in that dress?" Her smile turned into a saucy grin. "I bet Blake loves it."

"Blake does love it," he replied, sliding closer to Gabi so they were touching, and rested his hand on her thigh "He loves it very much. He'd love it even more on the floor of our bedroom."

Gabi crossed her legs and clenched her thighs together to ward off her arousal. His idea made warmth spread through her nipples, and the slide of his palm along the soft material of her dress sent a potent wave of goose bumps over her flesh.

Leah chuckled. "OK. OK. That's enough. Don't scandalize my virginal ears, or eyes for that matter."

Blake leaned into Gabi, grazing his teeth along her earlobe as his hand rose higher on her leg. Her pussy clenched, needy and persistent. They weren't alone, and still, her body screamed for her to crawl on top of him and take him, right here, right now.

Leah cleared her throat, and his palm paused at the top of Gabi's thigh.

"You need to stop," Gabi murmured under her breath. Her body wasn't equipped to handle the sudden spikes of adrenaline, anxiety, and arousal. Underneath her ribs, her heart palpitated, threatening to burst from her chest.

She needed a distraction.

"Where were you?" she asked, tilting her head to look him in the eye. "When I was getting ready, where did you go?" It was a diversion tactic.

One she should've thought through. She didn't mean to pry. She only wanted to get her mind off stripping him of every article of clothing to see the bare, tattooed man underneath.

He stared at her, his brows pulling together slightly. "I needed space to think." His hand slid from her leg, placing a field of distance between them.

"I didn't mean to poke my nose into your business."

Talk about a one-eighty. Her insides felt shredded from whiplash.

Blake didn't respond. He sat there, his expression turning to concern, or maybe he was anxious, she wasn't sure. They'd been open and honest for years, and although she promised she was all right with his secrecy, the thought of him keeping something from her now, when they were face to face, hurt like hell. She knew the darkness in his life, knew his fears, and had helped him through his weakest moments. Yet now, he had something to hide from her?

She shook her head. No. She was being selfish. The last thing Blake needed to do was placate her insecurities.

His breath brushed her neck, making her betraying body burst into tingles. "I went to the VIP area on the third floor so I could think without worrying you."

She pressed her lips together and nodded, not meeting his gaze. "OK."

"No," he spoke softly, gripping her chin and softly guiding her attention back to him. "You've been my protector for years. You've fought my battles, dealt with my demons, and been the one to keep me strong." The firm line of his lips and intense gaze brooked no argument. "I want to stand on my own two feet for once. I want to fight my own battles and prove to myself that I'm not weak anymore." He stroked a hand through the hair at her cheek, his gaze following the movement as he placed it behind her ear. "Everything's fine, angel. You don't need to worry."

She grabbed his hand, resting her cheek into his palm briefly before bringing it to her lap. "I really didn't mean to pry." She leaned into his shoulder. "You were making me…*hot*, so I asked the first question that popped into my mind to distract you from your little game."

He chuckled. "Well you should be proud, because it worked."

She winced. "I'm sorry." Why couldn't they find a balance? They were either on a high or on a low. There was no in between. Maybe this was what life with a famous rock star would be like—never-ending drama and excitement.

He placed a soft kiss on her lips, stealing her breath with his tenderness. "You never, ever need to be sorry for caring about me. I appreciate your concern more than you'll ever know. It's because of you that I can now stand on my own two feet."

The corner of his lips lifted in a grin, and he leaned in again, placing his mouth against hers. His tongue licked across her lips, demanding entrance to devour her completely. A hand moved into her hair, clutching, until she was at his mercy, while his other hand, *oh, his other hand*, slid up her leg, to the apex of her thighs.

Leah cleared her throat, loud, startling Gabi from her fast descent into slutty whore-ishness. She pushed at the hardness of Blake's chest, breaking the scorching connection.

He chuckled, releasing his dominant hands and sat back in his chair. "Leah, you're no fun."

"Don't worry, Blake," Mason called from the other end of the limo, raising his scotch glass in salute. "I enjoyed the show."

Heat crept into Gabi's cheeks. She didn't blush. She rarely got embarrassed. So why all of a sudden was she feeling like a teenager? *Oh, yeah, probably because she was acting like a hormonal adolescent.*

"I think I even glimpsed a slice of tiny, white panties."

Gabi groaned and focused out the window. They were teenagers trapped in the bodies of men, she was sure of it.

Chapter Fourteen

BLAKE STARED OUT the limousine window as it pulled up at a small airport—a different one from where they landed yesterday.

"Damn it," Leah mumbled and scooted to the door. "OK, guys. We've got a crowd."

Gabi flinched beside him.

He placed a comforting arm around her shoulder, holding her tight. "Were we followed?"

"Not sure. The company we're flying with could've told a few friends who told a few more friends. It happens all the time."

She had nothing to worry about. Their security detail would be out there, in front or behind the limo. It wouldn't take long for them to control the small group of people gathered at the fence leading to the tarmac.

"We're stopping here?" Alana asked, turning her wide eyes to Mitch. "I thought we were going out for an early dinner."

"We are," Leah interrupted. "We're just going someplace special. I thought it would be a nice surprise."

"We're catching another plane?" Alana's gaze darted around the faces in the limo, and one by one, everyone focused somewhere else—on the floor, out the window, at the ceiling.

"Helicopter, sweetheart," Mitch answered, his voice lacking the nervousness Blake would've expected.

"You knew?" Her voice rose in excitement.

Mitch cleared his throat and shrugged. "Leah mentioned it, but I wasn't really listening."

Alana slapped him playfully on the chest, turning her focus out the window to the ocean blue helicopter standing in the middle of the empty tarmac.

"I'm going to hop out and see if they're ready for us to leave." Leah opened her door, setting off the screaming fans.

Their security detail moved to stand broad-chested around the vehicle. One of the guards leaned into the open door, offering his hand to Leah, and closing it as soon as she climbed out. Together, they strode to the nearest building and walked in through the automatic glass doors.

"Don't fret, angel." Blake kissed Gabi's hair, inhaling the sweet floral scent. He couldn't help acknowledging that he enjoyed seeing her like this, needing his guidance and reassurance for once. It chipped away a piece of his self-loathing to finally feel needed instead of needy.

Minutes later, Leah strode back to the limo, opening the door briefly before sliding back in. "They're ready to go."

The *whoop whoop* of propeller blades reiterated her statement, the noise growing faster with every second.

"Let's get this party started." Sean scooted along the wall seat, down to Leah. "Lead the way, gorgeous."

Leah quirked a brow. "One word—inappropriate."

He grinned back, unapologetic.

"I'll get out first," Blake spoke to Gabi, "and you can follow straight after."

She nodded. The door opened again and they slid along the seat, moving from the quiet interior of the limo to the rush of noise outside. The wind blew, spurred faster by the spin of the rotor blades while the small group of fans began to chant. The cacophony grew as Gabi moved to her feet and Mason came out from behind her.

"Oh, my gosh," Gabi winced. "This is crazy."

Crazy, yes. But an everyday occurrence when they toured or travelled together. When they were on a break, Blake, Ryan, and Sean didn't usually have to deal with paparazzi or rabid fans. Mason and Mitch were the ones who got slammed twenty-four-seven.

"Where are you going?" a woman called, leaning around one of the security guards who stood in line with the others making a human fence. "Are you two getting married?"

Gabi's hand jerked in his hold, and she shot him a glance. Her eyes were wide, her mouth agape. He'd imagined the same thing earlier. He was in a tux. She was in a white dress. *Cream* he mentally clarified. The shade didn't matter, she still looked like a breathtaking bride, and he kind of wished she was.

"No," Blake turned his gaze to the woman. "We're not getting married." And holy shit, he hoped that didn't turn up on the front page of a gossip mag.

"Then who is she?"

Blake ignored the question and followed Leah and Alana to the back of the vehicle. The others went to the crowd, posing for photos, signing autographs, and hopefully clearing up any wedding questions in the process.

"Time to go," Leah called, staring pointedly at Mitch and tapping her watch.

Everyone snapped to attention, except Alana who stood beside Leah, completely ignorant to the underlying importance. As a group, they strode over the tarmac, hunching over as they approached the helicopter, and were greeted by a man in black formal pants, white collared shirt, and tie.

"G'day," he yelled and pulled the main door to the chopper open. "Climb aboard and we'll talk inside."

Sean led the way, keeping his head lowered while he stepped into the main cabin. Once they were seated in rows of pairs, the pilot pointed to the back of Gabi's seat, indicating the headset hanging over the back of the chair.

"Put these on," he mouthed, then pulled the door closed with a thwack.

Blake settled the headphones over his ears and positioned the microphone piece in front of his mouth. Static hushed softly, dimming the heavy whoop of the rotor blades.

"You're so naughty for not telling me about the helicopter," Alana's voice spoke loud through his headset.

Blake turned his questioning gaze to Gabi who had her lips pressed in suppressed laughter. Did Alana not realize everyone could hear her?

"Don't worry, you can punish me later," Mitch replied.

"Whoa, whoa, whoa!" Mason turned around in his seat at the front and pointed to his headphones. "Headset, dickhead. As much as I love imagining Alana nekkid, picturing your lily-white ass getting punished is making my balls shrivel. *Comprende*?"

Laughter echoed through Blake's headset, and the pilot turned from his seat at the head of the helicopter with a sheepish grin. "Sorry, guys. I haven't had a chance to say my spiel yet. My name's Paul, and I'll be your pilot today. The flight will take approximately an hour and a half to get to our destination. If you have any questions along the way, please feel free to ask. Now, I should've mentioned straight away that the headsets are geared up to allow us *all* to communicate. If you speak to the person beside you, we will all hear it." He smiled at Alana. "So just be aware."

"Yeah, thanks for that, Captain Obvious," Mitchell muttered.

Blake glanced over his shoulder, past Sean and Ryan, to Mitch and Alana at the back. She made eye contact, cringed, then pointed to herself and mouthed the word "Idiot" before sinking into Mitch's chest.

"I'm sure Mason or Sean will say something equally embarrassing or inappropriate in the next five minutes, so don't worry about it, Al," Blake offered.

She rolled her eyes, "Yeah, thanks."

Gabi turned from the window beside her to grin at him. She smelled like heaven, her sweetness filling his lungs on each inhalation. Her lips were dark, luscious, and tempting. He ached to kiss her, to slide his tongue into her mouth, and breathe in her moan of submission. But he couldn't. If he started, he wouldn't stop, and he already had to suffer through at least another five hours before they would be back in their hotel suite.

"Ok, guys, let's get this bird off the ground," the pilot announced.

The heavy rush of propeller blades increased, and Blake entwined his fingers with Gabi's. They drifted off the ground, slowly ascending into the Melbourne sky. Gabi's mouth parted as she focused out the window. He loved the wide-eyed innocence that softened her already sweet features when she experienced something new. It filled him with pride that he was actually doing something worthy, instead of constantly dragging her down. They were meant for each other. Had fitted together like two lonely puzzle pieces. And there was no way he would allow Michelle to get between them.

Everyone remained quiet as they soared over the ocean, following the coastline while the sun lowered to the horizon.

"It's beautiful," Gabi murmured, leaning over him to look out the window on his side. The sky filled with varying shades of pink, purple, and orange, draping the landscape in a warm glow.

"I wish I would've brought my camera," Alana sighed.

"Shit, I knew I forgot something," Mitch added. "Sorry, babe."

The pilot noted places of interest along the way making the time pass quicker—*"That's the highway heading out of Melbourne.... That harbor leads to the port city of Geelong... Right there is Torquay, which marks the start of The Great Ocean road."*

Daylight slowly faded and Gabi nestled into Blake, the warmth of her hand moving around his waist. He spread his arm around her shoulders, holding her close, mentally counting down the minutes until they could be alone.

"Up ahead are the twelve apostles," the pilot announced. "I know we don't have a lot of light left, but you should be able to catch a few of them before night settles in."

"What are the twelve apostles?" Ryan asked.

"A collection of limestone rock formations protruding from the water. It's quite stunning during the light of day. Although, there aren't actually twelve left. The southern ocean has caused some of the stacks to fall."

Minutes passed, the sky now filling with shades of dark blue and a slash of soft pink on the horizon.

"There." The pilot took the helicopter down toward land and headed toward the coast, giving them a view out one side window.

Gabi straightened, his body immediately missing her warmth as she stared out her window. Blake could see the outline of a large rock formation, standing tall in the middle of the crushing waves. Moments later they passed another and another, all of them sticking out of the water like tall soldiers.

"Wow," Leah gushed from beside Mason. "They're gorgeous."

"We should've come earlier," Alana added. "It would've been nice to see them at sunset."

Nobody commented. They all knew they needed the darkness of night to set the scene for Mitch's proposal.

"Maybe next time, sweetheart," Mitch offered.

The coastline sunk under the darkness, the soft glow of the helicopter equipment the only light in the dark cabin.

"We're almost there," the pilot offered. "Right on time."

Mitch cleared his throat, and Blake glanced over his shoulder to find his friend tugging at the collar of his shirt. Not even the dim light could hide his nervousness.

"I think I'm going to be sick," Mitch murmured, and everyone turned to face him. He looked up in surprise, and then frowned. "Fuckin' headset."

"Are you OK?" Alana asked in a rush, leaning back to scrutinize his face.

"I'm fine. I forgot about the damn microphone. Just keep looking out the window, we'll be there soon."

She smiled and rested into him. "There's nothing to see anymore, only darkness."

"The place we're staying at should be visible from the air," Leah offered. "It's an immaculate property on the coastline. I was told it looks gorgeous from the ocean at night."

"Really?" Alana sat up straight and peered out the window across the tiny aisle.

Everyone followed her gaze. Gabi leaned over Blake, Ryan pushed against Sean and Leah did the same to Mason.

Below, on a blanket of darkness, stood a paddock size message in flickering lanterns—*Marry me, Allie.*

The silence was palpable. Thick and heavy, as everyone waited for a reaction.

Then there it was, a ragged indrawn breath, a whimper, followed by Alana turning slowly to stare wide-eyed at Mitch, her hand clutching her chest.

"Allie," Mitch started, and then cleared his throat. "You are my happiness."

Blake raised an eyebrow and gave an approving nod. Maybe his friend wouldn't fuck this up after all.

"My every thought, dream, and fantasy revolves around you. You make me whole, and I can't go back to living without you in my life. Will you marry me?"

Blake's heart clenched with pride, happiness, and yeah, a little jealousy. Mitch and Alana were perfect for each other. An undeniable match from the moment they met. He wanted what they had—a relationship without distance or skeletons haunting them from the past.

"Yes," Alana whispered, nodding her head. "God, yes."

Gabi sucked in a breath beside him, and he pulled her close, needing to know she wasn't going anywhere. They may not have forever, just yet, but they had tonight.

Mitch pulled a jewelry box from his pocket and opened it, carefully taking out the ring. His hands shook as he straightened Alana's fingers with his own. "Shit!" He fumbled, the ring slipping from his hand and falling to the floor. It landed silently, twirling and spinning until Mitch moved to his knees and slapped it down.

Someone groaned.

"He was almost in the clear, too. Poor, dopey, fucker," Sean murmured.

Mitch picked up the ring and glared at Sean as he pointed to his headset. "I can hear you."

"Oops, sorry," Sean winced.

Alana chuckled, her bright beaming smile lighting up the interior of the helicopter.

Mitch turned to his woman, inhaled a breath that hissed into Blake's earpiece, and slid the ring on her finger. "I love you."

There were more indrawn breaths; one from Gabi, another from Leah. Then Mitch leaned in to kiss Alana… and jerked straight back when their microphones tangled.

"*Fucking* headset," Mitchell growled, yanking the earphones off.

Alana lowered her headpiece to rest around her neck and mouthed something that made Mitch grin from ear to ear. When their lips finally met, the interior of the helicopter exploded with applause. A wolf-whistle pierced Blake's ear and he swore under his breath.

"Shit, sorry," Ryan spoke over the noise.

"My congratulations to the happy couple," the pilot announced. "And we're now coming in to land."

"They can't hear you," Leah replied.

One by one, the rest of them turned to face the front of the helicopter as Mitch and Alana turned their celebratory make out session into something that bordered dry-humping.

"I wish they could hear us," Mason drawled, "then I could tell lover boy to keep his dick in his pants until we get off this damn thing."

Chapter Fifteen

"Yo," Blake said in greeting to the guy holding open the front door of the Oceanside house. The kid, barely in his twenties, wore a waiter's suit, his posture straight, chin forward. Everything from the neck down spoke of professionalism. It was his face, with the gaping mouth and bulging eyes that gave away his awe.

"You organized all this?" Gabi asked Leah from behind him.

"Mitch was specific with what he wanted for tonight. I just made the phone calls."

"Wow. It's amazing."

"Oh, my god!" Alana's high pitched voice carried down the hall from the entryway.

Blake turned to face her, along with everyone else and found her standing in the doorway, staring down at her hand.

"It's… It's…"

"A ring," Mason muttered.

"It's gorgeous," Alana gushed. "I couldn't see it properly in the helicopter. It was too dark. But, oh my. It's… I'm speechless."

She rushed into Mitch's arms, smothering him with her appreciation. "I think we need some privacy," Mitch murmured between kisses and lifted her off her feet. "Leah, where's the bedroom?"

The man at the door cleared his throat and pointed. "The main bedroom is down the first hall to your left."

Mitch and Alana took off without a backward glance.

"And I hope you guys have a loud enough stereo system to drown that shit out," Sean added.

Blake leaned against the wall and waited for Gabi to bridge the distance between them. The house was lavish—rock star lavish. Everything gleamed, from the polished tiles to the array of vases and framed artwork. A waitress holding a tray of champagne flutes strode toward them, her black skirt and white collared shirt, formal and flattering.

"Champagne?" Her smile was bright and flirty. No surprise there.

"No thanks." He waved away her offering.

Gabi stepped into him and grabbed his hand. "I'm fine as well, thank you."

Blake looked down at her, equal parts frustrated and flattered that she wasn't drinking because of him.

"On second thought," he raised his voice as the waitress began walking away, "I'll grab one." He took a flute from the tray and handed it to Gabi. "For you, my angel."

"I said I was fine."

"I know you did, but you only said it because of me, and I don't want that."

"I don't need to drink to enjoy myself, Blake."

He shut his mouth to stop a growl from escaping and pulled her into the start of another hallway. He pressed her back against the wall and rested a hand near her head, leaning into her. "I want to be clear, Gabi. I stay sober because I *want to*, not because I have a problem with alcohol. So there's no need for you to stop drinking."

Her lips were pressed together, the empathy in her blue irises sinking under his skin while one hand clutched her champagne flute and the other held her purse.

"So the only thing your sobriety achieves is making it harder for me to take advantage of you."

The side of her mouth curved, and she rolled those gorgeous eyes at him. "As if you ever needed help in that department."

He shrugged. She was right. Whenever they were together, he took on the role of horny frat boy, and she turned into a malleable sex kitten.

"You're fun to watch when you're tipsy." He remembered the night they met, how she danced with uninhibited sexual grace and made him harder than stone from the mere sway of her hips.

She cleared her throat and broke eye contact to take a large gulp of her champagne. When she lowered the glass, she looked up at him through tinted lashes. "Yeah, I was told you like to watch."

Warning. Warning. That shit didn't sound good.

He quirked a brow and ignored Sean, Mason, and Ryan as they walked past, striding down the main hall. "Your tone implies a hidden meaning that I'm not quite comfortable asking about."

She chuckled and ran the hand holding her purse around his neck. "A little birdie told me that you like to watch." She closed her mouth, working the plump bottom lip against her teeth.

"*Who* told you that?"

She shrugged, lowering her gaze. His heart did a little two-step, advising him to tread lightly. He didn't spread bedroom gossip, never had, never would. There was only one voyeuristic experience he'd taken part in over the last year. One that hadn't made tabloid headlines because all parties involved were here tonight.

"Hey," he lifted her chin. "Did Mitch say something?" If that motherfucker had opened his mouth and upset Gabi, he'd find himself in a world of hurt.

"No," she gave a half-hearted laugh. "Forget it, I shouldn't have said anything."

"Then it was Alana," he assumed. There was also Leah or maybe Sean, Mason, or Ryan but he was pretty sure they wouldn't put their balls on the line by sharing something private that didn't involve them.

"She didn't say it to cause trouble," Gabi defended. "It was a slip up. A bad word choice that had me jumping to conclusions. So she had to fill me in."

"And now you're worried." Her inability to make eye contact spoke loud and clear.

"No," she shook her head, lowering her focus to try and hide the truth.

"Right," he cleared his throat and pressed harder into the wall, placing his hips against hers. How the hell had that conversation started? The need to know clawed at him. He ignored it, focusing on what really mattered—Gabi's insecurities. He knew all about feeling inferior and never wanted her to experience it. Especially when there was no need.

"Alana's a great person." He scrutinized her, waiting for the moment when she would make eye contact again and start believing him. "Yeah, she's attractive. But for starters, she's with Mitch, and secondly, she doesn't compare to you. She's not even close."

Her blue gaze turned up to meet his.

"There's no one else for me, Gabi. There hasn't been for a long time, I just hadn't realized it."

She leaned into him, pressing the heat of her lips against his mouth for a scorching second before pulling back.

"I'd never cheat on you," he whispered, needing her to know the truth. "Please trust me enough to believe that."

Her head snapped back, her brows now tightly knitted together. "I do. It's not that." She shook her head. "It was the whole kinky sex thing."

"The whole kinky sex thing?" he asked, stroking the wisps of hair from her face.

"You seem to like…different things. Voyeurism. Exhibitionism. I'm not sure I can keep up."

It was his turn to pull back in shock. He'd never associated those words with his sex life before. He didn't have any specific kinks. He simply loved sex, no matter what form it came in. "I've had my share of threesomes and one night stands with groupies, but I'm pretty straight when it comes to the whole bumpin' uglies thing, Gabi. I honestly have no idea what you're talking about."

She stared up at him, the whites of her eyes gleaming from the recessed lights overhead. "Pretty straight?" She recoiled. "Threesomes? Having sex in the ocean. On a plane. That isn't straight for me." Her voice squeaked. "That's pretty freakin' crazy in my world."

He laughed, unable to hold it in.

She glared at him. "Don't laugh at me!" Her hand fell from around his neck and she moved to walk around him.

He grabbed her wrist, stopping her in an instant. "The threesomes are a thing of the past. Mitch was my wingman, sometimes Sean, but we haven't done that in years. OK?"

She glanced at him from the corner of her eye and gave a slight tilt of her head in acknowledgement.

"And the whole ocean-plane thing had nothing to do with me being kinky and everything to do with how much I want you." He pulled her into his arms, uncaring that the champagne sloshed from the glass. He worked his pelvis against her abdomen, proving his point by rubbing his hardening cock into her. "I'd fuck you right now if I thought you'd let me."

"For starters I don't 'fuck,'" she hissed. "I make lo—"

"I hate to break it to you, angel, but what we shared in the ocean wasn't making love. It was fucking. It was sexy as hell, wet, dream worthy, fucking. And same goes for on the plane. Tonight however," he leaned in and whispered in her ear. "I'll make love to you and show you the difference."

"Where is everyone?" Leah's voice echoed down the hall.

"I guess that's our cue," he spoke against Gabi's lips, ignoring the throb in his groin that became more insistent with every passing second.

She circled his waist with her arms. "I'm going to miss you."

Bam. Direct hit, straight through his heart. It would be worse for him once she went back to Queensland. She had work and a life to occupy her time, whereas everything he did reminded him of Gabi. His music. The nights spent alone while the guys went out drinking. Even his dreams would taunt him.

"It won't be for long." He focused on the necklace he'd given her and loved that she rarely took it off.

"I know." She nodded and placed her purse under her arm before reaching for his hand. "It'll be worth it in the end."

It would be. He would make sure of it. One day soon, they'd all be celebrating Blake and Gabi's engagement, their commitment to forever. It was inevitable, something he wouldn't let slip through his fingers. He only needed to wait for the right time. "I'll make sure it is, sweetheart. I promise."

Chapter Sixteen

The night continued like a fairytale that Gabi couldn't believe was reality. The waitress and waiter—the man who originally greeted them at the front door— had served canapés, champagne, and mixed spirits until Mitch and Alana finished "celebrating." Then a chef prepared a mouthwatering crab, avocado, and mango tower for an entrée, and stuffed quail with baked vegetables for the main meal.

By the time they finished eating, Gabi was buzzing from the alcohol Blake kept plying her with. Each time he handed her a new champagne flute, he'd wink and give her a devilish grin that spoke of naughty things she couldn't wait to experience.

After dinner, Leah announced they had another hour before the helicopter returned. Mitch and Alana went on a private moonlight stroll along the beach, while the rest of them stayed inside chatting, laughing, and drinking.

"Come out onto the balcony with me." Blake tugged her outside onto the wooden slats that made up the floor. He'd discarded his jacket earlier in the night and rolled up his shirt sleeves to expose the skin she loved so much.

The cool coastal breeze was warmed by four portable patio heaters that stood evenly spaced along the wooden railing. At either end of the balcony stood a staircase leading down to a pool sparkling from underwater lights. The rush and ebb of the ocean sounded in the distance.

"I'm counting down the hours until we're back at the hotel, you know that, right?" he murmured in her ear, pressing his body into hers against the railing.

The fire from the portable heaters warmed her cheeks, increasing her alcoholic buzz and adding to the lava rushing through her veins. Her core pulsed in reply, her nipples hardened, and it was only through sheer determination that she didn't moan.

They were in plain sight for everyone inside to see, yet hiding behind the broad expanse of his shoulders, she didn't care. She wanted Blake too much to worry about the opinions of others tonight.

"I'm not sure I can wait that long," she teased.

His hand came up to trace the necklace he'd given her, causing more blood to flow to the needy parts of her body.

The sound of the glass sliding door opened and the heavy thud of footsteps followed.

"Christ, you guys are driving me insane," Ryan spoke softly.

Blake glanced over his shoulder. "Suffering from blue balls, buddy?"

"Blue balls and chafed palms," Ryan muttered and started descending the stairs, moving out of view.

Gabi's eyes widened. Didn't these men have a social filter?

"Poor guy." Blake ran an arm up her back, stopping at the base of her neck to hold her tight. "Now where were we?"

She groaned at the tingle that ran down her spine and placed her hands on his waist. "I think you were trying to slowly kill me with pleasure."

He chuckled and grazed her chin with his teeth. "I missed you today."

Gabi sucked in a breath. His touch always found her erogenous zones, making her shiver with a mere brush of his fingers, or mouth, or tongue.

"God, woman, I can smell your arousal," he growled.

"Well, stop touching me," she replied, breathless, weightless and totally hoping he'd ignore her statement. She closed her eyes, sinking into the dreamy sensation taking over her body, then groaned when the glass door slid open again.

"Sorry, guys…didn't mean to interrupt." Leah pulled the door closed behind her and strode toward them. "Have you seen Ryan?"

With a heavy sigh, Blake glanced over his shoulder. "He took the stairs a few minutes ago."

Gabi poked her head around Blake to look at Leah. Her forehead was creased with concern, her lips pressed firmly together.

"Everything all right?" Gabi asked, sensing an uncomfortable undercurrent.

"Yeah." Leah swallowed. "Just checking on all my little chickens."

"Have you spoken to him yet?" Blake asked.

Leah narrowed her gaze and glowered. "Blake," she chastised.

"Spoken to me about what?" Ryan came into view at the top of the staircase, his phone alight in his palm. Silence hung heavy in the air while he glanced between Leah and Blake. "Spoken to me about what, Leah?"

Blake swore under his breath and Leah turned to face Ryan. "We need to talk."

Ryan shrugged. "Then talk. Blake obviously knows what you're about to say, so go ahead."

"Umm," Leah shot a glance to Gabi, then Blake, her eyes widening in panic. "We should do this in private."

Ryan stepped forward and slid his phone into his jacket pocket. "Come on, Leah. Spill."

She let out a shaky sigh, her gaze finding Blake's for a fleeting second before turning back to Ryan. "It's just gossip and entirely unfounded at the moment. I didn't want to bring it up unless the claims were true."

Ryan crossed his arms over his chest and raised a brow. When she didn't elaborate, he huffed, "What claims?"

"One of the tabloids back home is saying they have proof of Julie cheating on you—"

Ryan's boyish features transformed to a mix of heated fury and shock. "What?" He stalked forward, his hands fisted at his sides.

Gabi's stomach hollowed, and she turned to grip the rail, focusing on the darkened beach. She didn't want to be here. She had no business being privy to something so private.

"It's a load of rubbish. They won't validate their claims," Leah continued. "They're only digging for a story."

Ryan let out a self-deprecating laugh. "If they have no proof, then why the fuck am I the last to know?"

Gabi glanced over her shoulder, surprised by the vehemence in Ryan's tone.

He threw his hands into the air. "Jesus Christ, Leah, how dare you tell Blake before me?"

Leah startled, her mouth gaping for a brief moment before she snapped it closed to swallow. "Nobody else knows." She lowered her voice, "I didn't want to hurt you unnec—"

"Oh, OK." Ryan nodded with sarcasm. "So I should be happy that you only told Blake before me?"

Blake tensed and dropped his hands from Gabi's body. "Back off, Ryan. I know this must be hard to hear, but it's not Leah's fault."

Ryan turned his scathing glare to Blake, making Gabi shrink under the fury in his eyes. "You think this is fair, do you?" He stepped up to them, getting in Blake's face. "You're meant to be my friend. My fucking *brother*. And yet you kept this from me. For how long, Blake?"

"Calm down."

"*For how long?*" Ryan raised his voice.

"Only early this morning!" Blake spat. "Damn it to hell, Ryan. I know you're cut up, but Leah's been going through some pretty heavy shit. She didn't want to hurt you for no reason. We all know how hard it is for you to be away from Julie."

Ryan poked Blake in the chest. "You don't know shit."

Gabi covered her mouth with a gasp. They were going to fight, and she couldn't stand to see either of them hurt.

The click of Leah's heels tapped against the wooden patio floor, followed by the glass door sliding open. "Mason. Sean," she called. "I need you."

"Great." Ryan backed away. "Get everyone else involved." He shook his head and turned on his heels. "I'm outta here."

"Where are you going?" Leah cried. "The helicopter will be back in half an hour."

Ryan ignored her, striding to the top of the stairs before jumping down more than one at a time and going out of view.

"What's going on?" Mason asked, following their gaze to the end of the balcony.

Blake stepped forward, giving Gabi space to breathe. She felt horrible for Leah and Blake and most of all her heart ached for Ryan. The thought of leaving the person she loved tomorrow had already been tearing her apart, yet Ryan had been doing this for years.

Leah let out a shuddering breath and lowered her head. "Oh, god, what have I done?"

Blake went to his band manager, gathering her in his arms and holding her as she began to weep. As Leah's tears continued to fall, Gabi inched along the railing, moving silently to the other side of the balcony. She didn't belong in this moment. Blake was comforting and finding comfort with Leah…not her. She needed to clear her head and put things into perspective. It was a friendly hug, nothing more. Her brain could rationalize it, and still, she felt insignificant.

Bloody alcohol.

At the final step, she tiptoed onto the gravel path and let the inside house lights guide her to the gate at the front of the building. The rush of the ocean called to her, and she was thankful to find a sandy trail running along the outside of the fence. She undid her shoes, carrying them by the straps, and leisurely walked into the darkness.

The path steepened, with wooden planks forming makeshift steps to ease the way. Above, the yellow moon glowed full and bright, making the reed covered dunes visible. When she made it to the beach, she stopped and so did the beat of her heart.

Up ahead, Ryan sat in the sand, his hands wrapped around his indrawn knees, his gaze focused on the water.

"Ryan?" she asked softly. She glanced over her shoulder, wondering if she should turn back and leave him alone with his thoughts.

He didn't answer.

On silent feet she moved beside him. "Ryan?"

"Shit!" His head jerked up. "You scared the crap outta me."

"Sorry. I didn't mean to."

He scoffed and turned his attention back to the waves. "I should be the one apologizing."

"No, not at all. You have good reason to be angry."

"Yeah?" He shucked his suit jacket and laid it down beside him. "Wanna sit?"

So sweet, so thoughtful, even when he was falling apart. "Thank you." Straightening her dress over her bottom, she sat on his suit coat and brought her knees to her chest.

They sat in silence, watching the white foam burst to life with every breaking wave.

"You know," Ryan started, his voice low. "For a brief second, I felt relieved when Leah said Julie had been cheating."

Gabi turned her gaze to face him, resting the side of her head on her knees.

"I don't think I'm in love anymore."

She froze, not sure what to say. Apart from the information Blake had shared over the years, Gabi didn't know much about this heartbreakingly vulnerable man. Yet, everything inside her screamed to move closer and wrap a warm arm around him. Just like Blake had done to Leah.

"We're not happy anymore. We're barely even friends."

Gabi opened her mouth, but no words came out.

"I feel like a failure."

"Don't." She straightened and shook her head. "Marriage isn't easy."

"No, it's not, but loving someone shouldn't be so hard."

Ryan continued to stare at the water in silence. Heartbreak emanated from him. She didn't know what type of woman would let a wonderful guy like Ryan fall out of love with her. If it was Gabi, she would fight with everything she had to keep him in her life.

"You and Blake have something special going on, don't you?"

It was Gabi's turn to stare at the water in contemplation. What she had with Blake went beyond special. However, she wasn't sure if they could make it through the alone times.

"He's a great guy," she replied.

"And?"

She gave an unenthusiastic chuckle. "I love him." She glanced at Ryan, who waited for her to continue. "He means the world to me. I'm just scared—and insecure."

She dug her heels into the sand and watched her feet disappear. Her face heated, knowing Ryan still stared at her.

"I get the scared part. Blake freaks me out sometimes, too." Ryan leaned over and nudged her shoulder with a laugh. "Unfortunately, I think the insecurity will be a battle for anyone who decides to take on one of us guys. I know my wife hates the thought of groupies. But hey, I've never cheated on her. Not once, in all the years we've been together."

The burr of a helicopter sounded in the distance, growing louder over the rush of the ocean.

Ryan sighed, "I really don't want to go back up there."

She couldn't blame him. She didn't want to go back herself. Thankfully her alcohol buzz had lessened. Now she only had to calm her irrational thoughts and she would be fine. "Come on." Gabi stood and picked up his suit jacket, doing her best to dust off the sand. She held out her hand and he took it, allowing her to pull him to his feet. "Let's get this over and done with."

Chapter Seventeen

BLAKE STOOD BEHIND the glass doors overlooking the balcony, staring into the darkness. Where was she?

He'd fucked up. Again. The fight with Ryan was his fault, and when Leah had stopped crying against his pounding chest, he'd turned in search of the comfort of Gabi's arms, only to find her gone.

"Where the hell is everyone?" Mason asked the quiet room, the faint whoop of the helicopter getting closer by the second. He sat on the kitchen bench, his feet swinging back and forth.

"Hopefully they'll come back now that our ride's here," Leah spoke from her seat beside Sean on the couch. She was still upset, nestled into Sean's side, sniffing with every breath.

Footsteps echoed up the hall, followed by a feminine giggle.

"Stop it," Alana chastised, coming into view beside Mitch in the reflection of the glass.

"Didn't you guys go for a walk?" Mason asked.

Blake turned to face them, ignoring the way his anxiety increased with every minute that Gabi was away.

Alana glanced at Mitch, then flushed and looked away.

"We took a detour." Mitch smirked, wrapping his arms around Alana's waist, making her squeal and squirm.

"Let me guess, to the bedroom?" Mason muttered.

Alana pushed from Mitch's arms and walked around the couch to

Leah. "Where are Ryan and Gabi?" Her gaze narrowed. "Leah? What's wrong?"

"Everything's fine," Blake interrupted, pivoting back to the window. They owed it to Ryan to keep the gossip private. If Ryan wanted everyone to know, he could tell them himself.

"Everything doesn't look fine." Alana scooted in beside Leah while Mitch came to stand beside Blake.

"What's going on?" Mitch murmured.

Blake turned back to his friend and plastered a fake smile on his face. "Nothing for you to worry about, bro." He stepped forward and yanked Mitch close for a quick man hug. "I haven't had a chance to congratulate you yet. I'm real happy for you both."

Mitch clapped him on the back. "I'm happy for you, too, man. It seems like you've found the right lady."

Blake gave a jerky nod. "Yeah, I have."

"Well, I hope she never realizes how much of a tool you are."

"Yeah." Blake laughed but didn't feel the humor. "Me too." Karma must have fucked up somewhere along the line because Blake definitely didn't deserve to have Gabi in his life.

Mitch glanced around the room and frowned. "So where is she?"

I have no fucking clue.

Something moved in his periphery and he stepped forward without thought. *Gabi.* She was outside, walking along the fence surrounding the yard with Ryan beside her, his suit jacket over her shoulders.

He let out a deep breath, releasing the tightness in his chest. *Thank god.*

She tilted her head to focus on the house and met his gaze. The soft smile she sent him almost knocked him off his feet.

"Uh, why is she with Ryan?" Mitch asked.

"Long story." Blake opened the glass sliding door and moved onto the balcony. Gabi and Ryan walked out of view, and moments later the side gate clanged. When footfalls sounded on the steps, his heart ramped up a notch. He'd been worried. He hadn't realized how much until his body flooded with relief at seeing her again.

Ryan reached the top step first—his eyes filled with remorse—and jerked his head in greeting. "Where's Leah?"

"Inside."

"Right. I might keep my distance for a while. I'll meet you at the chopper." Ryan moved to walk past him.

Blake placed a hand on his friend's chest, halting his progression. "Look Rye, I'm sorry I didn't say anything, and Leah didn't mean to hurt you either. I knew she was worried about something, and I hounded her until she told me."

Ryan ran a hand through his tangled shoulder-length hair. "I understand."

Yeah, Ryan was the most understanding guy Blake knew, which made the situation harder to bear. Blake dropped his hand and watched him walk away, leaving down the stairs on the other side of the balcony. Once his footfalls died under the burr of the distant helicopter noise, he turned his focus to Gabi who stood waiting at the top of the stairs.

"You had me worried."

She padded toward him in bare feet, her high heels hanging from her hand. "I needed to take a walk and clear my head."

"You were running from me." He kept his expression impassive, hiding the hurt that gripped him by the balls. He'd hoped she'd gone in search of Ryan, instead of leaving to get away from him.

She came forward, her big blue eyes dark with widened pupils. "No." She shook her head slightly. "I was overwhelmed. I needed time to think."

His palms itched to touch her, to swipe Ryan's jacket from her shoulders and replace it with his own. "Did I do something wrong?"

Gabi stepped into him, running her arms around his waist. "You didn't do anything wrong," she whispered, her voice almost drowning under the turning propeller blades in the field beside them. "I think I was in shock at seeing you and Ryan almost come to blows. It scared me, that's all."

"Why didn't you tell me? When I turned to find you gone, I didn't know what to think."

She nestled her head under his chin, hugging him tighter. "You were busy…with Leah."

He stiffened. When Ryan had stormed off earlier, Blake had been consumed with guilt. He'd been the cause of all the anger and had instinctively gone to comfort Leah. It was his fault she was crying.

"Leah's a part of the family," he spoke his thoughts aloud.

"I know." Gabi nodded against his chest.

"She's like a sister to me."

"Yeah… I know that, too."

He ran an arm around her back, running his hand up and down the material of Ryan's suit jacket. "The last few days have been crazy, haven't they?" Meeting for the first time was monumental enough. Add to that all the other external influences that had been flung their way, and it made for a highly emotional situation. He was surprised one of them hadn't cracked earlier.

"Mmm-hmm."

And tomorrow will be worse.

"Was that what you were worried about?" she asked, pulling back to peer up at him. "The secrets about Ryan's wife, was that what you had to deal with earlier?"

He stared into her hopeful eyes. His answer should've been an easy "No," yet he paused and contemplated if it would be better to take away her worry with a little white lie.

"It was part of it." The words didn't sting as much as he expected. In reality, it was kind of the truth. The issues with Julie's fidelity had hovered in the back of his mind.

Her lips curved in relief, and she snuggled back under his chin. "Can we go home now?"

Home.

If only he could take her back to his apartment in the US. Things would be much simpler there. He'd tie her to his bed and take care of her every want and desire, never letting her leave.

"Yeah, angel." He kissed the top of her head and inhaled the sweet smell of honeysuckle. As he straightened, Leah caught his eye from inside the glass doors. She mouthed for him to "hurry up," then turned on her heel and walked from the room. "I think everyone else has made their way to the helicopter."

Gabi stepped out of his arms. "Just let me get my shoes on." She bent her tight ass over in front of him and tied her straps.

When she stood, he grabbed for her hand, pulling her close so he could speak in her ear. "Remember what I promised to teach you when we get back to the hotel?" She sucked in a breath and shivered. He ran a finger down the sensitive skin of her neck and followed the trail with his tongue. "I thought so."

Blake was thankful the flight back to Melbourne didn't take as long. Travelling over land instead of the ocean cut half an hour off the trip, which was a bonus when no one was talking.

After takeoff, Gabi nestled her head against his shoulder and hadn't spoken a word since. Alana and Mitch were in the back of the helicopter, snuggled together, eyes closed. Mason and Ryan sat together in front of Blake, Ryan leaning against the window while Mason stared out the opposite side. And Sean was in the front seat beside Leah, his arm resting comfortingly around her shoulders.

The limo ride was equally entertaining.

They arrived at the Crown a few minutes past one in the morning with no crowd in sight. A few gasps of recognition sounded when they strode through the lobby, but hotel security kept people at bay.

The elevator ascended in silence—all of them too tired or uncomfortable to speak. When the doors opened on their floor, Leah stepped out first, her head low as she said a quiet, "Night, guys."

Blake followed, holding Gabi's hand with Mitch and Alana walking out behind them. They all had king suites, while Mason, Sean, and Ryan shared the bigger room upstairs.

"Late breakfast in our suite at eleven?" Mason asked.

"Sounds good," Mitch called over his shoulder.

"Yeah." Blake dropped Gabi's hand and walked backward, watching as Ryan placed a foot out of the elevator.

Leah didn't answer. She'd already begun striding in the opposite direction to her suite.

"Hey, Leah," Ryan called, his face haunted, his lips in a thin line.

Leah paused, and then slowly turned on her heels. She looked at Ryan, remaining quiet while her fingers clutched at the purse in her hands.

"Do you mind if we talk?" He took another step, moving out of the elevator and allowing the doors to close with Mason and Sean still inside.

Leah pressed her lips together and nodded. Without a word, she continued down the hall, not stopping for Ryan who jogged to catch up.

Blake watched them enter her suite and tensed at the guilt that ate away at his stomach. Why the hell had he opened his mouth?

"They'll be fine," Gabi whispered from beside him, entwining their fingers. "Come on." She tugged his arm, and they walked the remaining steps to their door.

Gabi took the key card from his hand and unlocked the suite. He followed her down the dimly lit hall, around the small dining and kitchen area to their bedroom, and dropped onto the end of their king size bed. She flipped on the light and closed the curtain, shutting out the world.

He tugged at his tie, loosening the restrictive material, and then started on his shirt buttons. The hours of silence had given him perspective—not a favorable one. Why was he such a fucking failure? He'd caused a rift between his friends, ruined his last night with Gabi, and on top of all that, he had Michelle to deal with.

"Talk to me," she said softly, lifting her hands to unclasp her necklace and place it on the top of her closed suitcase.

He pushed to his feet, caught her hand, and dragged her back to the bed to stand between his knees. She was the light in his life. The brightness that made all the darkness easier to bear.

"What do you want me to say?" He was numb, his limbs, his chest, his mind. The only thing he could feel was his heart and the warmth it held for his angel.

She ran a hand through his hair. The delicate fabric of her dress swished against his thighs. He watched it glint in the bedroom light, clinging to her curves, hugging her breasts. Her scent filled his lungs—sweet and feminine, with the finest hint of her arousal.

Moments ago, he'd been dead inside. Now, in an instant, she had his blood heating and his cock thickening.

She lifted his chin and peered down at him. "I want you to tell me what I can do to make you smile again."

A crooked grin pulled at his lips. "That's a loaded question."

Her cheeks lifted. "And one you could've used to your advantage, but now you're already smiling. My work here is done." She turned to walk away. He reached for her hips, and she squealed when he pulled her back into him.

He tightened his thighs around her, staring her down, daring her to move while he undid the belt of his pants and lowered his zipper. "Take it off," he demanded, indicating her dress with a jut of his chin.

She raised a brow, raked her haughty gaze down his body, all the way to the erection tenting his boxers, and swallowed. Hard. A second later she complied, reaching behind her back to undo the zipper. He widened his legs, giving her room to move and felt his pulse kick up a gear at the seductive way she flicked the straps from her shoulders, allowing the dress to fall to the floor.

"Now what, *Master*?"

Chapter Eighteen

GABI PRESSED HER lips together, fighting back a laugh. It was a relief to see the happiness back in his eyes. Although keeping his friends amused and entertained was his M.O., he carried the weight of the world on those broad shoulders. For tonight, she wanted to make him fall asleep smiling, relieved of all his worries.

"Come here." He wrapped an arm around her waist and pulled her against his chest. "Kiss me."

She obeyed, lowering her head to meet his upturned face. Their lips brushed in a delicate sweep, and she moaned when his tongue sought entrance to her mouth. His other arm snaked around her back to the clasp of her bra, working it one handed until it came undone. Then both hands drifted lower, cupping her ass in a firm hold.

A ragged breath escaped her and she clung to him, palming his lightly stubbled cheek with one hand while the other went into the hair at his nape. His chest rumbled, the masculine sound beading her nipples and sending desire to pool between her thighs. He made it so easy to love him, physically and emotionally. No other man compared. No other man even existed.

He pulled back, sending her reeling, making her pull tighter on his hair to remain standing. "Take off your panties. I want to taste you."

She whimpered at his words, at his large dilated pupils, and the way his hands were working her ass like he was kneading bread.

"Now, Gabi." He dropped his grip on her.

She fumbled backward, her gaze still glued to his, and let her bra straps fall down her arms to the floor. His nostrils flared, sending a blanket of goose bumps over her body while he yanked off his unbuttoned shirt and threw it away.

With shaky fingers, she grabbed the elastic of her white lace g-string and pushed it down her thighs. She stood before him, completely naked except for her cobalt blue high heels and a nervous smile.

"Damn, you make me hot," he murmured.

She felt the same way. He stole her breath, her heart, her insecurities, and made her soar. Even now, with a foot of space between them, she could feel his touch. The sight of him was something she would never forget, no matter how far he travelled or how long he stayed away. He was a man without physical flaw. His arms were corded with muscle, the intense colors of his tattoos turning her core molten. Then there was the dark stubble that marred his smooth skin and the ruby lips that made her shiver with promise.

"I adore you," she whispered.

His nostrils flared again, and when he pulled her closer this time, he rose to his feet, pushing her down to lay on the mattress.

"You don't want me to take off my heels?"

He knelt on the mattress between her parted thighs and held her hips, pushing her higher on the bed. "Hell, no." Palming the back of her shoe, he lifted and nuzzled her ankle. "So fucking hot." His mouth ran a trail up the side of her calf, stopping at her knee. His gaze slid up her legs, lingering at her parted sex, then rose to her face. "Ready for a lesson in love, angel?"

She bit her lip and nodded. "I'm always ready for you."

He smirked, making his features all the more devilish before leaning down to softly blow against her swollen nub. "Lesson one." His tongue came out to flick her clit, sending an instant burst of pleasure to ping through her body. She arched her back, her hands frantically searching for something to cling to.

"I wouldn't taste you slowly if we were fucking." He lowered his mouth to her slit, leisurely licking her from top to bottom and back again. Then he drew her clit into his mouth and sucked. "I'd devour you with your legs around my neck, making you scream my name."

She encircled his back with her legs, the heels of her shoes clinking together, and squeezed her eyes shut. The tender way he worked her with his tongue made her wish they were fucking instead of the evil way he currently tortured her. The flicks against her clit were light, teasing, and holy heavens, they made her belly flutter.

"If we were fucking…" He ran his finger along the small expanse of skin between her pussy and the entrance to her bottom, adding pressure with each pass. "I would've lubed my fingers with your juices and teased your ass, making you squirm until you begged me to penetrate you there." His touch went lower, to her tight hole.

She tensed and opened her eyes with a start. "Blake."

He raised his head from her mound and chuckled. "You wouldn't want me touching you there?"

She shook her head.

"I'd make sure you liked it."

She didn't doubt it for a second. Right now, her interest was on penetration of a different kind. "When are you going to stop talking and actually make love to me?"

He leaned down, nipping the tender flesh on the inside of her thigh and quirked a brow. "In a hurry?"

Yes. No. Her mind wanted this to last forever, while her body screamed for completion. "Please, Blake." She moved to rest on her elbows. "I need you."

"And your wish is my command." He scooted from the mattress and stood at the foot of the bed. With quick, efficient movements he pushed his trousers and boxers to the floor, exposing his erection.

"You're beautiful," she murmured, taking the time to appreciate every part of him. She loved the soft definition of his stomach, the underlying hint of a six pack. However, it was his pecs and arms that made her mouth dry. They were sculpted, as if from stone, and sinfully wicked with the ink that adorned them.

"No, sweetheart, *you're* beautiful." He slid over her body, leaving a kiss on the inside of her thigh, a graze of teeth against her hip, a lick of his tongue over her nipple. "And tempting." He sank his mouth onto the low of her neck, suckling and licking. "And made only for me."

She let her head fall back and moaned at the sensations spiraling through her body. Her nipples tingled. Her stomach tightened, and between her thighs was the most delicious throb that only Blake could relieve.

She wrapped her thighs around his waist and ground her pelvis into him. The friction was light at best and did nothing to alleviate her need. And still he continued to bathe her with kisses, his hands gliding over every curve, loving her, adoring her in a way she'd never experienced before.

Blake knew how to fuck, there had never been any doubt. But the way he loved her, cherishing her with tiny kisses and soft growls when he found a sensitive spot on her body, reaffirmed the deep emotion he spoke of.

He'd been her secret friend for years, listening to her share things she couldn't voice with people who surrounded her on a daily basis. He comforted her, made her laugh, turned her on, and now he was fulfilling her dreams, loving her in a way that would never be compared.

She relaxed into the mattress, releasing her grip on the covers to touch him in return. She ran her fingers up the smooth skin of his back, trailing her nails along his shoulder blades. He responded to her touch with harder kisses, softer flicks of his tongue, and the nuzzling and grazing of his teeth.

"You mean everything to me," he murmured in her ear. "I mean it, Gabi. There's no one else. There never will be."

She closed her eyes briefly and filled her lungs to capacity, floating on a cloud. This would be the moment she cherished. The time when she was naked in Blake's arms, being loved by his body and his words. "I feel the same way."

He pulled back to stare down at her, climbing just a little higher so his pelvis rested against hers. A smile pulled at his lips, subtle, yet it made her toes curl. "You're my happiness."

He kissed her lips, sliding his tongue into her mouth and dancing it over hers. His erection nudged her entrance, teasing, adding more torment to her already tortured body. He leaned over her, reaching for the bedside table with an outstretched hand and retrieved a condom. The packet was torn apart in seconds, the protection placed over his cock with equal virility. Then he was poised at her pussy again, the head of his shaft nudging her entrance in tiny increments.

She kissed his jaw, his mouth, his neck, each caress of her lips slow and gentle, like the undulation of his body. "I love you." Her heart was overflowing with emotion.

He palmed her breast and tweaked her nipple. "Doesn't count. You should know better." His smile was made of heaven and happiness. Nothing in life had ever gripped her in such a consuming hold like the slight tilt of his lips. "But I'll take your love anyway I can get it, Gabi."

Then his mouth found hers, taking her breath, making her cling to his shoulders for spiritual grounding. This kiss was demanding, and in one hard thrust he was inside her, sliding home. Their moans filled the room, the noise increasing as his hips began to move, gliding in and out with slow deliberation.

"Touch yourself," he commanded. "I want to feel your fingers on your clit."

A whimper escaped her lips. She'd always needed that friction to achieve orgasm, yet at this moment, she felt ready to explode without it.

"Do it."

He continued to thrust, his hips rocking in a languid motion as her hand slid down to where they joined. She felt for him, letting her fingertips brush against his cock while he moved.

"Not a good idea," he ground out.

She made eye contact and quirked a brow while she encircled the base of his shaft. He closed his eyes and growled, his head tilting back slightly.

"Ahh, damn you feel good." He pumped harder, once, twice, then stopped. "You've gotta move your hand, sweetheart."

With reluctance, she withdrew and moved her touch to the top of her mound. His lips found her ear, sucking her lobe into his mouth, his breath coming hot and heavy down her neck. "Never forget me, Gabi. I couldn't take it if you moved on while we were apart."

She turned her head and gazed into his dark irises, finding renewed anguish lurking in their depths. "You're a part of my life, Blake. One I can't live without. I'll never forget you. It isn't possible. I love you too much."

He rested his forehead against hers, keeping eye contact while he thrust and withdrew. "I want to make you happy."

She chuckled softly. "You're currently doing a really great job."

He let out a whisper of a laugh, his eyes brightening for a moment before sorrow settled back in its place. "My angel," he whispered, then closed his eyes and ground into her.

Their hips rocked together, the friction igniting her impending release. She arched her back, thrusting her breasts out to rub her nipples against the fine sprinkling of hair on his chest. "So close..."

He rocked harder, faster, opening his eyes to stare down at her. Determination replaced his pain and a fine sheen of sweat covered his skin. The low of her belly tightened, her core convulsed and with his next hard plunge, he sent her over the edge, crying out with the ecstasy that took over her body.

Her ears buzzed, and she was sure her grip was tight enough to draw blood. But she couldn't help herself, couldn't regain control with the liquid fire coursing through her veins. His moan vibrated against the walls, the sound of his release spurring her a little longer as her pussy clamped down on his length.

Thrusts turned into gentle rocking which faded away until Blake collapsed at her side, pulling her with him. Gabi sucked in air, trying to regain her steady breathing while her gaze ran over him. His lips were flushed, ruby red and swollen. His normally spiked hair lay limp against his forehead. His shoulders were slumped, the angel over his heart rising and falling in rapid movements.

"Why did you stop?" she asked, working her finger over the lines that made up the angel's wings.

"Hmm?" He raised a brow.

"Your tattoos. When we first started talking, you were getting them all the time. Some you told me about, like the snake." She traced her finger along the scaly body until it ran round to the back of his arm and out of view. "But others I had no clue, like the angel." She placed a kiss over his heart and loved the way he shuddered under her lips. "Then you stopped."

"I didn't need them anymore."

She raised her gaze from his chest and frowned. "What do you mean?"

He ran his arm around her belly and pulled her closer. "They were reminders—of the mistakes I've made and the things I need to hold onto to keep me grounded. The pain also helped. Getting a new tat was like a punishment for my fuck ups." He shrugged. "Then I found you." He raised his arm and tilted it so she could see the script writing on the inside of his forearm. *You saved my soul. Gave me new meaning. Fought against my demons, while I lay sleeping.*

"Those are Reckless lyrics."

He shook his head. "Those are *your* lyrics. The song is about you."

She swallowed to douse the tightening in her throat and gripped his wrist to read the writing again.

"I owe you my life, Gabi. I wouldn't have made it through without you. I had no one else to help me, and after we met in the chat room, I didn't want anyone else. Nobody could've given me the support you did. And when we spoke for the first time," his face brightened with a smile, "I knew, without a doubt, I wouldn't go back again. Because I had you."

Her hand fell away. Yes, she'd known he'd been alone in his struggles, but hadn't fathomed how much her support had meant.

Blake narrowed his gaze. "Too much?"

She shook her head.

He ran his hand through her hair, brushing it behind her ear, his sight following the movements. "I stopped marking myself when I no longer needed to." His lashes lifted and his dilated pupils ensnared her, tightening her chest. "I stopped with this," he pointed to the angel.

Again, words escaped her. She didn't know how to respond, or move, or breathe. He'd blown her away with his brutal honesty. She let out a ragged breath, then wished she hadn't when Blake stiffened. "I wish I'd known," she said in a rush, trying to ease his concern. "Then maybe we would've met sooner."

He gave a shake of his head and placed a kiss on her forehead. "I don't. I wasn't good enough for you back then… I'm still not. But at least now I've overcome one of my demons, and I can focus on trying to be the man you deserve."

"Blake." Her voice held a warning. "Please don't do that." She tilted her chin and placed a soft kiss on his lips, feeling his softening flesh slide from her body. "You need to forgive yourself. We both have insecurities, and we can't focus on those things. We need to trust each other and let go of the doubt. From now on, it's just you and me, as equals, OK?"

"Yeah. OK." He spoke into her mouth and swept his tongue against hers. "I can do that."

"Good." She went to deepen the kiss but a yawn overtook her.

"Oh, yeah, that's great. Tell me not to feel insecure, then yawn in my mouth. That really boosts my ego."

She chuckled and snuggled under his chin. "Sorry. I couldn't help it."

He kissed her temple and slid off the mattress. "Go to sleep."

Her eyelids drooped while he walked around the bed, removing the condom. Water ran in the bathroom, then the lights flicked off and moments later he was tugging at the bed covers and sliding her limp body to lie on the cool sheets. "Goodnight, angel." He spooned in behind her, resting the hardness of his chest against her back, nestling his face in her hair.

Gabi moaned, loving the feel of his possessive arm around her belly. "Love you."

"Mmm, still doesn't count," he murmured. "But nice try, sweetheart."

Chapter Nineteen

GABI SAT ON a plastic chair late the next morning, trying not to cross and uncross her legs too often while she stared straight ahead. The guys of Reckless Beat, along with their crew, were buzzing around the stage, running cables, setting up speakers, tuning instruments. It was like watching a colony of ants prepare for a storm. Everyone had a job, and they all worked together in smooth synchronicity.

"It's hard to believe that sixteen thousand people will pack this arena in a few days." Alana spoke beside her, snapping her out of a naughty daydream involving the stage, loud music, and Blake's "instrument".

Gabi cleared her throat. "Yeah," she croaked. Damn, the sight of Blake in a plain white T-shirt, hair spiked, tattoos on display, torn jeans, and wrist cuffs…just—damn. The way he cradled each of his guitars, one after the other, with confident reverence and the concentration that creased his brow as he tuned the strings. The mere preparation had her heart palpitating. She didn't want to contemplate how her body would react if he started to play.

Alana giggled. "Mesmerizing, isn't it?"

Gabi dragged her gaze from the stage to give Alana a brief smile. "Definitely. They all seem so…" There wasn't a word worthy of their description—the mix of self-assurance, intensity, and sexuality.

Alana turned back to the stage with a laugh. "Hot."

"Yeah, *very* hot."

Too mouth-wateringly desirable. Any hot-blooded woman wouldn't be able to resist the allure of seducing these men by any means possible. And once Gabi went home, she wouldn't be able to beat them off with a stick.

"Test. One. Two," Mason spoke over the microphone, sending his voice ricocheting through the empty arena.

"Sounds good," one of the crew yelled, giving a thumb's up.

"I wish I could see them play… properly I mean," Gabi voiced her thoughts and sighed. "I guess there'll be time in the future." Ticking that item off her bucket list would have to wait a while. She didn't have long before she had to catch her flight to Queensland.

"You've never seen Blake play?" Alana's voice rose, and her knees pivoted to touch Gabi's. "You can't leave without hearing at least one song. Hold on a minute." She stood and took a step toward the stage.

"Wait!" Gabi grabbed her hand and pulled her back. "What are you doing?"

"They're almost set up. I'm sure they wouldn't mind playing at least one song before you leave."

"No," Gabi shook her head. She didn't want to interrupt the flow. They had a routine, a schedule, and it was all coming together nicely. And besides, she would only embarrass herself when she orgasmed in her chair. "It's fine. Really."

"What's going on?" Mitch's voice came over the bustle of noise, and Gabi glanced up to see him standing at the edge of the stage, looking down at them.

"Gabi hasn't heard Blake play," Alana called.

Blake lifted his head at the sound of his name and frowned. "What was that?"

Mitch's lips twitched, and he turned to Blake, talking too soft for Gabi to hear. She held her breath while they spoke, the tightness growing in her chest until Blake moved his focus to Mason and asked, "Have we got time for a song?"

Mason shrugged. "I'm set."

"Sean, how about you?" Blake asked.

Gabi couldn't see Sean at the back of the stage behind his drum kit, but she heard his reply of, "Yeah. I'm good."

"Rye?" Mitch jerked his head in question.

Ryan strummed his guitar, one hand sliding over the fret board as the sound pierced the air with a nerve tingling riff. His fingers moved with precision. Gabi squinted to catch every detail, her heart pounding with the impact of each note. Then he gripped the whammy bar and the seductive howl that followed sent adrenaline coursing through her veins.

When the noise faded, Mason positioned himself in front of the mic. "A simple 'yes' would've sufficed, smartass."

Another guitar sounded from a different direction, piercing her chest with its ferocity. Gabi snapped her attention to Mitch. He was poised on the edge of the stage, staring down at Alana as he tried to outdo Ryan, playing faster, harder, and longer. One by one, the crew grabbed plastic chairs, all of them sitting to watch the impromptu performance.

As Mitch continued, Leah came out from side stage, striding toward Mason, her tablet computer under her arm. With an air of authority, she grabbed the microphone stand and cleared her throat. "Come on, guys."

Mitch slapped his palm over the strings, the sudden weight of silence hanging heavy in the empty arena.

"Thank you. Now if you've stopped stroking your Johnsons, can you please play something proper for Gabi? She has to leave for the airport in fifteen minutes." Leah fixed her sights on Mitch. She was professional and determined in her navy tailored suit, her blonde hair loose and falling over her shoulders.

There was a brief pause, then a cymbal crashed, loud and earsplitting, followed by the hard beat of drums at a breakneck tempo. Sean thrashed from his seat at the back of the stage, pounding hard, his arms flying from the high hat to the floor tom, moving in a constant blur before abruptly stopping.

"Sorry," he called out. "My Johnson felt left out."

Leah shook her head and thrust the microphone stand at Mason before striding from the stage. Gabi couldn't tell if their band manager was genuinely annoyed or acting with the usual air of underlying humor. She hoped it was the latter. Nobody had discussed the argument from last night, and both Ryan and Leah had kept their distance, remaining quiet all morning.

"I think we're ready," Mason announced, his voice smooth and seductive. "What song, Emo?"

Blake pointed to his groin and mouthed the words "blow me" before turning to Gabi. Their gazes connected, creating a chain reaction of sensations that ran through her limbs. Her stomach flipped, her nipples tightened, and her mouth dried out to the point of pain.

She adored this man. Always had. And seeing him on stage, in a place where he felt most confident, made her all the more addicted to his charm. He was at home up there, and it was invigorating to see him so alive.

"Angel of Mine," he announced and continued to stare at her while Mason glanced between them.

Nobody knew it was her song. Christ, until last night she'd thought it was written about a friend of Blake's, just like everyone else had. Now Mason was scrutinizing them, his questioning gaze seeping under her skin in search of the truth.

"OK, let's rock this," Mitch announced.

"Ready, Mace?" Sean called, holding his sticks above his head.

Gabi held her breath, waiting.

There was a beat of silence.

"Yeah, I'm ready," Mason answered, palming the microphone in the stand, his gaze focused on her.

Gabi let out the breath congealing in her lungs and smiled in relief at Blake. He grinned back and mouthed the words *I love you.*

Gabi ignored Alana's gasp and mouthed the words back. *I love you.*

"Thanks gorgeous, I love you, too," Mason replied.

Gabi pierced the lead singer with an unconvincing glare. She couldn't help that her lips were twitching. Mason had a way of being so sickeningly arrogant that it became appealing. He smirked at her, his brown eyes gleaming, yet his expression held no flirtation. He was teasing her like a friend, treating her as part of the family, showing her she belonged. She didn't think many people would've experienced the caring side of Mason, and she was glad to be one of the lucky few.

Sean tapped his sticks over his head—one, two, three—forcing her to concentrate. In the next beat they began to play, the mix of guitars—rhythm, bass, and lead—along with Mason's voice and the drums, making the arena walls vibrate.

With trembling hands, she inched forward in her seat, sitting on the edge to get a better view. Blake stole her attention, hypnotizing her with every move of his fingers, the flex of his tattooed arms and the flick of his cuffed wrists.

Lyrics echoed in the back of her mind, and for the first time, after falling in love with this song a lifetime ago, the words now held new meaning.

You saved me from myself, from the drowning and the pain.

As much as she mentally commanded, Blake didn't look at her. From the first moment his fingers strummed the guitar strings he remained focused on his instrument. His head hung, his eyes closing for long moments at a time.

Sweet angel mine, keep me from the darkness, soothe the acid in my veins.

When Mitch stepped forward for his solo, Blake glanced up and she sucked in a breath at the naked vulnerability in his gaze. She could see how much this song meant to him, could feel it echo inside herself.

He focused back on his guitar, backing up and deepening the piercing sound that emanated from Mitch's guitar, making it slice through her chest with its ferocity. The intimacy of the lyrics, the brutality of Blake's life was laid bare for millions of people to hear. Yet nobody knew it was about him. Them.

As Mason repeated the chorus for the final time, Gabi moved to her feet. The song ended with a drawn out guitar note, and by then, she was walking forward, her legs moving without thought as she headed to the portable staircase standing alongside the stage. Her heart pounded against her sternum, growing more frantic with each step.

Blake's stare followed her, making her weak and vulnerable, strong and certain, all at the same time. She watched him yank his guitar strap over his head and thrust his guitar at Mitch when he walked past, striding toward her. They met at the top of the staircase, and without a word, they moved into one another, his arms going around her waist, hers around his neck, their lips meeting in the middle.

He stole her breath, her heart, her love and gave his back in return.

He kissed her as if he lived for the taste of her. He held her like she was his anchor and he needed grounding. His hands delicately stroked her back cherishing every inch of skin he touched. And still she wanted more. She couldn't get close enough, couldn't kiss hard enough, but she tried, with every sweep of her tongue and every caress of her lips.

His hands slid to her ass, cupping, and then lifting her off the ground. She wrapped her legs around his waist, clinging to him, not caring who watched. They only had now. Tomorrow she would be alone, distraught, and heartbroken. Nothing would stop her from enjoying these last moments together.

"Why don't you guys take this out back?" Leah's voice called softly. "You've got ten minutes."

Blake broke the connection, his face a mix of anguish and undeniable lust.

"He only needs two," Sean sniggered.

Blake rested his forehead against Gabi's, their chests heaving together in a fierce rhythm. Then without warning, he turned, her ass grasped in his hands and walked them into the side stage corridor. The area was dark, silent, and led to a small room in the back. He rushed them inside, kicking the door shut with his foot.

He collapsed against the door, pulling her body with him. "I can't do this," he murmured. "I can't say goodbye."

"Shh." She placed a finger over his lips. "Then don't." She couldn't stand to hear it anyway. "Every day will bring us closer to where we want to be. It's only a matter of time."

She loosened her legs from his waist and let her feet fall to the floor. Her mouth found his, her tongue licking his bottom lip. A growl rumbled in his chest, enticing her to do it again and again. "Show me how much you love me," she begged.

"Gabi." Her name was a plea. "I'll never be able to show you. You'd never believe me."

She ignored the heartache in his tone and ran her lips down to his chin, then along his jaw. She nuzzled his neck, sucked his skin into her mouth, marking him.

He sucked in a breath and ground the hardness of his shaft into her pelvis. His hand worked between them, fumbling in his pocket, pulling out a condom. As he undid his belt buckle, she kicked off her shoes and yanked at her pants, lowering them to the floor along with her underwear and kicking them away.

They grasped at each other, their hands and lips and tongues stroking and rubbing and caressing. He lifted her off the ground, placing her bottom on the small waist-high table and pushed between her legs.

Gabi fisted his shirt in her hands and raised the material, dragging it over his stomach and pecs until he quickly placed the corner of the condom packet between his teeth and yanked the shirt over his head. He pulled down the front of her silk camisole, exposing her bra and lowering the cups to grasp her breasts in his hands.

He groaned, working the underwear covered erection that peaked from his opened zipper, against the apex of her thighs. "Touch me."

She complied, lowering his underwear to expose the heavily veined skin of his cock and taking it in a tight fist.

He hissed and dropped his hands from her breasts, ripping open the condom packet with his teeth and spitting the wrapper to the floor. "This isn't gonna last long."

"Good," she panted. She wanted hard and fast and brutal.

He sheathed himself with fierce jerks that made her pussy clench. Gripping his cock in his fist, he placed the head of his shaft at her entrance, and in one savage thrust he sunk home, tearing a cry from her throat.

She clung to him, her hands gripping his taut biceps as her legs encircled his waist. The table rocked with his movements, pounding against the wall, harder and harder.

"Oh, Blake… Oh…" She closed her eyes, delirious with lust.

He reached for her bra again, lowering the cups to tweak her nipples. Pleasure speared down her center, pooling in her sex, making her buck against him.

"Gabi," he warned, one hand leaving her breast to trail around her back and grip her hair. He tugged, exposing her neck, making her helpless.

The *bang, bang, bang* against the wall increased as his head lowered to her shoulder. She wanted to come, she was right there, on the cliff's edge but she wouldn't go without him. Not this last time.

She tilted her head, moving her lips to his ear. "I'm a slave to the way you fuck me."

He pulled tighter on her hair, causing her core to clamp down on his cock.

So close. Oh, so close.

"Angel." The endearment was a breath this time, softly spoken against her skin.

Her body broke out in goose bumps, the tingling sensation starting at her neck, spreading over her chest, and finally sinking to her core, pushing her over into the peak of ecstasy. She sucked in a breath, moaned his name, and held on while wave after wave of pleasure pulsed through her.

"Fuck," Blake yelled, holding her tighter, sinking harder while they both moved together in orgasm.

She writhed, arching her back, raking her nails down his skin until the haze of lust started to taper and their movements calmed, slowed, then stopped.

"Every minute will feel like a week without you beside me." He pulled her into his chest, cupping the back of her head with his palm. "It's going to be he—"

A light rap sounded at the door and Gabi stiffened.

"I'm sorry, guys, but Gabi's car is waiting," Leah said.

"We'll be out in a minute," Blake spoke over his shoulder.

This was it. The moment they'd been dreading. Her heart threatened to crack under the weight of inevitable loneliness. She circled his ribs with her arms, hugging tight. "I don't want you to come to the airport with me."

"What?" He jerked back and stared down at her, his eyes frantically searching hers.

She didn't want an audience for their goodbye. She needed to do it here, while things were perfect. Intimate. "Let's do this now. That way you can help the guys set up, and you won't have to go all the way to the airport and back."

"Fuck that, Gabi. I want to go with you."

"Think about it." She placed a palm against his cheek and rested her forehead against his. "There will be hundreds of people. It will be busy and messy and rushed." She shook her head. "I don't want that."

They were both hurting and Gabi preferred to suffer in private than have the threat of paparazzi or screaming fans barging in on their goodbye.

He stepped back, gripping the condom before pulling from her body.

"Give me a minute." He disposed of the condom and zipped up his fly, fastening the belt while she scooted from the table and tugged on her underwear and pants. After righting her clothes, she looked up to find him standing tall, his dark, tortured eyes staring back at her.

Wordlessly, he opened his arms and she went to him, falling into them, feeling his love and adoration cover her like a blanket. He kissed her hair and held her close, not letting go. "We'll see each other in a few weeks," he promised. "Once the tour is over, I'll be on the first plane back to you, OK?" He grabbed her shoulders and pulled back so he could peer down at her. "We'll make this work."

She nodded her head. "I know." She was determined to make their relationship last, no matter how hard the path would be. The comforting fact was that she could see the same determination mirrored in Blake's eyes.

"And we'll be able to talk the same as we always have. That won't change."

She smiled at him. He was beginning to ramble and it was cute. "I know." She ran her hands around his neck, committing every detail of his face to memory. "I don't plan on letting you go easily."

He grinned. "I don't plan on letting you go *at all*." He placed a gentle kiss on her lips before retreating with a sigh. "Where are your things?"

Her heart clenched. "Leah was taking care of them."

"OK." He reached for her hand. "Let's do this."

She straightened and shook her head, blinking away the moisture that began to form. "No. Say goodbye to me now. Please. I can't handle doing this in front of the others."

His hand squeezed hers and his Adam's apple bobbed with a deep swallow. "God damn it, Gabi. This is so fucking hard."

She raised her chin and shook her head. "No, it's not. We're not going to let it be hard. We'll just do it quick and painless, as if we'll see each other again tomorrow." She stepped into his body and smiled up at him. "I'm going to kiss you, and then I'm going to walk away."

He peered down at her for a long moment, staring at her hair, her eyes, her mouth. "All right."

Gabi licked her bottom lip and slowly reached up on tiptoes. "I love you, Blake Kennedy."

He grinned for the briefest moment. "I love you, sweet angel."

She placed her mouth against his, and her nose began to tingle with the threat of tears. The kiss was feather-light, tender, and with all the strength inside her, she pulled away.

"Bye," she whispered and turned in his arms to leave.

Her feet were heavy, her limbs aching as she took the first step. His hand gripped hers and pulled her back, ripping a sob from her chest. He tugged her into his arms and cupped her face with his palms. His lips smashed against hers, hard, doubling her heartache, multiplying her pain. Their tongues tangled and her hands went under his shirt needing the warmth of the expanse of skin above his heart.

She clawed at him, sweeping her tongue back and forth over his, loving the way he cradled her lovingly in his hands. Tears blazed down her cheeks, scorching her from the outside in, only increasing the way her stomach somersaulted from passion and equal parts misery.

Their lips parted on a heated gasp, and she didn't allow herself to falter. In a heartbeat, her hands were out from under his shirt, and she was striding from the room.

"See you soon, angel."

Chapter Twenty

I TOLD MY parents about you. Gabi pressed send on the text message and seconds later her phone rang.

"Hey, angel. I miss you." Blake's voice sounded tired.

"I miss you, too." She missed his voice, his touch, his love, and barely twenty-four hours had passed. "And thank you for the lilies. The florist delivered them this morning."

"I hope you liked them."

"I always do." Blake had sent her flowers three years in a row and each time it gave her strength to face the day.

"So what happened with your parents?"

She inhaled and slumped back onto the bed. They had acted according to plan—apprehensive, protective, and disapproving. She hadn't planned on telling them about Blake, had argued with herself all Tuesday night about it. But when she arrived at their house on Wednesday, she knew she wouldn't get through the day without releasing the bubble bursting to break free.

If she couldn't be with Blake, then she needed to talk about him. And it wasn't like her parents couldn't use a distraction. She'd gone with them to the cemetery, had held her mother while she sobbed at Greg's grave, and watched her father stand tall and proud as he focused on his son's headstone. Gabi had made morning tea, helped with lunch, then cleaned up the mass of dishes to start again at afternoon tea. And when they sat down for another coffee, the words flittered from her lips. *"Mom... Dad...I've met someone."*

"I told them I'm seeing someone."

"And?" He growled, "Come on, sweetheart, you're killin' me."

She chuckled. Nothing was sexier than that guttural sound he made. "I suppose it ended better than expected."

"Which means?"

She could hear banging in the background, guitars being tuned and people shouting. "Are you working? Is this a bad time?"

"Christ. No. Just tell me!"

"I can hear noise in the background. I don't want to disturb you."

"We're about to do a full rehearsal with the supporting band. I'm not playing for over an hour, though, so tell me. Now, woman!"

OK, she'd procrastinated long enough. "My parents were...*concerned* about your career. Which I suppose is warranted. What parent wants their only daughter dating a rock star? In the end, though, I think I won them over. They want to meet you... Well, I think dad actually wants to grill you until you cry, but at least he didn't vow to get out his shotgun."

Silence.

"Blake?"

"That's great." His tone said otherwise.

"I don't understand. I thought you wanted to meet my parents."

"I did... I *do*." Awkward silence. "Now that it's actually going to happen, I'm kinda shitting myself."

Her cheeks lifted with a wide smile. "I'm not looking forward to it myself. But you'll be fine. They'll love you. Eventually."

"Ha ha. Very funny. I gather you didn't tell them how we met or what I look like."

"Uh, yes and no. I told them we met online."

Gabi cringed, remembering the way her father responded, *"I hope it wasn't one of those cheesy relationship sites."*

She'd wanted to smile and say, "No, Daddy, the website was all about drug addiction." Instead, she bit her tongue.

"I told them the basic details. Your career, where you live, and most importantly that you make me happy. For now, that's all they need to know."

Baby steps were the key.

"Well, I'm glad they know. Did today go all right otherwise? I've wanted to call you every second."

Gabi closed her eyes and rested her head back on a pillow. Anniversaries were always tough. This year had been worse because of her ping-ponging emotions and the way her heart yearned for Blake's comfort. "I got through the day."

"I wish I was there with you."

She crinkled her nose and pressed her lips together. Not a single tear had fallen down her cheeks today. She wouldn't start blubbering now. "I wish you were here, too." God, how she wished he was here. A simple hug from Blake would soothe everything, the exhaustion, the heartache, the grief. "Remind me again, how long until you finish your tour?"

"Too long, angel. Too god damn long." Blake stared at the grey cement floor and focused on the image of Gabi in his mind. The hours apart had made him determined. He was going to make his life a fucking fairytale, all for her, the woman he loved—his best friend.

His first hurdle was Michelle. He'd stayed awake until early morning, writing a list of contacts, making calls to the US and asking favors from people who owed him nothing.

Thank god for the celebrity status draw card.

People had vowed to keep an eye out for potential acting positions. Some even offered to look in different media avenues that might appease the demon bitch.

"Will you call me before you go on stage tomorrow?" Gabi asked.

"Definitely." He toed a stone with his black boot and watched it roll along the floor. This distance shit really sucked. How the hell did Ryan do it? "I'll call you first thing in the morning and every fifteen minutes afterward, if you want."

He'd do it too, if he thought she wouldn't grow tired of him in the process. He was dying to be with her again. Even the lingering scent of her shampoo on his hotel pillows drove him insane. Housekeeping had wanted to change the sheets this morning, and he'd had to turn them away, clinging like a little bitch to the one piece of Gabi he had left.

Her laugh echoed through the phone, the feminine, free-spirited sound warming his heart and shattering it all at the same time. "I think once before the show will be enough," she said. "It's already too hard to concentrate on anything other than you without the promise of calls every fifteen minutes."

He couldn't concentrate for shit. The band's promotional obligations had started this morning with radio and television interviews, and Blake had been too distracted when asked, "What have you been doing since arriving in Australia?"

Apparently, "Gabi" wasn't the correct response.

Leah hadn't been amused. Not that it changed her already sullen mood. She still hadn't recovered from her argument with Ryan, and neither one of them would talk about it.

"I'll let you get back to work."

Gabi's voice kick started his heart into a faster tempo. All night his conscience nagged at him to tell her about Michelle. The few hours sleep had only increased its potency. He couldn't do it now though, not on the anniversary of her brother's death. Blake probably wouldn't tell her until they were face to face again, and hopefully then the problem would be resolved. No, it *would* be resolved. He'd make sure of it. Until then, he had to deal with keeping the information from her.

"OK. I'll speak to you soon."

"I love you, Blake."

One side of his lips lifted in a grin. He'd never get used to hearing that. "You know, angel, I think that one actually counts."

"It always counts when I say it."

He sure hoped so, because right now her love was the only thing keeping him sane.

Chapter Twenty-One

"I don't want your pity job, Blake." Michelle bitched over the crackling cell connection.

After a week of waiting for one of his contacts to pull through, he'd finally got the call. The part wasn't much, a small stint in an upcoming paranormal sitcom, but it was a job. A paying job, and something that would get Michelle's foot in the door…and out of his ass.

"We made a deal, and I'm sick to death of waiting. I've got nothing. Nothing, Blake! No money. No job. No social life. Either be here the day after your last concert—and yes, I do know when that is—or the deal is off."

Blake clutched the hotel balcony railing and ground his molars until his jaw threatened to pop. "Don't push me, Michelle. You seem to forget, I'm not the only one that'll be publicly shamed with those images."

Her threat had shadowed him for too long, making him edgy. It didn't help that he was already falling apart from being away from Gabi. He found it hard to breathe when he wasn't around her and he didn't want to break her heart by postponing their catch up at the end of the tour. "Take the fucking job."

"You take the fucking job!" she screeched.

How the hell had he ever been attracted to this woman? She was bat-shit crazy.

He closed his eyes and silently counted to ten, letting the slight Adelaide breeze ease his anger. Reckless Beat was flying to their final tour destination of Perth tomorrow for a week of performances. That gave him seven days to find a way to calm the wicked bitch of the West and get his happily ever after. Call it intuition, but whenever he thought about Michelle, and in return Gabi, a deep unrelenting ache settled behind his ribs.

"Fine. I'll keep looking for something else," he snarled.

"No, you won't. That wasn't the deal. *I* will find the acting position *I* want. Your job is to get my face back in the magazines."

He couldn't allow that. He needed to appease her before it got that far. Giving her money and dealing with her ranting was one thing. Hurting Gabi with images of him with his ex wasn't acceptable. He wouldn't be able to stand seeing the woman he loved with another man, no matter how innocent it was. So he wouldn't do it to her.

"And if I can't do that? What then?" Blake held his breath waiting for the inevitable answer.

"Then you leave me no choice."

He scoffed. "I've had no choice from the start. Why can't you take the job? Yes, it's a small part, but at least it's something. It'll make a better news story than seeing us talking at social events."

She laughed, and the maniacal sound gave him goose bumps of the shit-scared variety. "We won't be talking, Blake. We'll be making headlines, drawing attention, and doing whatever's necessary to land me a *big* role in an upcoming movie. Not a piddly little snap shot in a no-name sitcom. So stop wasting time phoning friends."

Padded footsteps sounded behind him, and he turned to see Alana's worried gaze staring back at him from the other side of the sliding screen door.

"I've gotta go," he muttered and ended the call. As he placed his cell back in his shorts' pocket, Alana stepped onto the balcony, a coffee in her hands.

"Everything OK?" Her hair was ruffled from sleep, her body covered in a pink silk bathrobe.

"Fine, Allie." He smiled and leaned back against the second story railing, feigning a calm he didn't feel.

She broke eye contact and sat down on one of the wooden chairs lining the window, staring into her coffee. "It didn't sound fine." She shot him a quick glance from under her lashes, and then looked back at her mug.

He shrugged. "It's nothing." He wanted to follow up with "please quit asking," but she didn't deserve his anger. "Just an old acquaintance causing a few minor problems. I've got it sorted."

She sipped her coffee and focused on him over the rim. When the mug came back down to rest in her hands, she continued to stare. "I lack a lot of life experience, Blake, but I'm not stupid. I can tell you're in trouble. I only hope you'll come to me or Mitchell for help if you need it."

Blake worked his jaw and bit the inside of his mouth until he tasted the coppery tang of blood. Gabi had always been the one to share his burdens with. The one he relied on to lighten the weight of his problems. Going to Mitch or Alana would feel like a betrayal to the woman who had stood by him through the hardest times.

"Thank you." He pushed from the railing and stood tall. "Everything will work itself out. I'm not worried." Again with the lies. Every time he uttered mistruths the weight of guilt became heavier.

She took another sip of her coffee and nodded, focusing her attention through the balcony posts to the nature park below. "How's Gabi?"

Direct hit.

"Gabi's…great." His words lacked conviction. Hell, *he* didn't even believe his tone. "I miss her." He missed her, yearned for her, not only in his bed but in his arms, her scent in his lungs, her bright smile in his mind. Yet he'd stopped calling her as often. Every time they spoke he felt like he was betraying her. "I think I need to cancel our plans after the tour finishes. I've got things I have to sort out at home."

Alana glanced at him from the corner of her eye. "Gabi has a soft heart, but I'm sure she'll understand if you explain the reasons to her."

He nodded. There was nothing else to do. Gabi did have a soft heart. One he knew would break if she found out about Michelle. Trust was a big thing for Gabi, and he'd broken that trust. She just didn't know it yet. Hopefully she never would.

"Yeah. She'll understand. It doesn't stop me missing her, though."

Alana gave a sad smile.

"Oh, surprise surprise," Mitch opened the screen door and stepped onto the balcony, placing a kiss on Alana's forehead. "Fancy finding you two alone together."

Alana flashed her fiancé a wicked grin. "Morning, sweetheart."

Mitch grasped her chin and kissed her lips with force. "Mornin'."

Jealousy was a trait Blake despised, yet it clawed at him anyway. He was happy for his friends, but having the ease of their relationship shoved in his face only made him ache more for Gabi. "I'll see you guys later," he muttered and opened the screen door to go inside.

"What's wrong with B?" Mitch asked softly.

"I don't know," Alana replied. "But I'm worried it's something big."

The days passed like months, the weeks like years, until Gabi contemplated putting her degree on hold to follow Blake. For the first ten days after leaving Melbourne, they'd spoken on the phone and used every other form of social media possible to keep in touch—Skype, Snapchat, Facebook, Twitter, you name it, they were on it. And still it hadn't been enough. For over a week, she'd woken to heartfelt emails counting down the time until they would be together.

Then things slowed.

Blake no longer answered her Skype calls, and when he returned them, their conversations were unemotional and vague. He no longer sent her pictures. Didn't comment on Facebook or send her tweets. When she questioned him about it, he apologized and made excuses about being tired and run down.

She got that. Really, she did. His life was filled with late nights, adrenaline filled concerts, and a never ending line of public appearances. It would be daunting, yet he'd lived like that for years, and not once had he cut her off like this. Something had changed, she just didn't know what.

Had he met someone else? Tammy had been hinting at that outcome for a few days but even her close friend wouldn't come out and say it.

Her phone buzzed in her pocket, and she eyed her university lecturer before pulling it out and checking the message. *Blake—We need to talk. Are you free?*

Dread consumed her stomach and filtered out to her limbs. He should know she was in class today. She'd told him in another one of her emails that he hadn't replied to.

With her throat tightening, she quietly packed up her text books, grabbed her handbag and ducked out of the classroom. She placed her things on the hallway floor and began scrolling to his number when her phone started buzzing with a silenced incoming call.

She stared at the screen while her intuition begged her not to answer. Was he calling because he thought she was in class, hoping she wouldn't answer? Did he plan to break things off in a voice message? Well too bad, she had no intention of letting the call go through to the answering service.

She connected the call and placed the phone at her ear, jutting out her chin. "Hello."

"Gabi? I—I didn't know if you'd answer."

He didn't want her to answer, more like it.

"I stepped out of class," she replied, withholding the hurt from her voice. "You haven't answered my calls in so long I didn't want to miss the opportunity that you might actually want to talk to me." She may have hidden the hurt from her tone, but her resentment came through in technicolor. She'd been beside herself for too long, bottling up the hurt and insecurities to let it simply go unsaid.

"I know." His voice was low, breaking her heart a little with each softly spoken word. "I'm sorry. I've had problems back home that kept me distracted. I was hoping they would've blown over by now."

"What happened? What's wrong?" Her heart rate increased causing her hands to tremor slightly. She could hear the hurt in his tone, could sense the inevitable bad news she knew would affect her.

"Nothing…Nothing you need to worry about, anyway. But…"

He heaved a breath and she held hers. Waiting. Panicking.

"I can't meet up with you once the tour finishes, angel. I'm so sorry."

She closed her eyes, wishing away the pain. The days apart had been one long and unending struggle. She felt detached from her heart. Alone and incomplete. The only thing that kept her going was the countdown to when they would be together again, when the missed calls and unanswered emails would no longer matter, because they were together.

"I—I understand," she lied.

She had no clue what she'd done wrong or what had changed between them. Were they breaking up? If so, he needed to come out and say it. She didn't want to be dragged along for days, or weeks, or months, wondering where they stood.

"Is this the end, Blake? Just tell me if it is. Tell me now so I don't hold on." Her voice broke, betraying the emotion clogging her throat. Annoyance tangled with the hurt and confusion. He'd never left her in the dark before, had never kept things from her or hidden himself, even in the worst of times. Having him do it now, after they'd been together physically, hurt more than she thought he would ever realize.

"No, Gabi!" His sudden answer soothed some of the tightness restricting her chest. "This has nothing to do with us. I still want to be there with you—that's all I want—I just can't at the moment. As soon as I fix the mess, I'll be on the first plane back to you."

Silently, she let out a heavy breath and rested against the cold wall. "I hate when you keep things from me. You never did before. How bad can your problems be when you've told me so much in the past?"

She wished she could see his face, to read his reaction.

"Please don't worry about me. That's the last thing I want. For once, I'm going to sort out my own mess." He chuckled, but the humor didn't reach her. "I'm not used to cleaning up my mistakes. I've always had you to rely on."

She nodded to herself. He continued to bring up the need to fix his own life, and she had to respect that, no matter how much it hurt to be left out.

"I want you to be proud of me," he whispered.

Air shuddered from her lips and she stared at the ceiling, widening her eyes in the hopes the burning would fade. "I've always been proud of you. I wish you knew that."

"I do. I also need to do this to feel like I actually have a set of balls. Real men fix their own shit, ya know?"

She chuckled and sniffed. "OK."

"And I'm sorry for being distant. I've wanted to speak to you every day, but my mood is contagious. I don't want to drag you down. Once I have my life under control, things will go back to normal, and I'll be on the first flight back to you."

"Please don't take long." She shouldn't have added to his burden, yet she missed his friendship too much to let the words go unsaid. Being without him physically was something she lived with for years. His support and kindness was completely different.

"I received an email from Alana about the engagement party," she spoke quickly, hoping to change the subject. The invitation came a week after Gabi left Melbourne, with the celebration set to take place in New York, not long after Reckless Beat arrived back from tour.

Blake was silent for a moment before asking, "Do you think you can come?"

"I wish I could."

"Me too," he whispered. "Hopefully by then I will be on my way back to Australia."

"And miss their engagement party?" Was he serious? The Blake she knew would never miss an event like that. He wasn't making sense. First he couldn't speak to her or return her emails, now he wanted to miss a monumental event to fly back to her?

Doubt darkened the back of her mind, and she shook away her suspicions before they had time to fully form. "You can't miss that. We'll be together soon enough." She spoke the words, even though she lacked the enthusiasm to back them up. Every second that passed unnerved her, making her frantic to see Blake in person.

"Yeah. But soon enough feels like forever."

Soon enough meant nothing to Gabi. She didn't know what problems he had to deal with at home.

"Do you forgive me for backing out of our plans?"

She sighed, long and loud. "Yeah." She didn't have a choice.

"I'll make it up to you." Cheeky flirtation accompanied his words, warming her heart.

"Don't worry. I'll hold you to that."

He laughed, and she could picture him smiling on the other end, his dark eyes glistening, his muscles flexing as he reclined in a lounge chair.

"OK, angel. I'll let you go. Sorry for interrupting you during class. Once things settle down, I'll let you know."

Her heart flipped, clenched, dropping to the soles of her feet. She wanted to know when she would speak to him again, and with equal measure she didn't want to sound needy. "All right, bye."

She waited for his farewell and ended the call. Grabbing her books and handbag off the floor, she walked to the classroom door. The lecturer spoke loud, pointing to the white board behind him with a wooden ruler. There was no way she could concentrate now. Not when her mind pinged like a pinball machine.

Stepping back, she started down the hall, heading for the car park. When she got home she would email one of her classmates for notes. Then she would email Alana. If Blake couldn't give her any answers maybe Mitch's fiancé could.

Chapter Twenty-Two

Blake's fingers hovered over the email send button. Eight days had passed since he last spoke to Gabi, and now he was home, sitting in the Reckless Beat jet while it taxied into Teterboro airport. She'd emailed him every day, her messages growing more concerned the longer he went without replying, yet he still didn't know what to tell her.

He re-read the email he still hadn't sent—*Hey, angel. Sorry I've been distant. I just wanted to let you know I arrived safely and hope to be back with you soon.*

Love Blake.

"What's wrong?" Mason asked from the seat beside him.

Blake glanced up and met the stares of each band member along with Leah and Alana as they scrutinized him from their seats. They all knew something was wrong. They just assumed it revolved around being away from Gabi.

"Nothing." He focused back on his phone and pressed send. The email was lame at best, but at least he was keeping in touch. He couldn't stand speaking to her, hearing the hurt in her voice, especially when he couldn't ease her pain. It wouldn't be long now and his problems would be over. He'd have coffee with Michelle once or twice, be seen in the same nightclubs and create a few national headlines—making sure nothing was exciting enough to make the global gossip mags. Then bam, the devil spawn would leave him the fuck alone.

Until then, he needed to continue to keep his distance from Gabi. She needed to concentrate on her studies anyway, and he'd gone too far for her to find out about Michelle now.

"Nothing? Like the same 'nothing' that's kept you grumpy for the last three weeks?" Mason asked.

"Or the same 'nothing' that has you swearing your ass off on your cell? To people you refuse to name," Mitch added.

"Leave him alone," Alana spoke softly. "He'll tell you when he's ready."

Leah moved forward in her seat. "We're worried about you, Blake."

"There's nothing to be worried about," he answered, trying not to shuffle in his chair under all the attention. "I miss Gabi. End of story."

"So why didn't you stay in Aus?" Leah frowned. "Your band commitments are over for a while. You didn't have to come back with us."

"I've got stuff I need to sort out at home. Once that's organized, I'll be on the next flight back to her." He shrugged. "It's no big deal. I just miss her, that's all."

The jet pulled to a stop, and one by one they unclicked their seatbelts, letting the conversation drop. While he stood and gathered his carryon luggage, Ryan came up beside him.

"It's hard, isn't it? Leaving them behind, I mean. I've done it for years, and it never gets easier." Ryan patted Blake on the shoulder. "I hope whatever you have to deal with at home isn't too serious."

Blake turned to Ryan and nudged him with his shoulder. "No, everything's cool. I've got a newfound respect for you though. The whole long distance thing sucks. How do you do it?"

Ryan scoffed, "Obviously not very well. My marriage is hanging by a thread."

"You'll pull through. Have faith."

"I honestly don't think we will." Ryan shrugged. "And I'm not sure if I want to anymore. What's the point? Apart we're miserable, and together isn't any better. I'm beginning to think that catching Julie cheating will be a good excuse to make a clean break."

Blake jerked back in surprise while his friend turned and strode to the opened cabin door. Had he been too consumed with his own issues to notice the enormity of what Ryan must have been going through?

"I'm a fuckin' douche," he muttered to himself and grabbed his iPad from its position between the chair cushions and patted his jeans pocket for his passport. "Hey, Rye, wait up."

Blake was the last to descend the aircraft staircase, shading his eyes from the early morning sun. An airport shuttle waited for them a few feet away, and he climbed on, disappointed to find Ryan already seated next to Mason.

Marriage had always meant a lot to Ryan, so Blake couldn't let the conversation slide. They'd have to talk later, once they caught up on sleep, and the comfort of home soil made their problems less exhausting.

The bus drove them to the customs building where they went through the usual security protocol. Within minutes they were all hustling to the front doors manned by two of their usual security staff.

"Another big crowd?" Leah asked.

One of the men shrugged. "Not too big."

"OK, guys, let's make this a quick exit. I want to get home." Leah walked outside and waited.

The standard burst of noise that accompanied their fans, erupted when they walked from the building. Females held up signs dedicating their love, men yelled, and cameras flashed—nothing new or out of the ordinary. Except for the woman breaking from the crowd.

One of the security guards lunged for her, his hands sliding over her slim waist as she jumped out of his reach. She ran toward Blake, throwing her thick, dark glasses and baseball cap to the ground, releasing a mass of silky, strawberry blonde hair.

Shit.

Michelle pounced on him, wrapping her legs around his waist. He had no choice but to grab her hips to steady himself and fumbled backward until he stabilized her weight. She clung to him, her thighs gripping him tight, her hands running around his neck.

"Get the hell—" His words died under her lips, the clash of her mouth hard and unyielding against his. He jerked back and dropped his hands from her body, letting her fall to her feet. Cameras flashed, people cheered, and none of it penetrated the wild *thump, thump, thump* of his chest while he wondered how he would explain this to Gabi. "Mother fuc—"

"Now, now," she whispered, placing a finger over his mouth. "Is that any way to greet your girlfriend?"

He stepped back, gaining distance to breathe. Mason strode toward them, his gaze darting from Michelle, then back to Blake. "Is this the 'nothing' you were talking about?"

There wasn't a rock big enough for Blake to hide under. Everyone stared at him, photographers, fans, security, Mitch, Leah, Alana, and Sean. The final kick to the balls came when he caught Ryan's scathing gaze. "Remind me not to let you near my wife."

"Now this is the type of attention I was talking about," Michelle purred, the side of her lips lifting in a menacing smile.

He wanted to throttle her. To wrap his hands around her neck and wring the life from her. She stepped into him, placing her hands on his chest. All he could do was stand there, too shocked to figure out how to handle the situation without making a bigger mess.

"Get the fuck away from me," he growled under his breath.

"Oh, sweetie, the photos have already been taken. No point worrying about it now." She rubbed her breasts against his body, and he cringed. "It wasn't so bad, was it?"

He ignored the question, sidestepping her and continuing to the limo. All he could think of was Gabi. How she would react. What she would say. And how her beautiful face would contort in pain when she saw the inevitable photos.

"Blake, wait," Michelle called over the bark of questions from fans.

He continued to walk in long strides across the tarmac, climbing into the waiting vehicle and pulling the door shut.

Inside, silence reigned, thick and uncomfortable.

"Gabi's going to be devastated," Alana whispered to Mitch, loud enough for everyone to hear.

Yeah. Gabi *would* be devastated. And the worst thing? Blake had a feeling this was only the beginning.

Chapter Twenty-Three

GABI WOKE TO the chime of her phone alarm and winced at her stiff neck and pounding head. She'd gone to bed early. Falling asleep every night worried about her relationship with Blake had paid a toll on her health and nothing seemed to lighten her mood. All she needed were answers. Some direction. A little insight.

She was stuck in limbo, not sure if the emotional distance he'd put between them was because of the issues he faced or simply because he didn't know how to end things between them. Reaching for her phone on the bedside table, she silenced the alarm and frowned at all the notifications lining the top of her screen. Twitter, email, Facebook, missed calls, messages. All the icons stood side by side.

She flicked her finger over the screen and clicked the first notification—a text message from Tammy. *Gabi call me asap, honey.*

The missed calls came from her parents and…Tammy.

Yet again, nothing from Blake.

It was too early to return any calls so she navigated to Twitter and searched her favorite hashtags. #recklessbeat and #blakekennedy were all she bothered to follow, and today, the stream was alive with recent tweets.

#blakekennedy glad to see you back with Michie. That woman's damn fine.

Her heart stuttered, and she sat up straight in bed. There had to be a mistake. Or maybe she was still asleep.

#blakekennedy goes BANG! Barely steps foot off the jet and already has a woman literally running for him. I bow to the master of p*ssy.

Gabi couldn't breathe over the tightening of her throat. She skimmed down the Twitter feed, reading similar comments, most mentioning something between Blake and Michelle. Some included links to photos, and curiosity demanded she take a look, even though her mind begged her not to.

#RecklessBlake Heartbroken to see you reunite with Michelle at the airport. But happy for you both. Took this pic…

Her blood pounded loud in her ears while she clicked on the image link. In the next beat her chest constricted and she covered her mouth with a gasp. "Oh, Blake, what have you done?"

The photo showed a side view of him standing, his hands holding the slim waist of a woman, her legs around his hips, and his mouth against hers. Gabi knew instantly who it was. *Her.* Michelle Clarkson. Blake's ex. Or what the Twitter feed now clarified as his new girlfriend.

Gabi dropped her phone, holding her knuckles against her lips to stop herself from throwing up.

He wouldn't do this to her.

How could he do this to her?

She slid to the side of the mattress and placed her feet on the floor. He wouldn't. Not Blake. Not after everything they'd shared. He had more decency than to play with her emotions.

So why hasn't he contacted you?

Rationality taunted her, weighing her down. She didn't want to think about that. If she did, she would lose the grip on her wavering restraint and fall into a place she couldn't recover from.

Maybe this was the reason he'd been distant. Had he been playing Gabi for a fool? Or was Michelle the situation he wanted to sort out by himself? *Yeah, it looked like he was sorting her out good and proper.*

"Oh, god," she choked.

Her phone vibrated on the bed, flashing with an incoming call. She froze, unsure what to do if Blake's name was across the screen. Inching forward, she raised her chin and peered down.

Tammy.

Of course it wasn't Blake. Another fist slammed through her chest. Even though she wouldn't know what to say to him, she wanted him to care enough to call. Having his reunion with Michelle plastered all over the internet wouldn't have escaped his notice. Or, oh god, what if he didn't care?

Maybe he was too busy fucking the whore.

She ran for the bathroom and fell to her knees, heaving over the toilet. Her stomach clenched and bile choked her throat, yet nothing came out. Minutes passed with her head hanging limp, tears burning the back of her eyes. She needed to get ready for work: Shower. Dress. Eat—if she could force food over the sickness that consumed her.

It wasn't as if she hadn't expected something like this. Blake had always been too good to be true. This was reality finally helping to open her eyes.

Pushing to her feet, she padded into her bedroom, grabbed her clothes off the dresser and went back to place them on the basin beside the shower. Her nose tingled, and she sniffed it away, refusing to cry. Tabloids thrived on creating gossip. This could be another celebrity scene blown out of proportion... Or was she weak and naïve for searching for unlikely excuses?

Stop! Blake's mouth on another woman would never be acceptable for her, no matter what way the press spun the story.

With numb hands she turned on the taps and stepped under the shower's spray. Rumors wouldn't defeat her. No. She was stronger than that. *They* were stronger than that. Blake only arrived back in the US less than twelve hours ago, and if something as monumental as their relationship hung in the balance, she was sure his first priority would be to get in contact with her.

She closed her eyes and the Twitter image glared back at her from the darkness. He'd had his eyes open.

Blake had been kissing Michelle with his eyes open!

A glimmer of hope sparked to life in her dying heart. She straightened her posture and tilted her head back under the water. No man ever kissed a woman he cared about with his eyes open. It had to be a set-up. Blake was going to call her. She could feel it. He would call or email or Skype and explain everything.

She just needed to try harder to convince herself of that.

Blake pressed the channel button on his television remote again and again and again. He had no clue what played on the screen, but the action kept his hands busy and away from his cell phone. One day had passed since returning home, and all he'd done was hide from the world in his apartment.

"Have you called Gabi yet?" Mitch walked into the entertainment room, sat beside him on the leather couch, and handed over a can of soda.

Blake shook his head. He couldn't call her. Listening to the hitch in her breath as he told her about Michelle would send him over the edge. And would she even believe him? This morning's tabloids had described a heartfelt reunion between old lovers. Far from the seething, hate filled homecoming it had actually been. All he wanted was to make Gabi happy. To keep her bright eyes glinting and her gorgeous smile wide. He wanted to make her proud, yet everything he did was a disappointment.

He'd spent every waking moment praying she hadn't seen the photos. It wasn't a stretch to wish she hadn't. The hype on Twitter and Facebook had grown and dissipated like a mini gossip whirlwind, however, the photos would always be on the internet if Gabi knew what to search for.

"She hasn't called or emailed since I returned to the states, so I'm taking that as a good sign that she hasn't seen the photos. And I told her I'd be out of contact for a while because I've got stuff to deal with, and she has work and school to keep her busy."

"You need to call her." Mitch cracked his can and rested back into the cushions. "Allie's havin' kittens worrying about her."

Allie was having kittens? Blake let the stress and anger and fear take hold, allowing his blood to boil with annoyance, his heart to thump with pain. He slammed his soda can on the coffee table and threw the remote, watching it slide against the polished wood and fall to the carpeted floor. In a burst of uncontained emotion he pushed to his feet. "Allie needs to mind her own fucking business."

He took two steps, beginning to pace, before he stopped. *Shit.* He'd finally lost his mind. His friends had been frantic planning their engagement party, yet Mitch continued to find time to stop by and check on him with Alana always sending food.

Blake ran his hands through his hair, pulling, trying to alleviate the emotional pain with physical. This needed to stop. He needed to take control of his life. Only every time he tried, he seemed to fuck it up more. It was time to come to terms with his future. He was going to lose Gabi, or his position in Reckless Beat. Or both.

Mitch cleared his throat and slowly Blake turned to meet his friend's glare. "Sorry," he muttered. "I didn't mean—"

"To be such a dickwad?"

Blake inhaled a deep breath and swallowed. "Yeah."

"Well, think yourself lucky that Alana didn't hear it. I'd have to kick your ass. And although you deserve it, and I'd definitely enjoy it, you look like you're suffering enough."

Blake gave a half-hearted laugh. He did deserve a beat down. The pain of a few broken ribs would be a blessing in comparison to the turmoil that kept him up at night.

"What's going on, Blake?" Mitch waved his hand lazily up and down in his direction. "This isn't you. I don't even know who this is anymore."

The disappointment hit him square in the chest, almost causing him to stumble back. "Me either," he whispered. He'd lost himself when Gabi went back to Queensland. Now he didn't know how to find himself again. Not without her guidance. "I'm in trouble."

Mitch raised a brow and leaned forward, placing his can on the coffee table. "What kind of trouble?"

Blake continued to pace. He had no idea where to start or if he should even reveal his past. There was too much to tell, too much to hide.

"If you need help, you know you only have to ask. Whatever it is, we can fix it."

Blake scoffed. If only it were that easy. He knew once the skeletons were out, Mitch would look at him differently, and what would it achieve? There was nothing anyone could do. Yet he couldn't take the pressure anymore. He needed to lean on someone.

He was such a weak prick.

"Are you into them both? Is that it? You've got a thing for Gabi *and* Michelle."

Blake stopped dead. "No. *Hell no*. I don't want anything to do with Michelle."

"Then what's with the drama? Just tell her to back off."

Blake shuffled to the couch, sat, then leaned forward to place his head in his hands.

"You're starting to worry me," Mitch murmured. "I've got this ugly ass feeling in my gut, and the more you put off telling me, the more it freaks me out."

Blake squeezed his eyes shut, trying to clear his mind. His head was confused, his heart too heavy. He couldn't see past the image of Gabi, her eyes filled with tears, her mouth contorted in pain. He would do that to her. He would tear her apart.

"She's blackmailing me." He opened his eyes and straightened when the weight lifted from his shoulders.

"Blackmailing you?" Mitch drew out the words. "With what?"

Leaning back, Blake pulled his cell from his pocket, scrolled to his messages and clicked on the image Michelle had sent. He handed it to Mitch. A picture spoke a thousand words, which was convenient because Blake couldn't utter a sound.

He waited, his chest growing tighter with every passing second that Mitch didn't comment. The silence became deafening, ringing in his ears until the cell was handed back to him.

Damn it. Blake shouldn't have dragged anyone else into the situation. It was his battle to fight, his fuck up to fix. It was weak and selfish to lay his troubles at anyone else's feet.

He was about to open his mouth and beg Mitch to forget what he saw, when his friend's voice broke the silence. "Tell me what I have to do to help you fix this."

Chapter Twenty-Four

Two days had passed since the reunion gossip took over cyberspace. Maybe three. Gabi was too emotional to remember.

And still Blake hadn't contacted her. Not by phone, or email, or Skype, or Twitter, or carrier pigeon. The more time that passed, the less heartbroken she became. Anger was now her best friend. Not even Alana could answer her emailed questions. It seemed Blake didn't want to talk to anyone about his problem.

She'd plastered on a brave façade for what seemed like an eternity and faced her parents and friends head on, along with their questions of Blake's fidelity.

"It's a publicity stunt," she'd answered to her mom and dad's carefully worded enquiries.

"He's going through some private issues back home that I can't discuss," she'd explained to Tammy. At least that hadn't been a lie. She couldn't discuss it with her friend because Gabi had no clue herself.

Everyone had glanced at her with sympathy, as if she was delusional. Perhaps she was. It seemed even more likely now that she sat in front of her laptop, poised on the brink of purchasing a one way ticket to New York.

On her way home from work yesterday, she'd driven past a billboard that announced the start of an international airlines major flight sale. Coincidence? Maybe. Fate being a conniving little bitch? Most definitely.

Overnight, Gabi had resigned herself to seeing Blake as soon as possible. Even if he called now and explained each of the thousand burning questions haunting her, it wouldn't be enough. Her insecurities had gone past rational thinking days ago. She needed to see him. To read his expression and not quit pestering him until he caved and told her what the hell was going on.

She'd emailed her university lecturer and left a message for her boss. Neither one of them would be happy with her sudden disappearance, but it was only a matter of time before she ruined her grades or got fired in her current state of distress.

Everything came together nicely in her mind. Her passport was valid. She could pack her suitcase today, work tomorrow, and once her shift finished, she could take the last available flight to Sydney, waiting in the airport until her connecting flight to the US arrived.

There.

Easy.

And the icing on the pathetic excuse for a twenty hour flight was the timing for Mitch and Alana's engagement party. *Yay me.*

It seemed too irrational, even in her crazy state of mind, to spend her entire savings on the trip without speaking to Blake first. Pride had taunted her, demanding that she wait for him to make first contact, yet the appropriate time for him to do so had already passed. Yes, she needed to see him, but not if he planned on breaking up with her as soon as she arrived.

Before she could contemplate the outcome, Gabi reached for her phone and scrolled to his number. Even though the international call fee would send her broke, she pressed the button to connect.

With the first ring, her skin broke out in a sweat, and she wiped her damp palms on her pajamas. The fact that it was ten in the morning and she was still in her nightwear spoke volumes about her motivation, but that was the least of her problems.

The call connected and the split second of silence stopped her heart. The female's voice that followed shattered it completely.

"Hello," the woman said, her voice low and sleep-roughened.

"Uh…hello." Gabi choked on her words.

A woman was answering Blake's phone. A woman with a voice so husky it sounded like she'd been deep-throating for hours. With less thought than it took to make the call, Gabi pressed disconnect.

"Bloody hell!" She squeezed her phone and clenched her stomach at the emotions threatening to explode. "Argh!" A scream burst from her lips and her mobile went flying across the room. The loud crack when it hit the plasterboard made her crumple to the floor. She crawled on hands and knees to pick it up. "Please don't be broken. Please don't be broken. Please don't be—Motherfucker!"

The screen was smashed, and a chunk of plastic was missing from the back, exposing the electronics inside. This was exactly what she needed—in a completely facetious sort of way.

It didn't stop her from stalking on her knees to her laptop and slamming her finger down on the Enter button. There! Tickets purchased. It was one thing to drag out the breakup of a short relationship with your long-distance girlfriend. It was another to ruin a highly dependent, long standing friendship.

Blake had some explaining to do, and Gabi wouldn't rest until she knew what the hell was going on.

"New York, here I come."

Alana swept into Blake's dining room, placing a tray of cookies down on the table. He watched as she smiled at Michelle who sat across from him, then walked around Mitch at the head of the table, and came to Blake's side.

Her skin was pale; her beautiful features more tarnished from the flu than when she'd first entered his apartment an hour ago. She shouldn't even be here, but Mitch insisted on being his wingman when he confronted Michelle, and apparently, Alana refused to stay home.

She leaned into him, and he tilted his ear toward her to better hear her hoarse, whispered tone. "Your phone rang while I was in the kitchen. I'm sorry, I thought it might be a business call and I could take a message—"

Blake leaned back and realized her lack of color came from anxiety, not illness. "That's fine, Al, no problem. What did they want?"

Her gaze shot to Mitch, then snapped back to Blake. She leaned closer, the heat of her breath brushing his skin. "When I picked it up, Gabi's name was on the screen. I'm so sorry, Blake. I know you've been keeping your distance from her, but I couldn't help answering."

He straightened, his heart beginning to beat like he was running a marathon. "How is she? What did she say?"

"I said 'hello,' and so did she. Then she hung up. I don't think she recognized my voice."

Of course she didn't. The hits just kept coming. Alana's voice was barely recognizable to him with the harsh scratching that accompanied her flu symptoms.

"OK." He nodded, keeping his voice even so Michelle wouldn't sense his panic. "I'll sort it out later."

Alana pulled back, her brow furrowed.

"Don't sweat it, honey." He gave her a halfhearted smile. "The situation couldn't get more fucked up if I tried."

A pained sigh escaped her lips. She turned and walked away.

Mitch leaned forward, his gaze focused on Alana's back while she fled the room. "What's going on?"

"I hate to interrupt," Michelle sneered. "But I've got an appointment in less than an hour. You asked me here to talk, so talk."

Mitch straightened in his chair, the side of his jaw ticking.

"Fine," Blake growled. "I asked you here because I've had enough. I'm drawing a line in the sand. You blindsided me at the airport, and I'm not taking the risk that you'll spring that shit on me again. I'll give you one more opportunity to claim whatever media attention you think you need, then this is over. I'm done."

Michelle's head tilted, her gaze slowly turning to Mitch. "He knows?"

"Yeah, I know." Mitch crossed his arms over his chest. "And I also plan on making your life a living hell if you share those photos."

Michelle smiled without warmth. "Honey, I'm already there."

"Yeah," Mitch scoffed. "I can tell by your manicured nails and designer clothes."

Her smile turned to a glare, and she pushed from the table to stand. "I don't need this."

"Sit. Down." The command barked from Blake's chest, loud enough to shock Michelle to plop back into her seat. "You have one opportunity—a club opening, a celebrity birthday, I don't care. Just name it so we can get this over with. And let me make this clear, we will be seen as friends and nothing more."

Michelle narrowed her gaze. "Do you think one public appearance at a stupid club opening is going to give me the attention I need? You've gotta be kidding. I won't agree to that."

Her response was expected and solidified his decision to move forward. "Then do what you have to, Michelle. Release the photos. I don't give a shit. I'm done." He pushed from his chair and stepped away from the table.

Moving forward was his only option. He couldn't continue to fear the future, and he needed to be back with Gabi. He would spend the next century regretting and apologizing for making the wrong decision, both to himself and the woman he loved.

"Wait," Michelle called.

He glanced over his shoulder and found her standing, her chin high and cheeks flushed.

"Fine." She raised her brows. "I've picked an event—Mitch's engagement party."

"Ha!" Mitch laughed. "That's funny." Then his face fell. "Wait, you're joking, right?"

Michelle rolled her eyes and focused her confident stare on Blake. "One night. That's it. The paparazzi will be buzzing, and I can butter them up with an inside scoop on the happy couple."

"No." There was no need to contemplate. It wasn't an option.

"We could make it work," Alana's raspy voice came from behind him. "Sorry." She smiled sheepishly when he turned. "I was listening from the hallway."

"No, Blake's right." Mitch pushed from his seat and walked to Alana's side. "It's our engagement party." He swiped the loose hair on her cheeks behind her ear. "I won't let her ruin it."

"She won't, will you Michelle?" Alana's tone was light, but the underlying venom was unmistakable.

Michelle's lips pulled into a sneer. "Of course not."

"Alana, no." Blake couldn't risk ruining their engagement party. "It's not an option."

Alana stepped forward, stopping a foot away from him. "Let us do this for you." She pinned him with her hope-filled gaze, her eyes sparkling with optimism. "If having her at the engagement party is all that it takes to clear this mess, we'll be happy to do it."

She bridged the distance between them and hugged him tight, resting her cheek against his shoulder. Something inside him fractured. He squeezed his eyes shut, fighting back his helplessness and circled his arms around her waist. He didn't want to let go. She reminded him of Gabi. Her scent. The soft material of her clothes, the warmth of her body, the way she didn't let him go. *Christ*. He couldn't do this.

He opened his eyes and met Mitch's glare of disapproval. "Back the fuck away, buddy."

The familiar playful banter made Blake smile. Through the darkness, disillusion, and hopelessness there would always be time to shit-stir with Mitch.

He kissed Alana on the temple and let her go. "We can finish this later, sugar."

Mitch raised a brow, and the corners of his lips twitched. "Let's finalize this so we can get outta here."

"Are you really willing to risk your special night?" Blake asked. He could laugh and flirt and joke with Mitch and Alana for the rest of his life, but right now he needed to be sincere.

Mitch shrugged. "If Allie's happy, then I'm happy. And besides, her gun toting mom is coming. So bringing along a skanky date is the last of your worries."

Blake winced at the memory of Mrs. Shelton and Michelle cleared her throat, which they all ignored.

"You sure?" Now that freedom was within his grasp, his heart began to stutter.

"Yeah, no problem." Mitch shrugged away the enormity of the situation. "You're my bro. I'd do anything for you."

Deep and meaningfuls weren't their style. In fact, it felt awkward. Really awkward. Blake grinned, hoping to break the discomfort. "Like letting me seduce your fiancé?" He had no interest in Alana sexually, but the thrill of teasing Mitch was too damn hard to resist.

"Like refraining from using my fist to break your face."

They both smiled and glanced at Alana who rolled her eyes.

"Well, now that your emasculating moment is over, can we work out the details?" Michelle hissed. "I need to get out of here."

"Oh, she's such a lovely little thing, isn't she?" Alana mumbled, reaching for Mitch to entwine their fingers. "We'll leave you to it."

Mitch patted him on the shoulder before walking from the room.

"Right," he swung around to face Michelle. "Let's get started on the rules."

Chapter Twenty-Five

GABI STARED AT herself in the elevator mirror, fighting the urge to run her nervous hands over the shiny silver satin of her gown. The charcoal fabric clung tight, accentuating her hips and waist, gracefully falling to her ankles. The dress wasn't new. Hell, after the money she'd spent on the flight and the one night accommodation at The Plaza, she'd never be able to afford retail again. But she was here now, currently descending to the Terrace Room where the engagement party would already be taking place.

Her stomach was woozy from the hours spent cramped on the plane, and the more she thought about making her entrance to the party, the more it churned. Her anger had vanished mid-flight, replaced with an eerie clarity. Tonight wouldn't end well. She could feel it in the ache of her bones and the shallow throb of her heart.

She even made sure not to call Blake and announce her arrival, giving her the element of surprise. His initial reaction to her appearance would tell her everything she needed to know.

Exiting the empty elevator on the second floor, she strode into a wide foyer smelling of sweet roses. The blooms were placed in large vases along a long gift-laden table. She made her way to the middle of the empty room and glanced through the archway to her left.

"Ma'am," a male voice greeted her.

Two security guards stood in the next room, each standing beside one of the four French doors holding out the laughter and chatter Gabi could hear coming from the other side.

"Are you here for the engagement party?" One of them stepped forward with a clipboard while fidgeting with the coiled cord running down from his earpiece.

Damn it. She hadn't anticipated security. "Yes," she answered, a little breathless. "I'm sorry I'm late. My flight from Sydney only arrived a few hours ago, and I needed to freshen up."

"All the way from Australia?" He grinned, his gaze lingering on the visible swell of cleavage at her neckline. "What name?"

"Ah." She froze and cleared her throat. "I'm Blake Kennedy's guest."

The man frowned and focused on the clipboard in his hands. "I thought I saw Mr. Kennedy enter a while ago with another woman."

Her mouth worked, and she felt the blood rush from her face. *Think. Think. Think.* She'd come too far to be turned away now, another woman or not. "He may have arrived with another guest," she spoke politely when what she really wanted to do was crumple against the wall. "I told him to meet me inside because I wouldn't make it on time." The lies slid from her lips, made easier because the guy wasn't looking at her, and the man standing beside the next door appeared half asleep.

"Mmm." He continued scrolling down the list. "Here he is."

He tapped his index finger near the bottom of the page, and Gabi stopped breathing. If there was another woman's name beside Blake's, she was screwed.

"It just says 'plus one.'"

Gabi lifted her chin and nodded, feigning excitement. "That's me."

He looked up again, this time scrutinizing her. "Right." He stepped back, giving the other security guard a glance before hesitantly opening the door behind him. Noise filtered into the foyer, a mass of people talking, laughing, and clinking glasses.

"Thank you." She ignored his skeptical gaze and sauntered forward, acting like she owned the place.

And boy, what a place. She stood on a walkway that ran the length of the room. Before her were huge archways bordered with a golden railing that gave a view to the mingling guests below. Beautiful people were bathed in the soft orange glow of a breathtaking chandelier in the center of the ceiling. And everywhere she looked hotel staff greeted guests with trays of food or wine.

Gabi really needed wine.

With shaky limbs, she walked along the walkway, close to the wall, hopefully blending into her surroundings. When she reached the sanctuary of the last archway pillar, she stopped, hiding behind it, and took a deep breath.

"Gabi!" Alana's familiar voice called.

Oh, shit. Gabi had no plans to flee, yet now that she'd been spotted it made the situation more real. More crazy.

She peered around the pillar and found Alana and Mitch making their way up the staircase.

"What are you doing here?" Alana's eyes were filled with excitement. She rushed forward in a sparkling ruby dress and enveloped Gabi in a hug. "It's so good to see you."

Gabi returned the embrace and glanced at Mitch over Alana's shoulder. He stood tall, his gaze frantically scanning the crowd below, his lips pressed firmly together.

"It's good to see you, too." Gabi stepped back and nervously ran her fingers along the necklace Blake had given her. Even with the threat of him moving on without her, she hadn't found the strength to stop wearing his gift.

Mitch stepped forward. "Hey, Gab. We're glad you made it." His words were hesitant while he glanced between her and Alana, a slight frown marring his brow. "Ah…does Blake know you're here?"

She wanted to laugh at his lack of subtlety. The panic in his tone made the tension grow inside her. Her body now simply waiting for the bad news to hit. "No." She shook her head. "I know I've turned up unannounced, but I needed to see him. I hope you don't mind."

"Not at all." Alana reached for Gabi's hands and squeezed, the three of them now hiding behind the archway. "Why don't you let Mitchell go find him while we catch up?"

Gabi stared into Alana's eyes, pleading. "No, please let me find him." She clutched Alana's hands while Mitch went back to nervously scanning the crowd. "I'm not here to cause trouble. I just need to find out what's going on. If he doesn't want to see me I'll leave, I promise."

Alana glanced over her shoulder at Mitch. His features softened and pity entered his expression. "Gabi, Blake's struggling to deal with a few things at the moment. He's—"

"I know," she interrupted. "I know he has things going on, and the secrets are what scare me the most. He's always told me everything." Her eyes began to burn, and still she didn't look away. She needed Mitch to know how serious she was. If she left, there was no coming back. "I can't sit around and wonder if he's shutting me out of his life anymore. I need an answer so I can move on."

Mitch searched her gaze, his shoulders slowly slumping. Finally, he let out a sigh. "Let me come with you. We can find him together."

Gabi released the breath tightening her lungs. "Thank you." She turned to Alana. "Thank you. I won't make a scene. I promise."

With a sad smile, Alana turned to descend the stairs. Gabi followed, taking each step cautiously, scanning the crowd while Mitch remained at her side.

"There." Mitch jerked his head to the other side of the room. "At the bar."

Gabi ignored the rampant beat of her pulse while she sought out Blake. Groups of people lined the bar. Men in suits, women in cocktail dresses, staff waiting for trays to be filled with drinks. Then there he was. She would've recognized his profile anywhere—the dark spiked hair, the broad shoulders.

"Let Mitchell go get him for you," Alana said.

Gabi shook her head, her focus remaining on the gorgeous man at the bar. Blake hadn't spared her the decency of a phone call. She wouldn't give him the opportunity to hide or come up with an escape plan. "No." She glanced at Alana and smiled. "I'm fine, thank you."

Gabi poised to take another step when Blake pivoted, turning to show his face. She paused, her foot hanging in midair. Was that really him? He seemed darker, harsher in the dim light. Maybe it was the distance between them. He didn't look like the fun-loving man she'd fallen in love with.

He raised a glass to his lips, and she squinted, making sure her eyes weren't deceiving her. Seconds ticked by in aching heartbeats, and not once did the vision change. Blake remained at the bar, sculling the dark liquid from a half full scotch glass.

"He's drinking," she whispered to herself, lowering her gaze to the floor. A knife of betrayal stabbed through her chest while her foot fell to the step below. He'd broken his sobriety without even mentioning it to her. What the hell? He always told her everything. And no, she wasn't his mother, but god damn it, she'd been his best friend for years.

"Shit," Mitch muttered beside her.

She glanced back to the bar and the force of Blake's gaze hit her like a burst of flames. His eyes were wide, his mouth now slightly ajar. Slowly, almost imperceptibly, his lips tilted in a grin and her blood heated in response.

That's all it took. One simple smile and the hurt dissipated, the pain flittered away, and in tiny increments her life brightened. She smiled back at him, her cheeks lifting, heating. He wouldn't be happy to see her if he no longer had feelings for her. He wouldn't look pleased by her presence if he had something to hide.

He stepped forward and her stomach clenched, waiting, wanting the comfort of his proximity.

Then a feminine hand grabbed his shoulder and he froze. His lips tightened, his chin raised, yet it was his eyes, the pity and the shame that made Gabi's skin shiver. She didn't need to glance at the woman who clutched his black collared shirt. Intuition and common sense told her who it was.

Michelle.

The viper moved around Blake, running her hands along his chest and encircling his neck, her long beautiful hair hanging low on her back. Gabi held the staircase railing to stop herself from falling. The pictures of them on social media had hurt. They'd sliced her open, leaving her vulnerable and weak. Seeing them in real life broke her foundation, shredding her soul into irreparable pieces.

Blake stepped back, ignoring Michelle's attention. That's when the heiress turned, following his line of sight to where Gabi stood on the stairs.

Mitch grabbed her elbow. "Maybe we should—"

"Don't worry, I'm leaving," Gabi rushed out. "I'm sorry for turning up unannounced." She turned to Alana, pasting a smile on her face even though the expression hurt. "I wish you both happiness for the future."

Before her throat closed, Gabi turned on her toes and used the railing for support to pull herself up the stairs.

"Gabi."

She ignored Alana and Mitch's calls, retracing the few steps she'd walked down, striding along the walkway to push through the French doors. She held her head high—even though her ankles wobbled—and made it to the elevator without looking back.

She ignored the security guards, the sweet rose scent that would always remind her of betrayal, and rammed her finger into the elevator button. "Hurry up."

"Gabi…wait!" Blake's voice carried from the main room.

She bit her lip, refusing to look over her shoulder and wrenched open the doors as they began to slide apart. Blake was her weakness, her heart, her everything. She couldn't sit through an explanation of why he decided to go back to Michelle. She'd deserved more than this from a man she'd stuck by for so long.

"Gabi," his voice grew louder, closer.

She rushed to the panel, frantically tapping at the button to close the doors. They moved with the speed of a snail on valium, one tiny inch at a time. When they were almost shut, a bang sounded from outside and Blake's face came into view through the tiny slither of space.

"Gabi, stop!"

She broke eye contact, unable to deal with the anguish tainting his features. He was so perfect. Angry, upset, frustrated, it didn't matter. He would always be gorgeous to her.

"God damn it!" His bellow echoed through the small room, ripping a choked sob from her mouth.

Once the doors were firmly shut, she pressed a numb finger against the button to the lobby and fell back into the wall. She needed fresh air. Well, as fresh as it could get in New York. And the bitter night chill would keep her mind away from the emotional pain.

Yeah, she was pathetic, completely and utterly ridiculous. Who the hell flew across the world to get an answer that had already been written on the wall? Anyone could've foreseen this. Yet she'd ignored her instincts and wasted her savings on the bonus of being humiliated in public.

The elevator jolted, and she raised her gaze from the floor when the doors opened. She took a moment to regain her composure, and then pushed from the wall, squeezing past a couple waiting for her to get out.

"Excuse me," she muttered and made it a few steps before the weight of Blake's betrayal had her slumping against the arm rest of the nearest chair.

Lying. Cheating. Drinking. That wasn't Blake. That was an asshole in the body of the man who owned her heart. She knew the real Blake. Knew how much of a kindhearted, compassionate, and sympathetic soul he was. Yet she didn't have the strength to confront the stranger who'd taken over.

"Gabi!" Blake's voice vibrated off the lobby walls.

She straightened, her body jumping to life as he stalked across the room from the hotel staircase, his chest heaving. He was menacing, his black silk shirt untucked, the first two buttons undone, his sleeves rolled to expose his tattoos. Stubble covered his jaw, and his eyes flashed with determination, enough to make her want to run.

She glanced toward the doors, trying to figure out if she could escape in time. No. Trying would be useless, especially in heels and an evening gown. The bright flashes of light from outside announced the awaiting paparazzi, resigning her to her fate. The last thing she wanted was to be humiliated on a global scale.

Raising her chin, she stood tall to face him. He strode toward her, slowing his pace the closer he came. He looked the way she felt, broken, tired, and miserable. She wouldn't feel sorry for him though. He deserved it.

"Gabi..."

Her name was breathy and so damn tortured that she wanted to whimper. Instead, she let it fuel her anger. He reached for her and she jerked back. An anguished crease marred his forehead while his hand fell limp at his side.

"Let me explain."

"Explain?" She let out a sardonic laugh. "No, I don't think so. The time for explanations passed weeks ago. I was just too stupid to realize. I hope you've found everything in Michelle that I must have lacked—"

"She's not—"

"*And,*" she snarled, "I also hope you enjoy your break from sobriety." Rage heated her cheeks, causing her nose to tingle. Why the hell did her body decide to turn on the waterworks when she was fuming? She didn't want to cry. She wasn't sad. She was fucking furious!

He stepped closer. "I'm not drinking." He lowered his voice and glanced over his shoulder at the gawkers.

"I don't care." She shrugged. "It's none of my business anymore."

He slid closer, bridging the gap between them and grabbed her arm in a light hold. She raised her chin and glared at him, hating that her heart ached as soon as his fingers brushed her skin.

"Smell my breath." He leaned into her, his lips hovering an inch from hers. "I'm *not* drinking."

For a brief second she enjoyed his nearness—his smell, his heat, his attention. And no, there was no scent of alcohol. That didn't matter. "I don't understand why you're bothering to try and convince me. I no longer care," she finished on a whisper and yanked her arm away.

Her flesh burned where his hand had been, and before she could walk away, she was back within his arms, his hands gripping her shoulders, yanking her forward. His mouth hit hers in an unyielding crush and his tongue licked the seam of her lips, sliding further when she gasped.

Shock left her weak and confused. She couldn't separate the pleasurable memories from their past with the current way he passionately kissed her. But the moan that vibrated from his chest broke the spell. She pushed away, fumbling backward on her heels as she panted.

"You bastard." She covered her scorched lips with a trembling hand. "You heartless, lying, bastard." Her voice grew with each word.

"Blake?" The unfamiliar feminine tone came from behind him, seconds before Michelle came into view.

Gabi retreated, not wanting to be anywhere near the happy couple. She always imagined his ex would be less appealing in person. That the glitz and glamour would fade in real life, but no, fate wasn't that kind. Michelle beamed with beauty, even under a truck-load of make-up and drug glazed eyes.

"I'm ready to leave, honey," she cooed, leaning in to press her glossy red lips against Blake's cheek.

He pulled away. "Not now," he growled.

"Yes, now." Michelle smirked at Gabi while she entwined her fingers with Blake's. "Don't make me explain to your little toy why I'm so eager to leave."

Gabi raised a brow and ignored the taunt. She didn't need fake boobs and lipo to know how the trolls of the Upper East Side worked. She'd watched Gossip Girl a time or two and knew that rich bitches fought their battles from the safety of their ivory towers. Gabi wouldn't stand a chance.

"Have fun." Gabi smiled sweetly.

Blake squeezed his eyes shut for a brief second before opening them again, fixing her with his gaze. "I'll explain everything."

Michelle tugged at his hand and huffed.

Gabi stared at the man she'd been in love with for years and found somebody new—someone she no longer wanted to know. She didn't need to reiterate her thoughts; the recognition was already in his eyes. With a slight shake of her head, she moved around him and strode to the elevators, ignoring the curious stares of hotel guests.

The time for fresh air had passed. She needed to have a shower, repack her things, and get some sleep before begging her airline for the first available seat out of JFK.

Stepping into the elevator, she pressed the button to her floor and mentally congratulated herself for not looking back. She could move on—start anew. Then the doors closed, signaling the end of an important part of her life. Her chest tightened with the beginning of the ascent, ripping a sob from her throat.

Blake meant everything to her. He was her strength, her happiness, her light, and no amount of denial or determination could convince her that she could live without him.

Chapter Twenty-Six

Blake stood in the lobby, shock freezing him in place while the elevator doors closed, taking Gabi away. He was reeling, tilting from confusion to astonishment at her appearance.

"Let's go," Michelle bitched from beside him, her words carrying a slight slur.

Good. He would drive her home, ticking off the final duty in their agreement, then come back to explain everything to Gabi in private. If it weren't for the stares of hotel staff and guests, he would've told Michelle to fuck off while he begged for Gabi to listen. But he couldn't ignore the blatant and unremorseful assholes that stood mere feet away, their phones pointed in his direction as they took photos or video.

Turning, he strode across the lobby toward the doors. Michelle's heels clicked frantically behind him, trying to keep up.

"Wait," she hissed. "We need to leave together. You owe me this."

He stopped and waited for her. When her hand gripped the crook of his elbow he clenched his jaw, concentrating only on the minutes until she would be out of his life forever.

The middle-aged concierge greeted them at the door. "Would you like your car brought around, Mr. Kennedy?"

Blake nodded. "Yeah. Thanks."

"It will only take a minute. Would you prefer to wait inside?"

"No," Michelle answered for him. "We want to see our fans before we leave."

Blake's nostrils flared. If she did something stupid now, he'd flip. He was done, exhausted, and willing to tell the world about her manipulative games.

"Not a problem." The concierge opened the door, setting off the flash of cameras and the roar of the crowd.

With Michelle on his arm, he descended the stairs into the cold night air. She pulled away once they reached the bottom, swayed a little, and went to the barrier holding back the crowd. A hotel security guard came to stand beside Michelle, providing a protective presence while she went to the first person with a video camera.

Blake tensed, his senses on hyper alert. He stood behind her, tight lipped, concentrating on every word that left her deceitful mouth. Minutes passed and confusion grew. She didn't lie, didn't cause a scene, and when his car pulled up, she grabbed the crook of his elbow and said her flamboyant goodbyes.

They slid silently into his white Camaro, and in seconds he was taking off, heading down the night darkened road.

"Turn left and go around Central Park."

He did as requested. "I'm done now, Michelle. I'll take you home, or drop you wherever you want to go, but we both agreed that this was it. No more games."

"Yeah whatever, asshole," she mumbled.

He gave a derisive laugh and shook his head. "Yeah, I'm the blackmailing, backstabbing asshole. I'm the one who wants to drag your name through the mud and ruin everything you've ever worked for."

"Fuck you!" She turned to him, pointing her finger near the side of his face. "You've got no idea what my life is like. You hold your head up like you're innocent and have nothing to hide, but you're exactly like me. You're just as weak."

"I'm nothing like you," he sneered and slowed his car below the speed limit. Her irrational state made him nervous. "Just tell me where you live so I can get you home."

"And what if I said I lived in the suburbs, over an hour away?" she purred. "What would you do?"

He clenched his jaw and turned down Central Park West, ignoring the way she changed from catty bitch to seducing psycho in the blink of an eye. "An hour drive would be worth it to get you out of my life."

"Fuck you!" she screamed and beat her hands against the dash.

He startled and swore under his breath. The click of her seat belt had him whipping his head around to see what the hell she was doing. "Put it back on, Michelle."

She ignored him, reaching for her purse with one hand on the door handle.

"Michelle," he warned, checking his rearview mirror and pulling closer to the curb.

Without a word, her door flew open and she pivoted to get out.

"Fuckin' hell." He slammed on the breaks moments before she jumped out and stumbled on her heels to the footpath. "Michelle, get back in the god damn car!"

She bent at the waist, piercing him with her evil stare and gave him the bird. "I'll walk home so I can 'get out of your life' sooner." She made air quotes with her fingers, then straightened.

"Damn it." He punched the steering wheel and pulled into a no parking zone. By the time he opened his door and got out, she was already striding into Central Park. "Michelle!"

She didn't stop, soon disappearing into the fading light.

He turned on the people walking past and glared. "Take a fucking picture," he snapped and reached back into the car to grab his cell phone. He dialed Michelle's number, heard the far off sound of her ringtone before she answered.

"I'll be fine, Blake," she sniffed, apparently succumbing to another mood swing.

He leaned his elbow against the roof of the car and rubbed his forehead. He couldn't take much more of this shit. "Don't be stupid. It's not safe to be walking alone at night."

"I'll walk to 65th and hail a cab. Don't worry, I'm out of your life now," her voice was choked. "Bye, Blake."

The line went dead, and he lowered his head to lean against the cool metal of the car roof. He should be thankful, yet no matter how much of a manipulative, coldhearted bitch Michelle was, he still worried for her safety. His phone buzzed in his hand, and he straightened, hoping she'd changed her mind. Nope. Mitch's name was on the screen.

"Yeah," he answered, sliding back into the driver's seat and placing his cell into the hands free console.

"Are you OK? Where are you?"

Blake checked his mirrors and pulled into traffic. "Michelle just jumped out of my freakin' car while I was driving and took off through Central Park. I don't know what the hell to do."

"Jesus Christ. Is she hurt?"

"No, just fucking crazy."

"And Gabi? Where's she?"

Blake pressed his foot down on the accelerator. "I don't know. I'm hoping she's still at the Plaza."

Silence, long and punishing.

"Do you want me to look for her?"

"No." Blake shook his head. "You enjoy your party and don't worry about me." Although things with Michelle hadn't ended the way he planned, they were still over. He'd upheld his part of the bargain, and she agreed to quit blackmailing him once they went their separate ways at the end of the night. His lawyer had all the legal paperwork to prove it.

One part of his nightmare was over. Now he had to focus on Gabi.

"I'm on my way back," Blake added, his blood pumping with determination. "I'm going to find her and make everything right."

Gabi wiped the steam from the bathroom mirror and fastened the remaining buttons on her flannel pajamas. She looked a treat—damp, scraggly hair, the skin under her eyes now red from crying, and her cheeks pale with exhaustion.

She already called her airline and secured a seat on a late morning flight to Sydney. All she had left to do was sleep, eat, and leave. Easy.

Hanging her towel over the railing, she shuffled to the bathroom door and stepped into the main room of the suite. Her feet hit the thick carpet, and in the next second, her stomach dropped.

"How did you get in here?" she whispered, her voice barely registering.

Blake stood in the shadows near the suite door, his shoulders slumped, his dark eyes hooded. He stepped forward, the dim lamplight revealing the mark Michelle's lips had left on his cheek. "Money talks."

Her lips trembled. "I bet. Now get out."

Another step forward. Another revolt from her stomach. She put up a hand, wanting him to stop. *Needing* him to stop.

"Out!" she yelled, her breath coming faster now, panting from her lungs.

Her limbs grew weak while she waited, the built up agony growing inside her. He didn't move, didn't flinch, merely stood there, his head tilted low, looking up at her through thick, dark lashes.

"Please," she begged.

He shook his head. "Not until you let me explain."

No. "I don't want an explanation." She wanted to stamp her foot. Instead, she strode past him to the door and jerked it open for him to leave. "I want to go back home and move on with my life."

He sighed, long and heavy. "I'll leave once you understand what happened."

"Can't you hear me?" her voice rose, wavering. "I no longer care."

He ignored her and walked further into the room. *Bastard.* She let the door slam shut and stormed after him, gripping the front of his black silk shirt in an effort to make him move. He raised his chin as she pulled hard, yanking at the soft material. A button popped, and she cried out in frustration. Her eyes burned, making her blink repeatedly until tears streaked down her cheeks. Yet he never moved. Never spoke.

She wasn't strong enough—physically, mentally, or emotionally. Heaving sobs wrenched from her lips, and her knees gave out. Before she hit the floor, his arms came around her, lifting her, comforting her.

"Don't!" she screamed. "Get your hands off me!" She pummeled his chest with her fists, hitting him with what little energy she had left.

He held her tighter, his breathing labored while he walked her to the nearest wall. Then he released her. *Thank god, he released her.* And she collapsed against the cold plaster, his hands coming to rest on either side of her face. He caged her in, his hard thigh pressing against hers. She felt him everywhere, on her skin, in her broken heart, overtaking her soul.

"Please…" she cried, closing her eyes, letting the heaving sobs escape. "What do you want from me?"

He touched her arms, encircled her biceps, holding her tighter with every passing second. His hair brushed her cheek. "The same thing I've always wanted, Gabi," he rasped into her ear. "Everything."

She opened her eyes to glare and pushed against his chest. "You can't have us both!" She wanted to be free of him, and yet, she wanted him to continue holding her, to never let her go. "Her lipstick is on your cheek for Christ sake!"

He swiped at his face, smudging the red marks on his skin. "Gabi," he whispered. "God, Gabi, please let me explain." He heaved a sigh and cupped her face with strong hands, making her look at him, making her see the hurt reflected in his glazed, dark brown irises. "Michelle blackmailed me."

She froze and shook her head in confusion.

He wiped the tear soaked clumps of hair from her cheeks. "I haven't been with her, angel. I swear to you. I haven't been with anyone."

"I don't understand." She sniffed and pressed her lips together to stop them from trembling.

His forehead rested against hers, his arms still holding her tight. The warmth of his breath brushed her mouth and for the second time today, she acknowledged there was no hint of alcohol.

"She has photos of me snorting coke. She threatened to hand them to the media if I didn't help put her in the spotlight. There is nothing between us, I promise. It was all for show."

Gabi remained silent and stared at him. The truth was in his expression, in the defeat and exhaustion that darkened his features, and still, it didn't redeem him in any way. All he'd done was explain Michelle's actions.

"And you couldn't tell me this earlier? Did you even wonder what it was like to find those photos of you and Michelle together? How absolutely devastated I felt? I've never experienced pain like that before." She glared at him. "When Greg died, it tore me apart, and I'd known beforehand that he was playing with his life. I'd known he might not make it through. But with you…"

She raised her chin and looked him straight in the eye, ignoring the tears that blurred her vision. "I never expected you to betray me like this. And for what?" She threw her hands up. "You know what? It doesn't matter. What's done is done."

"God, Gabi, I didn't know what to do." He closed his eyes and pulled back to shake his head. "I thought I could give her what she wanted and walk away without you getting hurt. I never expected it to turn out like this."

"You never expected this?" she accused. "That's funny. I never expected my best friend to betray me either." For a moment, guilt consumed her at the fresh wave of pain that washed across his features. Then she remembered what he'd put her through, how he'd broken her irrevocably. "I trusted you."

New tears formed and threatened to burst free. "Even when you kept me in the dark, I defended you. I stuck up for you when my friends and family hinted that you were a cheating, lying bastard." She pushed at his chest, and this time he let her go, stumbling back.

"I was humiliated." She swiped the dampness from her cheeks with the back of her hand. "You shut me out and made me believe you never cared. I spent my savings, risked my degree *and* my job, just to come here and find out something you could've told me over the phone." She moved forward, pushing into him, and thumped her fist against his chest. "You lied to me—"

He grabbed her wrist and pulled her closer, so they were waist to waist. "I never lied to you."

"No?" she sneered. "Well, hiding the truth is just the same. You betrayed me."

His chest vibrated with a growl. "I'm not perfect, Gabi, you know that better than anyone."

"I do." She nodded. "I just never thought I'd be on the receiving end of your stupidity."

She regretted the words before Blake winced from her brutality. Turning her gaze away, she wrinkled her nose, refusing to cry while his hands still grasped her wrists. The silence grew deafening, until she thought she couldn't take it anymore. Part of her wanted to apologize, while the other part needed him to suffer.

"This isn't you," he whispered. "And I'm sorry. I'm so sorry for everything. I'll make it up to you."

She shook her head, more to herself than to him. Hollowness consumed her. She couldn't see a way back to where they'd once been. To the perfection of what she liked to believe was true love.

He grabbed her chin, forcing her to meet his feral gaze. "Yes, I will. You'll love me again and you'll forgive me, too. I know you will."

His lips crashed against hers, firm and unyielding. A whimper tore from her chest, stripping her of her last defenses and leaving her raw. She hated him. Hated him for breaking their trust, for humiliating her, for going on with his life and ignoring her so easily. She never could've done that. And yet, she clung to him, her hands gripping the silk of his shirt, her lips kissing him back.

His tongue entered her mouth, lashing hers with fierce strokes. She didn't want to need him, but her blood heated anyway. Her body craved something she knew her heart couldn't handle.

"Don't." She pulled back, cursing her breathy voice that lacked conviction.

His lips burned a blazing trail along her jaw, down her neck, and to her collarbone. She wanted to cry out, to scream, to wail. She loved this man, yearned to have him inside her and in equal measure couldn't stand the anguish his touch brought.

He let go of her wrist and yanked at her pajama buttons, undoing some, ripping others. Then his hands were on her breasts, and the pleasure rallied against the knife embedded in her heart. She threw her head back and closed her eyes, the buildup of tears now running freely down her cheeks. Her fingers gripped his hair and his mouth latched onto her nipple, enticing a cry from her throat, this time one of pleasure.

Nobody would ever love her body the way Blake did. No man would ever compare, and it was that brutal honesty that made her bite her lip and enjoy this final goodbye. Being with him one more time wouldn't change what had happened. It wouldn't clear the mess of the past or mend the dishonesty. It would numb the suffering, though, if only for a little while.

He pushed the top from her shoulders and lifted her off the ground, walking her backward to the wall. Her feet landed softly against the carpet, and he gripped the material at her waist, crouching to gently pull down her pants and underwear until they pooled at her ankles.

He stared up at her from the ground. She ignored his tender gaze, and focused on the way he worked the few remaining buttons of his shirt and let it fall to the floor. The sight of him made her swallow. It would always affect her—the muscles, the tattoos, the angel adorning his chest.

She closed her eyes and tried in vain to remember a better time. A place when they'd only had the distance between them to worry about, not lies and blackmail and heartbreak.

"Don't close your eyes, angel. Don't shut me out." He moved to his feet, the harsh material of his slacks rubbing against her naked thighs. "Look at me," he whispered against her lips.

Slowly, she surrendered, lifting her lashes to the face of a man that would always own her heart.

"I love you, Gabi." He stared into her eyes, unmoving. "There is no one else for me. I won't let there be anyone else for you."

He was right. She'd been ruined. There would never be another man for her.

Turning her head away, she faced the curtain-covered window, not wanting him to know how right he truly was. She could handle their entwined bodies, not his softly spoken words. He kissed her collarbone, her sternum, her neck, and each press of his lips made her traitorous body hum. She arched her back, wrapped one leg around his thigh and hoped for a few fleeting moments she could distance herself from reality.

"Look at me." He nuzzled her chin.

She shook her head and ground into him, searching for his erection through his pants.

He moved his hips back, out of reach.

"Look at me, angel, or this ends now." His teeth nipped at her jaw, and a calloused hand ran up her waist to cup her breast. "The only reason you don't want to look at me is because you know I'm telling the truth. You know I love you. You know there's no one else."

When she didn't respond, he stopped moving and lowered his forehead to her shoulder. A ragged sigh escaped him. "I fucked up, sweetheart."

She pressed her lips together and frowned, stemming the burn in her eyes.

"Please forgive me."

"I will forgive you." Her response was choked. She *would* forgive him. She loved him too much not to. She just hadn't yet, and probably wouldn't for a long time.

He tilted his head to meet her gaze. "I'll wait. No matter how long it takes." His lips found her cheek, the side of her mouth, and his pelvis settled back against her. He kissed her softly, his tongue stroking over hers with delicate adoration, coaxing goose bumps to cover her skin.

"I'll treasure you, angel. I'll dedicate the rest of my life to making this up to you. Just tell me how. Tell me what I have—"

"Shh." She pressed her lips to his and gripped the buckle of his belt. Their tongues danced while she unfastened the clasp and helped him to shuck his pants. "Take me to bed."

He swung down, sweeping her off the ground. He carried her a few feet and laid her on the mattress. The hurt still lingered in his eyes, the pain still etched in his features. She ignored it as she cupped the back of his neck and encouraged him to climb on top of her.

She leaned back into the pillows, and he followed, nestling between her thighs. His erection nudged her entrance, thick and insistent, sliding through the dampness of her arousal. With a groan, he inched inside her, casually, with deliberate care.

He wasn't going to give her the fast road to heaven she wanted. He planned to drag it out, to love her slowly. She could tell by the way his hands lazily roamed her skin, relearning every inch, and how he stopped every few moments to gaze into her eyes, trying to read her thoughts.

She couldn't do this. Not slow and intimate. It pulled at her heart too much, made her want to forgive too quickly, and she owed it to herself not to let go of the betrayal. Pushing at his shoulders, she encouraged him to roll onto his back. He followed her lead and pulled her around to straddle his lap.

This gave her control. She stared at the cream plastered wall and rode him, grinding her hips with hard pulses, making him groan and reach for the headboard. That's when her gaze fell, landing on his chest and the angel adorning his pec stared back at her.

She faltered. Stopped.

The angel was a symbol of their friendship, of the loyalty between them—a loyalty that had crumpled. She wasn't strong enough to do this, to love him one last time before she walked away. "I'm sorry," she whispered and climbed off him.

"Gabi, wait." His arm came around her waist. "It's OK. We don't have to do this, just…"

She stiffened when his head came to rest against the small of her back, and he released a pained breath.

"Just let me hold you for a while."

Gabi sank back into the mattress, facing away from him, the warmth fading from her body, allowing the hollowness to seep back in. His touch made her weak, vulnerable, and no matter how much her head demanded she walk away now, her heart wanted one more touch, one more kiss, one more breathy whisper of love against her neck.

She climbed under the covers and Blake did the same. He spooned against her, placing his right arm over her waist, laying his hand against her belly. The tattooed word 'Reckless' stared back at her from along his knuckles, taunting her. Yes, she'd been reckless. With her heart, her future, and the one relationship that she couldn't stand to live without.

But how could she trust him again? The world thought he was in a relationship with Michelle. Fake or not, it still humiliated Gabi in front of her family and friends. He'd withheld the truth and made decisions that affected them both without consulting her. He broke her heart, consumed her with loss, and not once had he called to see what his actions had done.

She wasn't entirely delusional. Blake would always have her friendship. She knew losing him from her life would be unbearable. But at the same time, she couldn't imagine giving him back the power to destroy her heart all over again. Her body began to tremble and Blake's arm tightened around her waist.

"Don't lose faith in us, Gabi."

Too late.

Blake was the only man she ever wanted. The only love she'd ever craved. Yet now that the lies had settled and the truth had surfaced, his love no longer seemed enough.

Chapter Twenty-Seven

Blake had been awake since the first crack of sunlight filtered around the border of the hotel curtains. He'd spent hours staring at Gabi lying peacefully beside him, wondering how long it would take her to forgive him.

If only she'd let him make love to her. He'd wanted to make her feel good, to show her they were made for each other in the most primitive way, but she'd pushed him away. Even when he'd held her in his arms afterwards, she'd remained rigid, not relaxing until her breathing went heavy with sleep.

He owed her so much, emotionally and financially. She didn't have the money to jump on a plane and fly to the other side of the world, yet she had. For him. And how had he repaid her?

He sighed and rested back against his pillow. The money was an easy fix. He had her bank account details and would transfer funds when he got home. The emotional problems would take longer to mend. Much, much longer.

His phone rang, splitting the silence with the Jaws theme song and startling Gabi to consciousness. The tone belonged to Leah, someone who knew better than to call him at such an early hour.

"Sorry, angel." He scooted from the bed and grabbed his pants off the floor, reaching into the pocket to retrieve his phone. "I should've turned it off."

He contemplated hitting reject, but thought better of it. Leah didn't make a habit of calling without a work related reason. Clicking connect, he raised the phone to his ear. "It's kinda early, Lee."

"Where are you?" Her words were frantic.

"I'm umm…" He glanced at Gabi who had the sheet clutched to her chest, her eyes not meeting his gaze. "I'm still at The Plaza with Gabi. Why?"

"What happened last night?" There was a pleading tone to her voice, a mixture of panic and concern that unsettled him.

"I needed to speak to Gabi. Is this about bribing the hotel receptionist for a room key? I know it was wrong, and I'll speak to the manager if I have to."

"Blake…"

The silence that followed sent a shiver down his spine.

"Leah, talk to me."

"Turn on the TV."

"What channel?" He pivoted on his toes in search of the remote, finding it on the coffee table. "What's going on?"

"What happened between you and Michelle last night?"

Oh, fuck. She'd gone public. "Jesus Christ." He turned on the television and threw the remote back onto the table so he could rub his now aching forehead. He should've known better than to think Michelle had quietly left his life. "We need to talk."

"Oh, god, Blake, please don't tell me it's true."

His heart clenched. "I'm sorry. I was stupid but it was a long time ago."

"A long time ago?" Her voice broke. "Every reporter in New York is saying it happened last night."

"What?" His voice rose. "No. That's a load of shit. I haven't done drugs in years." He rushed to pick up the remote and scan for a news channel.

"Drugs?" Leah asked. "What drugs? I'm talking about the physical abuse against Michelle Clarkson last night."

He stumbled back, his calves hitting the coffee table and planting him on his ass as the television hit a news feed. A video of Michelle played on the screen. Someone was escorting her into the emergency department of a hospital, the sky still dark with night.

"Holy. Shit."

Gabi gasped from behind him, and he turned to find her gaze on the television, her face now pale, making the shadows under her eyes more pronounced.

"I don't want to ask, Blake, because I know you, and I'd never think you were capable of something like this, but I have to ask because it's my job. I need to know. Please tell me you didn't hurt her?" Leah's words became faster, between panted breaths as if she were running.

"No! God, no!" He would never hurt a woman. Not even one like Michelle.

"OK. Good. Glad to hear it. Now which room are you in? I'm on my way to the Plaza."

Blake recited the room number and stumbled to his feet, beginning to pace. Leah was going to kill him. Slowly. With something blunt. "Leah?"

"Yeah?" The echo of traffic came through the line.

"You better pick up Mason on the way. I've got some things I need to tell you both."

She sighed. "Sure. We'll be there soon."

He disconnected the call and turned, needing the reassurance that Gabi's presence always brought. Only she wasn't there. The soft click of the bathroom door hit him with the force of an uppercut. She'd seen the news feed, overheard his conversation, and yet, she still walked away.

―――⌒⌒―――

Gabi had taken her time in the shower, finally getting out to dress in the loose fitting jeans and comfortable jumper she'd swiped from her suitcase while Blake was on the phone. Now she sat on the lowered toilet seat, her thighs raised to her chest, her arms hugging them close, waiting for the minutes to tick by.

Morning hadn't brought the clarity she'd hoped for. Sleep hadn't taken away the pain. It was all still there, weighing down her chest, pulsing through her veins with every broken heartbeat.

She knew now that Blake hadn't cheated on her, but he'd shut her out. Betrayed her trust. And no amount of sleep would change that. He wanted to fix his problems by himself? Fine. With the tense call this morning and the topic of news on the television, it seemed he had a lot to deal with. So she would respect his wishes and stick to her plan, leaving on today's flight back to Sydney. No matter how much it pained her to turn her back on him.

"Gabi." Blake rapped softly on the door. "Leah and Mason are on their way over. I need to speak to you before they get here."

"I'll be out in a minute," she lied.

She already assumed Leah and Mason were on their way, and she planned to hide until they arrived. Even though curiosity demanded she find out what his latest problems were, it would be an opportune time to leave while Blake was distracted. She only hoped they wouldn't be too much longer. Although the thought of food made her nauseous, her stomach growled in frustration.

"Gabi, I need to use the bathroom."

Shit. "I'm coming." She sagged in defeat and stood. The partially steamed mirror taunted her. No amount of make-up had been able to hide her sorrow. It still clung to the puffy bags under her eyes.

With a deep breath, she pushed at the door handle and walked into the suite. She kept her gaze averted from Blake's dominating form, but his hand caught hers, pulling her back. He didn't speak. He simply tugged her into his chest, increasing her misery when he hugged her with gentle arms, resting his face in her hair.

She ignored his heat, the lingering scent of aftershave that she always associated with passion, and stared at the pocket of his black collared shirt. He'd put his clothes from last night back on, his tailored pants belted and buckled, while his shirt fell open, exposing his muscled stomach. He had no buttons. Well, he did, they were just strewn over the floor.

Time passed, each second making it harder to keep her hands at her sides. She wanted to claim his affection, to grasp it with everything she had and carry it home with her. Finally, she gave up trying to fight it. With heavy arms, she circled his waist, leaning her head into his neck.

Goodbye, Blake.

She clutched him tighter, listening to the faint beat of his heart, the pained exhalations of breath. In time they would regain the friendship that had been shattered—the trust that had been lost. She would forgive him, and they could go back to the way things were before they met in person.

A knock sounded at the door, startling her.

Blake didn't move, he only squeezed harder, moving his hand into the back of her hair. "I love you, angel."

Her breath hitched, smothered by another knock at the door.

"Blake?" Leah's voice called from the hall.

Gabi lowered her arms and stepped back with straightened shoulders. Without making eye contact, she went to her pajamas, grabbing them off the floor while Blake strode to the door. Quickly she shoved her clothes into the front pocket of her suitcase and rushed to the bathroom to retrieve her personal items.

Leah and Mason's voices filtered in while she grabbed her things—toothbrush, comb, make-up, and finally the necklace Blake gave her for her birthday. She held the charms in her palm and worked the chain through her fingers. The gift had given her strength over the past weeks. She had toyed with the turtle and guitar pick whenever they spoke on the phone and laid awake at night running her fingers over the smooth gold. Now the thought of putting it on tightened her throat.

Be strong.

Thrusting the necklace into her jeans pocket, she gripped the vanity. This wouldn't break her. She would go home, concentrate on her studies, work her ass to the bone, and move on with her life.

Oh, who was she kidding?

Blake *was* her life and had been for a long time. But she vowed to respect herself enough to gain the space needed to clear her head. One day soon, he would figure out his life. Hopefully by then Gabi would've gotten over the way he left her behind.

Clutching the beauty case under her arm, she strode back into the quiet suite and faltered. Blake sat on the end of the mattress, his head in his hands, entirely broken. Gabi swallowed down her need to go to him and glanced at Leah and Mason, finding them watching her with expressions mixed with concern and confusion. She ignored their scrutiny, giving Leah a brief smile before continuing to her suitcase, stuffing her personal items into the main compartment and re-zipping it. Then she reached for her ankle boots on the floor beside her and yanked them on.

"What are you doing?" Blake raised his head and pinned her with his gaze.

Gabi focused on her boots, pulling up the zippers before making eye contact. "I'm leaving." Thankfully her voice didn't waver. After the days of heartache, finally she'd gained the strength to carry on without tears.

Blake stood, his brow now creased. "Please, Gabi. Don't go. Not yet. Give me a chance to figure things out. Then we can talk."

She shook her head. Her mind was made up. A relationship was about sharing burdens, about sticking together through the hard times, the worst of times, no matter what. "No. I'm going home."

He moved to her, huffing in frustration. "*Please.*"

His plea almost undid her, almost stole her strength. Before she buckled, she reached into her pocket and sucked in a steadying breath. "Here." She pulled out the necklace and went to place it in his outstretched hand. "When you gave this to me, you told me the charms were to serve as a reminder of you when we were apart."

He pulled away, and she gripped his wrist with her free hand, firmly placing the necklace in his palm.

"I no longer want a reminder." She never needed one. He was always in her heart. Now the necklace choked her, weighing her down, taunting her with what she couldn't have.

"No." He thrust it back at her. "Don't do this. I'll sort it out. I'll fix things. Just give me some time." His eyes pleaded along with his words. "I can't do this without you."

She scoffed. Didn't he understand? Couldn't he see? "That's just it. The problems started when you tried to shut me out. We were supposed to be a couple. We were supposed to share everything. But you lied. You pushed me—"

"I didn't—"

"*No.* Let me finish. None of this would've happened if you were honest. I knew you had demons to battle. *I knew that.* I also knew how much it meant to you to be able to face them on your own. But keeping this from me… Letting me believe you were with someone else. Why the hell didn't you call?"

He stepped closer, and she stepped back.

"I didn't know how to tell you, and didn't want to do it over the phone. Your disappointment would've killed me."

She sucked in a shuddering breath, betraying the unrelenting hurt she tried so hard to hide. "I've always been proud of you. Always."

The trill of a cell phone broke the silence and Leah's soft voice answered the call.

"Angel." Blake reached for her, his shirt open, his chest and part of his heavenly tattoo on display.

She flinched and pulled away. "Don't."

If he touched her now, she'd crumple into his welcoming arms and would never be able to walk away. She still loved him, with all her heart and everything she was. There would never be another man to fill the gaping hole he left inside her. "I need time."

"Blake." Leah's voice interrupted. "I'm sorry," she gave Gabi a regretful smile, "we need to discuss this now. The label was on the phone, demanding answers."

Gabi lifted her suitcase to stand and grabbed the trolley handle, guiding it forward.

"I don't care," he growled, moving to block her path. "Gabi, I can't let you go."

She continued walking, pushing around him. "You already did."

Chapter Twenty-Eight

Blake stared at the door, his body numb except for the stabbing pain emanating from under his ribs. He no longer needed to fight. If he didn't have Gabi to protect, it didn't matter who found out about the darkness in his life.

Reckless Beat didn't matter. The band was his home, his sanctuary, but Gabi was his heart and soul. Without her, there was no point.

"Blake, we need to discuss this." Leah came up behind him and placed her hands on his shoulders.

Her touch should've brought comfort. He felt nothing—no hope, no relief, no peace. "I don't give a shit anymore," he whispered and meant it. "I'm done."

He turned on her, and she stepped back, her brow furrowed.

"Give Gabi the time she asked for. I don't know what's going on with you two, but you'll work it out. She loves you."

"She *loved* me," he corrected. The love Gabi once held for him wasn't in question. She *had* loved him. He'd known that. And now that love was gone.

Mason pushed from the sofa. "Come on, Blake. There's a shit-storm brewing and you're caught in the middle. We need to sort this out and address the media before it gets out of hand."

Shit-storm was an understatement. The taint of abusing a woman would never leave him, guilty or not. The question would always hover in the back of people's minds.

"I didn't do it," he muttered, sliding his fingers through his now greasy hair. God, how he wished Michelle had never entered his life. He never had much of a reputation to uphold, but damned if he wanted to go down in history as the drug addicted, woman abuser.

"I know that!" Mason spat, striding forward. "Do you really think any of us would believe you're capable of doing that? Christ, Blake, fuckin' man up." Mason got in his face and glared at him. "We're family. Your innocence isn't in question. We just need to get your story to the media before they start spinning shit that can't be fixed."

Blake glanced away, frowning hard to fight the tightening in his chest. "I can't—" He cleared his throat, pushing back the emotion. "I can't do this without her."

He should've known from the start that keeping her out was the wrong thing to do. She was his guardian angel, the one who fought his battles with ease and continuously placed him on the right track. She was his strength. His clarity. His everything.

"Don't worry about Gabi. That woman knows you've got a champagne flavored cock. She'll be back beggin' for more." Mason smirked, yet the arrogance didn't reach his eyes, instead concern hung heavy in his friends brown irises. "And if not, you can always go back to begging. I've never had to do it myself. Maybe you could ask Ryan for pointers."

Blake released a ragged excuse for a laugh and led them back to the sofa. Sitting back on the mattress, he waited for Leah and Mason to get comfortable.

This was it—the end.

"I was with Gabi last night." He stared at his feet and pressed his toes into the heavy carpeting. "She's my alibi."

Leah let out a relieved breath. "That's great. Why didn't you tell me straight away? The news kept repeating that Michelle hadn't made a statement, but the two of you were seen fighting in the lobby last night. There was even amateur footage."

"At least it's an easy fix with the media and cops," Mason added.

"I'll call hotel management," Leah stood, her relief palpable. "We can make a statement from the front of the building and stop the rumors before they spread."

"Wait," Blake murmured, glancing up to briefly make eye contact with Mason. God, this was going to hurt. He'd always looked up to the lead singer. He had has shit together all day, every day, when Blake continuously felt like he was flailing. "Michelle is blackmailing me."

"For what?" Leah frowned, retreating to drop back into the sofa. "With what? What would she have over you?"

Blake retrieved his cell from his back pocket and scrolled through to the picture message from Michelle. With a deep breath, he did exactly what he'd done with Mitch and handed the phone over.

Leah didn't say a word. Her disappointment was clear in the barely discernible way she shook her head.

"Show me." Mason grabbed the phone and stared at the image. "When the fuck was this taken? You look like a minor."

"A few months after I started with Reckless."

"Are you still using?" Leah asked softly.

"No." He shook his head and stared at her, trying to convey his sincerity. "I haven't touched drugs or even alcohol in four years… I'm sorry, Leah. I know this is going to create a nightmare for you, and that's the last thing I want. I hoped to fix the situation by myself. Obviously I can't even do that right."

He clenched his jaw and turned his attention back to his feet. "Michelle started me on cocaine the first night we met, and it didn't take long for me to realize I had a problem. I started craving the high—on stage, alone, even when I woke in the middle of the night to take a piss. That's when I found Gabi."

Silence. Leah and Mason didn't move, they barely even breathed.

"She was an online drug addiction counselor. Well, not even a properly trained counselor. She was just there to keep an eye on the chat groups and provide moral support when possible. The first night we spoke, she saved me."

He glanced up at Leah and winced at the tears in her eyes. He wouldn't cry. He wouldn't fucking cry. "With a few simple words, she gave me strength and helped me get through the hardest days… It was all her. Gabi is the only reason I'm here. Nothing else. I couldn't save myself. I never can. I'm too fucking weak. I owe her everything."

Leah stood, closing the distance between them and sat beside him on the bed. He swallowed over the growing lump in his throat and leaned into her as she ran her hand around his shoulders.

"Damn," Mason whispered. "I bow down to your secrecy skills, man. I had no clue."

"Me either," Leah whispered. "It shows how horribly lacking I've been in my position. I should've noticed…paid more attention."

"No." Blake shook his head. "This has nothing to do with you. I've fucked up enough in my life to know how to keep my mouth shut, and in the beginning I couldn't think past losing my position in the band. I would've done anything to keep it quiet."

"And now?" Mason asked.

Blake sucked in a deep breath. He was still hollow, numb and detached from the neck down. "And now, none of it seems to matter. All I want is Gabi's forgiveness. I can't see past losing her. She's all that matters to me." He raised his gaze to Mason. "I'm sorry, bro. I've fucked up, and I know having me kicked out of the band will cause a lot of extra work for you."

"Kicked out of the band? Like hell." Mason frowned. "That's not gonna happen."

Leah cleared her throat and released her grip on Blake's shoulder. "Unfortunately, it could. Blake's contract with the label has a morality clause for exactly this reason. Anyone seen to bring the label into disrepute or do anything that could harm sales can be in breach of contract. I've seen it happen before…mainly in groups with members that the label feels are interchangeable."

Meaning me.

"So, you're saying he could get the axe 'cause the label thinks we could find a replacement?" Mason sneered. "That's bullshit."

"That's life," Leah countered. "Reckless have always stood proud against the claims of drug abuse in the music industry. Hell, last time we were in Richmond, you visited the drug rehab center and the story was covered by the local newspaper. This won't go down easily, by the label or the community."

"It's OK." Blake shrugged. "I've come to terms with leaving."

"No. *Fuck* that!" Mason pushed to his feet. "It's not an option. If Blake goes, I go. Simple as that."

Blake's heart clenched, showing the first sign of life since Gabi left. He had no clue what he'd done to deserve friends—family—like this. If their roles were reversed, Blake would put his career on the line for any one of the Reckless guys, no questions asked. He simply hadn't expected Mason to do the same.

"Leah, call the label. Tell them what's going on and find out what they plan to do." Mason stood tall, his eyes flashing with anger. "If they plan to get rid of Blake, I'm walking. They can find someone else to earn them millions."

"It doesn't work like that." Leah sighed. "You're the lead singer, Mason, and under a tight contract. You can't walk away because you disagree with a decision they are legally entitled to make."

"I know I can't," Mason shot back. "But I can be in Time Square snorting coke off the sidewalk in less time than it takes to organize a press conference. And unlike Blake, I don't give a shit about my reputation. My low morality was cemented years ago."

"Christ!" Leah rubbed her forehead. "Just settle down. Who says this needs to go public anyway? Can't we continue to keep it quiet?"

"No." Blake sat in shocked silence, unable to believe the lengths Mason would go through to save him, but he couldn't continue to hide. "I can't live a lie anymore. I need to get it out in the open so I can move on."

Chapter Twenty-Nine

THE LOW HUM of the airplane drowned under the weight of Gabi's thoughts. She stared out the window, ignoring the deep blue ocean below. All she could see was Blake. The airline food had kept her occupied for half an hour, then she'd tried a movie, music, a documentary, not even episodes of The Big Bang Theory called to her.

Unfortunately, she had to come to terms with all the time she had to reflect before they landed in Sydney—hours in which she didn't have a phone or computer to keep her occupied. And her mind was the enemy. Already she'd begun to second guess her actions.

Leaving had been the right decision. She needed space and time to figure out all the things that didn't make sense. And at the moment, that was a lot of things—seeing Blake with Michelle, the way she touched him with familiarity, the way she'd kissed his cheek. Even though he'd told her it didn't mean anything, the shock had unbalanced her, affecting the way she rationalized everything else after that moment.

Maybe if she hadn't been blindsided things would've been different. Maybe if she had time to sit and think before checking out of the hotel suite and racing to the airport. Maybe…

Or maybe not.

Going home was the best option. It didn't have to be a permanent decision. She loved Blake too much to give up on forever, but right now the thought of being close to him made her ache with distrust.

"He did it for sure," the stout woman beside Gabi sneered aloud, her focus on the mini television screen that rested in the seat back in front of her. "Just look at him. Tattooed, dressed like death, and those eyes." The woman pushed the headset at her ears and shuddered. "Who knows what he's capable of?"

Gabi followed the woman's line of sight and her chest restricted at the image on the small screen. It was Blake, standing out the front of The Plaza hotel, microphones surrounding him. He wore the tan polo shirt Mason had been wearing earlier and dark smudges hung heavy under his eyes, weariness etched into his features.

With shaky hands, she reached for the headphones that rested at her neck and put them on. "What channel are you watching?" she asked, maneuvering the touch screen from the entertainment channels back to the main screen, then to the news.

The woman glanced at Gabi. "It's the first one, I think."

Gabi pushed her finger down on the first icon and sat forward while it began to load. "Come on. Come on. Come on."

Then there he was, standing before her, his lips moving with no sound coming out. *Shit.* She clicked on the volume, not stopping until it went up as far as it could.

"… made mistakes." His voice came through, rough and emotionless. "None bigger than those concerning Michelle Clarkson. But I didn't hurt her." He was hurting, though, she could see it in his tight lips and his lifeless eyes. Reporters burst to life around him, asking questions, waving their microphones in his face which he ignored with patient indifference.

"I stayed here, at The Plaza hotel last night and video surveillance can confirm that I entered the building hours before the doctors say Michelle was attacked."

"How is Michelle?" One reporter shouted.

"Who were you with?" Another asked.

Blake stared lifelessly to the left of the filming camera. "I haven't spoken to Michelle. As far as I know, she has yet to make a statement. And who I was with last night is nobody's business."

A sad smile tugged at Gabi's lips. He was trying to protect her, even after she'd walked away.

More questions erupted, and Blake spoke over the top of them, his words momentarily lost over the rush of voices. "...rumors that Michelle and I are dating. That is incorrect." He raised his chin and straightened his shoulders. The cameraman panned out, and Leah and Mason came into view on either side of him, their postures rigid. "She was blackmailing me with the mistakes of my past. Mistakes I'm ashamed of and fought hard to hide."

Gabi's pulse began to pound. Why was he bringing up his past? If the press knew he had secrets, they wouldn't stop until they were uncovered. Her throat tightened, and she swallowed to try and alleviate the ache. She didn't want this for him. No matter how angry and hurt she was, he didn't deserve this.

"I'm not going to hide anymore."

She gasped and covered her mouth with her hand. *No.* She shook her head, silently pleading for him to stop.

Blake cleared his throat while silence reigned around him, the vultures eagerly awaiting the news. "I was a drug addict. A fact that I'm sickened to admit."

Reporters inched forward, getting in his face. Gabi couldn't hear what they were saying because they all spoke at once, but from the disgust on Leah's face and the fury on Mason's, she knew it wasn't good.

Blake lowered his gaze, silently taking the assault. It wasn't until Mason leaned close, whispering something in his ear that Blake raised his focus, his jaw now tight, his eyes blazing with determination.

"At the start of my career with Reckless Beat, I began using cocaine for recreational purposes. Recreation turned into addiction, and although I realized my mistakes early, it took a while for me to return from the hell I'd sunk into." He spoke over the questions hurtled at him. "I kept this part of myself hidden from the people I loved and the band that has become my life. And I've done so for years."

Gabi's eyes burned. What would happen to him now? Would he lose Reckless Beat? Bloody hell, then what would he do? The lady beside Gabi muttered something unintelligible, and she ignored it, solely focused on Blake, wishing she was there with him.

"None of that matters anymore," he proclaimed, staring straight into the camera. "My loyalty to the band, my love of music—" He shook his head and wrinkled his nose. "None of it matters, because I've ruined the only thing in my life that means more to me than life itself. I've let down the woman who holds my heart and done the one thing I promised myself I would never do—hurt her."

The screen blurred and Gabi frantically blinked away her tears. When her vision cleared, Blake's head was bowed, his shoulders slumped. His chest heaved while he ran his hand though his tangled hair and glanced back at the crowd.

"I appreciate the support of Reckless Beat's loyal fans and hope that one day I can make it up to them. But for now, with my position as bass guitarist under jeopardy, I ask that you all hold me fully accountable for the way I've brought the band and our label into disrepute. And that you all please leave Mason, Mitch, Ryan, and Sean out of the drama I've caused. Thank you."

Blake turned, ignoring the questioning reporters and strode back into the hotel, Leah and Mason at his sides. The clip ended, returning to the news desk. Gabi lowered her earphones. Her heart pounded, protesting her decision to leave. She couldn't dwell on that now.

Blake had to fight this battle alone. She of all people needed to understand why. He always considered himself weak, even when he was the most strong-hearted, determined man she knew. He'd never believe her, never believe in himself. And no matter how much she yearned to run back to him, to help smooth out the pain in his life—this wasn't about her.

He needed to do this on his own.

Chapter Thirty

One week later

BLAKE HEARD A knock at the door and groaned. He didn't want to see anyone. Fuck, he didn't even want to move. His position in his favorite chair, reclined in front of the television, the footrest up, was where he wanted to be. Most importantly—alone.

The knock came again, louder.

"Hold on," he growled and pushed to his feet. He kicked past the empty pizza boxes and crumpled pieces of paper strewn across the floor before yanking the front door open.

"Holy shit. Did I knock on the right door?" Sean chuckled, turning to Mason.

"To be honest, I'm not sure," Mason replied. "Emo, is that you under all that hair?"

Blake rubbed at the beard covering his jaw and cringed. He hadn't shaved in…well, he couldn't remember, but he didn't give a shit.

"Lay off," Ryan said, pushing past Blake and into his apartment. "We all have aspirations. He can be a yeti if he wants."

Mitch snorted and gave Blake a half-hearted punch to the gut as he followed Ryan. "Lookin'…good, buddy."

Mason and Sean didn't ask for an invitation either, they simply strode into his apartment carrying bottles of soda and beer.

"Make yourselves at home," Blake muttered, slamming the door shut.

The guys had hounded him all week, calling daily, visiting too often, and constantly reminding him about the outside world even though he didn't want to be a part of it.

"I like what you've done with the place," Mason called from the living room. "It's very 'ghetto' and suits the new look you're sporting."

Blake gave him the bird and started picking up rubbish from the floor.

"So tell me the plan again," Sean leaned forward on the sofa, his focus on Mitch. "Do I get to hold him down while you guys shave that shit off his face, or do I get the blade?"

"Fuck off," Blake snapped.

"What's with all the paper?" Mason asked, looking at the hundreds of crumpled notepad sheets on the floor.

"Nothin'." Blake glared, taking his first load of garbage to the bin in the kitchen.

All week, he'd focused his waning energy on the emotions running through his mind—the regret, the heartache, the love. He wanted to write everything down, maybe compose a song, but the words he scratched along each page were shit.

The sound of paper crinkling came over the chatter, and Blake strode back into the living room, ripping the opened page from Mason's hand.

Mason rested back in the chair and frowned. "Were they lyrics?"

They were none of his fucking business. Blake closed his eyes, breathed through his annoyance, and crumpled the page into his fist.

"They're good, man," Ryan said from behind him.

Blake pivoted and snatched the paper Ryan held open. "Leave my shit alone!" Those pages were filled with pieces of his soul. The words were personal, intimate, and something he didn't want anyone to see. Especially not these teasing assholes.

"But you have so much of it to share," Sean chuckled.

Blake worked his jaw. He was going to lose his fucking mind. If they didn't leave, he would hurt one of them. All of them. It didn't matter how many. He just wanted to wipe those shit eating grins from their faces. "Why are you all here?"

The four of them looked at one another before focusing back on him.

"To help you clean up after your pity party," Ryan answered.

Mitch pinned him with a serious stare. "Michelle's attacker has been caught, the fans are all rallying behind you, and the fucking label has loved the publicity. So it's time to man up and move on."

Blake gritted his teeth. "No thanks. I'm fine."

"Oh, yeah, we can see that." Mason's gaze raked over Blake, taking in the old, dirty sweatpants and ripped T-shirt. "When was the last time you showered?"

"Is that an invitation to scrub my back?"

"I'm not usually into bestiality, however, if that's what it takes to make you human again." Mason shrugged.

Blake stood at the end of the sofa and crossed his arms over his chest. This was bullshit. He was a fucking grown man. He could grow a beard and forget to shower if he wanted to. Hell, he was a rock star. This behavior was how the public expected him to act on his downtime.

Mason cracked open a bottle of beer and inclined his head as he took a swig. "I don't care how long it takes to snap you outta this. I've got enough beer to last until tomorrow morning."

Assholes. Every single one of them.

"Fine. I'll shower." Blake turned and headed for his bedroom. "Then you can leave."

"Don't be stupid," Mitch chuckled.

Fifteen minutes later, Blake strode from his bathroom into his now clean bedroom.

"What the fuck?"

His bed was made, the clothes previously strewn across the floor were nowhere to be seen, and his window was open a crack, letting in fresh air. He threw his towel on the bed and stalked down the hall. His dishwasher hummed from the kitchen, and he poked his head in the room to find Sean stacking empty pizza boxes on the counter.

"Fuckers!"

He continued down the hall to the living room finding the floor now spotless and cleared of paper. Mason and Mitch knelt at his coffee table, flattening out the previously crumpled notepad pages and placing them in a pile.

No! Oh, god, no.

He felt his balls shrink. Nothing could've emasculated him more than having his friends read those discarded heartbroken rants. The things he'd written were deep—unintelligibly deep. And totally fucking embarrassing. The guys were going to think he was the biggest pussy on earth.

"Why don't you get Sidney to help you with these?" Mitch asked, patting the pile of pages.

Blake closed his eyes and let his head fall back. Did he really want to go that route? Calling the famous songwriter would mean he was deliberately sharing his weaknesses with the world. Hadn't he already done enough of that?

"They're good," Mason added. "Really good. Are they all about Gabi?"

Blake rubbed his hands down his now clean shaven face and let out a moan, which ended up sounding like a delirious laugh. Every word was about her, every thought, every memory, every regret. He'd hoped writing down his emotions would get her out of his mind, and they probably would've had a chance if he could make them fit together properly.

"Yeah," he admitted, and opened his eyes, waiting for their laughter.

None came. His friends only nodded and continued straightening his private pieces of paper.

"You'll be fine, princess." Ryan strode into the room, clapping Blake on the back when he passed. "We Cinderella'd your place and you look all purty again. It's only a matter of time before you're back to normal."

"You really should call Sidney." Mitch stood and jerked a thumb in Mason's direction. "Or get lover boy to call her."

"Love to," Mason answered. "Only I don't think it would work in your favor. That woman wants to gut me."

Blake snickered, and the guys all stopped what they were doing to look at him. "Oh, Christ, come on. It's not like I've never laughed before."

Mitch shrugged. "It's just good to hear, that's all."

Blake ignored the twinge of regret that turned his stomach. Even though he was miserable without Gabi, he needed to remember he had a lot to be thankful for. His friends were at the top of that list, followed closely by his position in Reckless Beat. He didn't know what he would've done if the label tore up his contract.

Walking to the couch, he sat in the corner, alongside Ryan. It was time to man the fuck up. Once the cloying thoughts were out of his mind, he'd be able to move forward. Well, at least he'd have the brain capacity to figure out how to take the first step.

Pulling his phone out of his pocket, he unlocked the screen and glanced at Mason. "Ok, then. What's Sidney's number?"

Chapter Thirty-One

Blake re-read Sidney's neat writing, his smile growing wider with every line. "It's good."

"Of course it's good." She smiled, her hazel eyes gleaming. "You've packed a lot of heartache and love into those lyrics. I think everyone will be reaching for the tissues when they hear you sing it."

He clutched the guitar in his lap tighter and swallowed his nervousness. Singing wasn't his forte. He was good enough to back up Mason on tour when the music was loud and fans drowned out his voice. However, singing alone, with only a guitar to keep him grounded, scared the shit out of him.

"Don't worry." Sidney patted his knee. "Truly, Blake, it sounds passionate and heartfelt. The woman you're singing about won't be able to resist falling in love with you all over again. Trust me."

He nodded, although not entirely convinced. "OK… Let's do this. I'll go get Mason." He stood, and not even the dark fringe covering Sidney's forehead hid her cringe.

"Are you sure *you're* up to this?" Blake asked, sitting back down. They planned on creating a video of his song—Gabi's song— and uploading it to YouTube. He couldn't call her, didn't know what to say if he emailed, but maybe his music would convey the emotions he had trouble getting out. The only problem was the sound. He could sing the song himself and accompany it with his guitar, but doing it in harmony with Sidney's sweet voice and Mason's smoothly popular tone would be magic. Sidney would have to suppress her loathing for Mason while they did it, though.

"Me?" She waved away his comment. "I'm fine."

Blake narrowed his gaze. He wasn't sure if Sidney and Mason had even spoken since the sex tape scandal. And looking at her now, with her innocent doe eyes and wholesome smile, he couldn't understand how a woman so sweet would've ever allowed herself to be taped getting naked with Mason, let alone Sean at the same time.

"Come on, Blake. Let's do this." She stood and strode to the studio door, hesitating briefly before opening it. "Hey, asshole," she called down the hall.

Blake cleared his throat to smother a chuckle. For the last two days, he'd worked with Sidney and not once had she been unprofessional. She was a true lady, one with manners and morals and self-respect.

"We're ready for you," she continued, then let the door close in Mason's face. In her sophisticated knee-length business dress and dainty black heels, she turned and walked back to the chair beside him. "See, I'm fine."

He grinned and shook his head. She could pretend to be fine all day. They both knew it was only a façade. He could see the hurt in her eyes and the denial in the weakness of her smile.

Mason yanked the door open and strode in. "Nice to see you too, wildcat."

"I wish I felt the same," she sneered. "Wait. No I don't. I'd be quite happy to never see your face again." She smiled, batting her thick black lashes. "Oh, I almost forgot." She leaned over and grabbed her handbag from the floor, scrounging through the contents. "I've got something for you."

Mason stopped a few feet away, leaning on the back of a wooden chair, watching her. She placed the handbag back down and flicked something small and shiny at his chest. "Go fuck yourself," she muttered, then lowered her gaze to the sheets of music in her lap.

Blake's eyes widened at the vehemence in her tone, not to mention her language. He'd never heard her swear before, and they'd known each other for years. Mason had that effect on women. They either loved him, or wanted to claw his pretty face.

Mason fumbled to catch the silver packet, and then held it up between his fingers. "I love the dramatics, Sid, but if I'm fucking myself, doesn't that kinda make the condom redundant?" He raised a brow.

Sidney didn't look at him. "With your propensity for sleeping with whores, I'd be protecting every part of my body against the diseases that thing—" she glanced at his crotch, then back to her work, "could carry."

Mason fixed Blake with a crooked grin. "Did she just call herself a wh—"

"Mason," Blake warned.

"You do remember that we've slept together, right?" Mason taunted. "If you don't, I can always call Sean. I'm sure he's still got a copy of the video."

Sidney's hurt gaze snapped to Blake, her bottom lip caught tight between her teeth. He wanted to comfort her. She didn't need it. In the next second, she raised her chin and her nostrils flared. Moving to her feet, she turned on Mason. "I remember. You were the biggest mistake of my life."

Mason's smirk increased. "Well, I definitely wouldn't be the smallest."

"Oh, that's cute." She took a step forward and smiled. "You think you've got something special between your thighs. Sorry to break the news, buddy, but you actually need to know how to use it for it to be useful."

Mason faltered, his brows furrowing before he leaned forward, inches from her mouth. "I distinctively recall you screaming my name as your tight pussy came around my cock."

Blake's focus flicked between the two of them like a tennis match. Each comeback spurred the other on, making them more livid. If he didn't know the circumstances behind the loathing, he would've guessed this was an anger filled mating dance.

Silence fell heavy in the room. Sidney clenched her fists, straightened her shoulders, and turned, moving back to her seat. Mason chuckled, the noise growing louder the longer she remained quiet.

Why was Mason being such an asshole? Couldn't he see she was hurting?

Sidney cleared her throat and met Blake's stare. "Can we hurry this along?"

Gabi sat at the reception desk, occupying herself with the *click, click, click* of her pen. She wasn't meant to be working today, but when another staff member called in sick, Gabi jumped at the chance to keep herself busy. Only she wasn't busy. She was bored. And boredom led to thoughts of Blake, which led to the cloying depression she'd been trying to ditch for days.

"Oh, my god," Tammy's voice came from the luggage storage room behind her, followed by foreign murmurs from a video.

"What?" Gabi asked, swiveling in her chair to face the doorway.

Tammy walked into view, her eyes wide and her phone in her hand. "Have you been on the internet lately?"

"Yeah," Gabi frowned. "I check my emails when we're quiet." She checked her emails every spare second of the day, always hoping to find something from Blake. Unfortunately, he'd listened to her appeal for time alone, and she hadn't heard from him since leaving the US.

"Umm." Tammy swallowed.

"What is it?" Panic started to overtake her, her palms now beginning to sweat. *Please don't let it be another Blake media scandal.*

"Get on YouTube."

Gabi paused, unable to determine if Tammy was excited or panicked, before swiveling in her chair to face her computer screen. She opened up an internet browser and typed the website address. "Now what?" Her fingers were poised over the keypad, her body tense, waiting to find out what was so important. If it was another cat video, Tammy would be in serious trouble.

"Type in, 'Blake Kennedy—Shattered Heart.'"

Gabi froze. She sat there, staring at the screen, her chest throbbing. She didn't know what to expect, but 'shattered heart' sounded laughably ominous.

"Do it, Gabi."

Tammy's hand came to rest on her shoulder, providing no comfort whatsoever. Again, Gabi felt alone, the numbness crawling under her skin, trying to take over.

"Fine. I'll do it." Tammy nudged around her to grab the keyboard. Her fingers clicked over the buttons, each soft tap increasing Gabi's anxiety.

"I don't think…" Her words drifted away when an image of Blake came on screen, an acoustic guitar cradled in his lap. He wore a black Reckless Beat T-shirt, his arm tattoos on display along with his leather wrist band.

His lips moved, addressing a beautiful, dark haired woman who sat beside him, with Mason at his other side. "Turn it up. Turn it up."

Tammy clicked on the volume, drawing her attention to the date the video was uploaded—yesterday—and already there were over twenty thousand views.

"Are you ready?" the woman's soft lilt whispered.

Blake nodded, brushing his fingers along the guitar strings. The delicate noise made Gabi's heart flutter, and she sat stunned in silence, watching his every movement. She loved his hands, the way they flowed effortlessly over the instrument, creating a heavenly sound. Then he began to sing, and the air rushed from her lungs.

"Wow," Tammy spoke on an exhalation. "Just…wow."

"Shh." Gabi didn't want to miss a thing. She'd never heard him sing before, not alone anyway. His voice was raw and gravel rich, the masculine tone entirely hypnotic. Mason and the woman backed up his vocals in a soft melody, repeating lyrics, heightening the emotion.

You're my passionate addiction, the only high I crave…

Blake stared at his guitar, his shoulders slumped, both hands working with synchronized beauty. She wanted to graze her fingers over the dark stubble lining his jaw, to run her hands through the thick lengths of his hair.

Colors have faded. Nothing matters anymore…

Her head told her to look away, yet her adoration for him wouldn't allow it. She missed him, loved him. So much it would never stop hurting.

I'm torn apart, broken and bruised, yet it doesn't compare to the way I treated you.

Mason tapped his foot, creating a tender beat while Blake sang louder, more emotional. The sound hummed in her ears, warming her frigid limbs. At one point his voice cracked and Gabi held her breath, unable to function through her sorrow.

I won't stay away. I'll be back for you someday.

Until then, you keep the shattered pieces of my heart in your hands.

Blake gave a final strum of his guitar and glanced at the camera. The corner of his lips tilted in a sad smile, his midnight eyes fathomless as he stared into her soul. Then the video faded to black and finally she could breathe again.

"What are you thinking?" Tammy asked.

Gabi shrugged and reached across the counter for a tissue. "He's a musician. Writing songs is a part of the job description." She didn't want to dissect his reasons for writing this particular song when she knew he didn't often contribute lyrically to Reckless Beat. Her mind had already started pounding with questions she couldn't answer, and after day upon day of suffering over him, she now craved the numbness she had become accustomed to.

"You're joking, right?"

"No, I'm not." Gabi pushed from her chair. "He hasn't bothered to call me since I left the US. Why should this change the way I feel?" Yes it seemed ridiculous, even to her ears, yet a simple phone call would've meant so much more. Gabi didn't wait for a reply. "I'm going to lunch."

Tammy nodded, still staring at her with pity. Damn, she was sick of that look—from her friends, her parents, herself when she looked in the mirror.

Grabbing her new phone off the counter, she strode outside. The thought of food turned her stomach. What she needed was the comfort of the ocean. As she made her way across the road to the steps leading to the beach, the warm sea breeze blew the hair from her face, but it didn't calm her. At the bottom step, she kicked off her shoes and wiggled her toes in the sand.

Still nothing.

All her life the sea had soothed her. The rush of the swell, the crush of the waves. It was home. Now it only served to remind her of what she'd once had. Blake's face taunted her every time she glanced toward the water. The sound of his voice echoed amongst the people when she swam. It no longer comforted her. Nothing did.

She missed him too much to let the pain fade away.

Heaving a sigh, she sat down on the sand in her grey suit skirt. She wished he would've called before releasing the video. Maybe then she'd believe he'd written it to win her back, not because of a publicity stunt.

Only he hadn't contacted her at all, and she didn't know what to do about it. If she called him, she'd regret it. She ran after him last time. She would never respect herself or any future relationship if she had to do it again.

Her phone began to sweat in her hand and she glanced down at the screen, hoping for answers. "I should move on." She spoke the words aloud, making the statement real. But how could she let Blake go? She believed he loved her, only his commitment didn't seem as strong as hers.

"Bloody hell." She had no idea how to fix things.

"Everything OK, angel?"

She stiffened. Surely that wasn't his voice. Slowly she glanced over her shoulder, and her breath caught at the sight of him. "Blake?"

His lips curved. "Yeah, gorgeous. It's me." He stood there, his hands in his jeans pockets, a casual black collared shirt untucked at his waist, and the silver studs on his wrist bands glinting in the sun.

"What are you doing here?" Her heart fluttered. *Evil, betraying heart.*

He shrugged, nervousness and apprehension marring his features. "I was in the neighborhood and thought I'd stop by." He stepped forward and reached out his hand, helping her to stand. "Tammy thought you might be down here."

When he released his grip, she wiped the sand off her ass, needing to keep her hands busy. He was so close, within touching distance. Her fingers itched to connect with him. She wanted to caress the dark smudges under his eyes and wipe away the exhaustion.

He raised a hand to brush away the hair blowing across her cheeks. "I'm sorry. I know you wanted time to think, but I can't stay away any longer." His dark eyes peered down at her, heating her blood. "I can't live without you anymore, angel."

She shook her head. "I don't believe you."

His brows furrowed. "What don't you believe? That I can't live without you? Just ask the guys, they're the ones who had to pull my life back together."

"No. I don't want to ask the guys or hear love songs on YouTube. All I need is for you to be honest and tell me."

His hand dropped from her cheek. "I've got a lot to explain."

"Yeah, you do." And she hoped like hell that it was convincing.

"Do you want to go someplace more private?"

She shook her head. She couldn't wait a moment longer to hear his reasoning.

"OK. Wanna sit?"

She nodded and followed him to the sand, sitting close at his side. He reached for her hand, and for long moments he remained quiet, his fingers running trails along the creases in her palm.

"I don't know what to say, Gabi. I don't want to make this worse. I can't stand the thought of you walking away for good."

"I need the truth. At the moment, I'm struggling to figure this out. Things between us had been fantastic and then you changed. You shut me out, and that's the one thing I can't understand. I never could've done that to you."

"I was sick of being the broken one," he spoke softly, his voice barely registering over the crash of the ocean. "And my fear of hurting you narrowed my thoughts. When Michelle blackmailed me, all I could think about was how you'd react. How disappointed and upset you'd be. So I kept it to myself, vowing to make it right without dragging you down."

"Your honesty would've hurt a lot less."

His face crumpled, and he nodded. "I…" He let out a derisive laugh and glanced away. "Truth is, I actually thought I was doing the right thing." His gaze came back to meet hers, searching. "You've always been my protector, Gabi, and for once I wanted to protect you—from me."

Her heart clenched. "I've never needed your protection, Blake. I've only ever needed you."

He turned his gaze back to the ocean, staring off into the distance. "I know that now. Hindsight's been painful." He raised her hand, bringing it to his lips to leave a gentle kiss on her palm. "I've made too many mistakes to count. And most of the time, I can't believe my own stupidity. I should've told you. I just couldn't stand to be weak again."

Gabi leaned into him, feeling the strength he didn't believe existed. "You need to stop letting your past define you, Blake. I wish you could see the brilliant man that I do."

His arm circled her shoulder, holding her tight. "You've been telling me that for years, and while we were apart, I had a lot of time to think about it. I realized I'm never going to make either one of us happy unless I forgive myself."

"And did you?" She pulled back to look him in the eye.

His mouth tilted at one side, the briefest hint of a smile curving his lips. "After a little ink therapy, yeah, I think I have."

"You got another tattoo?"

He nodded and pulled up the hem of his shirt, revealing the skin below the angel on his left pec. *Forgive. Forget. Finally be free.* The words were written in fine, black script.

"It's beautiful." She ran a finger over the raised flesh and his stomach clenched, the muscles defining under her touch. A skitter of excitement ran through her veins, heating the intimate parts of her body.

"Thank you."

She ignored the heat in his gaze and rested back into his shoulder. There would be time for intimacy later. Right now she only wanted to be held, to feel the strength of his love embracing her. He lowered his shirt and pulled her into his side, his fingers lazily stroking up and down her waist, giving her goose bumps.

"I'll make it up to you, sweetheart," he whispered in her ear. "Nothing matters more to me than making you happy for the rest of my life."

Gabi squeezed her eyes shut, overwhelmed with relief. This morning she'd been lost to heartache, and now, even if he hadn't said a word, she would've believed the regret and sincerity in his eyes.

"Never lie to me again." She kept her face hidden, not wanting him to see the smile she couldn't control.

"Never. I promise." He kissed her temple, turning her heart to flames. "Do you believe me? Can you believe *in me* after everything I've done?"

She snuggled into the darkness of his neck, inhaling the scent she associated with love and passion. They were made for each other. There would be more mistakes in the future, more hurdles to overcome and compromises to be made, but none of that mattered if they trusted each other. They could make it work.

"Yes." She couldn't elaborate, her heart was beating too hard, her stomach alive with a mass of butterflies and eagles' wings.

He held her tight, pressing his lips into her hair. "God, I've missed you." He kissed her again. "I've ached for you with every heartbeat." She believed him. She always would. "There's no one else for me. There never will be," he continued, breaking down her barriers.

Gabi peered up into his face. She read the sincerity in his eyes, the seriousness in the flat line of his lips. When she was in his arms, surrounded by his warmth and affection, nothing else mattered.

He lowered his gaze, focusing behind her shoulder. A bright reflection glinted in his pupils and the tinkle of something metallic sounded over the rush of waves. She straightened and pressed her lips together at the sight of her necklace tangled around his fingers.

"Taking this from you almost killed me." He paused, letting his words hit her with the brutal force of regret. "I'd never been more proud or happy than on those days when you wore this. I loved knowing a piece of me was on you, touching you." He turned his hand over, letting the necklace rest in his palm. "Take it back, Gabi. Please."

She'd given it to him in New York because she thought his betrayal had made it hang heavier around her neck. She was wrong. It wasn't the betrayal that strengthened the gold, it was his love—the reminder that he'd picked out a gift more perfect and heartfelt than anything she'd ever received before. The breathtaking birthday present had made her feel guilty for feeling betrayed by him. And at the time, she didn't want to have those emotions. She only wanted to be angry.

She slid her hand over his and grasped the necklace. The mere touch of warm gold soothed her heart. He watched her from the corner of his eye as she placed it around her neck and let it rest against her chest.

Blake leaned over, reaching into his pocket. This time he pulled out another piece of jewelry. One that was smaller, round, and sporting an emerald cut diamond in the center.

Holy dooley.

"It's not enough," he started, pivoting the band so the sun reflected off the dazzling rock. "Nothing I have will ever be good enough for what you deserve, but I want you to be mine, angel."

He turned his face to her, and she swallowed at the love emanating from him. She couldn't think, couldn't breathe. In fact every inhalation had been restricted since they first met in person.

He stood, taking her hand and pulled her to stand on wavering legs. Then he lowered again, down on bended knee and raised the ring between them. His eyes glistened with unshed tears, his lips slightly tilted in an adoring smile. "Sweet angel mine, I love you with everything I am, everything I've been, and everything I ever will be. Will you marry me and make my life complete?"

Gabi sucked in a shaky breath and held it, expanding her chest until it pounded. She felt the same. She loved him with everything she was and everything she ever would be… But this was too soon. Too fast.

"Please?"

A panicked chuckle bubbled from her lips and she dropped to her knees in front of him, cupping his cheeks with her palms. "Blake Kennedy, you're an incredible man who I love dearly. And I *do* want to marry you."

His face fell.

"I haven't said 'no.'" She shook her head in warning, and held him tighter. She stared into his eyes, the dark hue that almost bordered black. The color that always made her melt. "Before we become engaged, can't we first enjoy being a couple? I want to have fun with you, to learn more about each other without the stress of planning a wedding and a future."

He inclined his head and lowered the ring between them. She reached for it, grasping their hands together.

"Don't put it away." She smiled, cheeky and seductive, letting him know things between them would be OK. "I want to wear it. I want to be reminded of your promise every day, but for a little while, can I place it on my necklace?"

He quirked a brow and released the ring into her hand. "So it's a no *for now*?"

"It's a yes, with a delay. I want to earn this ring. I want us both to. And more time together will achieve that. We have a lot of things to figure out, and I don't want to rush a single second with you."

His lips tilted, the slight grin turning into a fully-fledged smile. "We're going to get married?"

"Yes, we are." She kissed him, holding him tighter, never wanting to let him go. "But first we're going to work for it."

Epilogue

"Who wants another beer?" Mason asked, walking into the kitchen of his Richmond, Virginia home.

"Me," Sean and Mitch grunted in unison.

Blake glanced at the two empty bottles beside him on the poker table and smiled. "Yeah. Grab another one for me, too. Thanks."

He never thought he'd get back to sharing drinks with his buddies. Hell, he never thought he'd have the strength to stop hating himself every time he glanced at a beer bottle. But he'd changed.

In the few months he'd spent living with Gabi, he'd learned a lot about himself. She'd convinced him to create new memories to associate with the buzz of intoxication. So that's what he was doing—relaxing, enjoying a good laugh with his friends while they celebrated Christmas Eve at Mason's secluded mansion. He only wished Ryan was here with them, instead of choosing to stay home with his wife.

"Here ya go." Mason handed Blake a chilled bottle of beer and sat down beside him. "How are you doing?"

Blake turned his gaze to Gabi who sat on the sofa with Alana, both of them occupied with a mass of bridal magazines. "I'm great... Thanks for letting us crash here for the weekend."

Gabi hadn't removed the engagement ring from her necklace, but things between them couldn't be better. They were in love—the heavy and consuming kind that provoked continuous PDA's that drove his friends crazy.

Mason cracked the lid of his bottle. "No problem. To tell you the truth, I kinda had an ulterior motive."

Blake quirked a brow. "If any of your 'motives' include Gabi, you can think again, pretty boy."

"No, it's nothing like that." Mason took a swig of his beer. "I've been running low on song ideas and thought having you guys around might help. I haven't even started on the next album, and any day now Leah is going to start hounding me for updates."

"Why don't you call Sidney?" Mitch interrupted, shuffling the deck of cards for another round.

"Yeah, that's an awesome idea. And while I'm at it, I could shove my dick in a blender, just for shits and giggles."

Mitch laughed. "It'd be more fun if you let her do it. I'd love to see her face light up."

"Leave her alone," Sean growled. "She's been through enough without you guys making fun of her."

Mason glared at Sean, both of them staring the other down. The crackle of the fire and Alana and Gabi's soft murmurings were the only noise to break the quiet discomfort.

"Touchy much?" Mason asked, pushing from his chair. "What happened wasn't my fucking fault, so shoot your filthy looks somewhere else."

Sean narrowed his gaze. "You've got serious ego problems if you think her ruined reputation isn't your fault."

"Your cock was in her too, bro," Mason spat, walking around the poker table.

"Yeah, but you were the only one with a camera."

Moments passed with everyone in the room on alert, waiting to see if the argument escalated.

Mason raised his chin, turning his gaze to Mitch. "Count me out of the next hand. I'm going to take a piss." He shot a final warning glance to Sean before striding from the room.

Sean didn't react. Mitch continued shuffling his cards. And Blake sat there, drinking his beer, content and a little giddy that his life wasn't the most dramatic for once.

"What are you smiling at?" Gabi sauntered up behind him, placing her arms around his shoulders to drape over his chest.

"Just thinking about how much I love you," he whispered against her cheek.

She chuckled, the delicate sound adding to his alcohol buzz. Life was too damn perfect. He overcame his demons, had the best job in the world, and eventually got the girl, too.

"You know," she murmured in his ear, the heat of her breath making his cock jerk to life, "I don't think it counts when you're drunk."

Minx. God he loved this woman.

Mitch watched them, his hands working the cards while his gaze focused on Blake's chest. "Nice bling, Gab."

Blake frowned. "What bling?"

Gabi cleared her throat and pulled back, taking the warmth of her arms with her.

"What bling?" he repeated and turned to face her.

She gave him a soft smile, the tops of her cheeks flushed and high. Her teeth worked her bottom lip, making his cock twitch as he searched her face for answers.

"I was trying something on for size." Her throat convulsed with a swallow as she held up her left hand, showing off the engagement ring.

Thump, thump, thump. His heart took off while his brain stopped functioning. He sat his beer down on the table and nodded, feigning a calm he didn't feel. "Are you trying it on for the day? Or maybe a bit longer?"

She shrugged, still gnawing on her lip, still driving his cock to madness. "I thought maybe permanently," she whispered, yet the words hit him as if amplified by a microphone.

He stared at her in silence, overwhelmed with disbelief and happiness. He wanted to run. He wanted to whoop. He wanted to take her in his arms and kiss her until he couldn't breathe.

Merry fucking Christmas, people. I just hit the jackpot.

Pushing from the table, he stood, never taking his gaze off the most beautiful woman he'd ever seen, and hauled her into his arms.

She squealed, her hands frantically clinging around his neck. "What are you doing?"

"We're going to celebrate… In private. And I'm going to show the woman I love, exactly how happy she's made me.

Gabi chuckled, sweet and hypnotic. "And what if she's not convinced?"

He grinned down at her, loving the way she beamed back at him, her eyes wide, her lips now glistening and inviting.

"Then I'll never stop trying, angel. I'll never stop loving you."

~ Please consider leaving a review on your ebook retailer website or Goodreads ~

~ Look for these titles from Eden Summers ~

Reckless Beat Series
Blind Attraction (Reckless Beat #1)
Passionate Addiction (Reckless Beat #2)
Reckless Weekend (Reckless Beat #2.5)
Undesired Lust (Reckless Beat #3)
Sultry Groove (Reckless Beat #4)
Reckless Rendezvous (Reckless Beat #4.5)

Vault of Sin Series
A Shot of Sin (Vault of Sin #1)
Union of Sin (Vault of Sin #2)

Concealed Desire
Sneaking a Peek
"Phantom Pleasure" Halloween Heat V

About the Author

Eden Summers is a true blue Aussie, living in regional New South Wales with her two energetic young boys and a quick witted husband.

In late 2010, Eden's romance obsession could no longer be sated by reading alone, so she decided to give voice to the sexy men and sassy women in her mind.

Eden can't resist alpha dominance, dark features and sarcasm in her fictional heroes and loves a strong heroine who knows when to bite her tongue but also serves retribution with a feminine smile on her face.

www.edensummers.com
eden@edensummers.com
http://www.facebook.com/authoredensummers
https://twitter.com/EdenSummers1

Printed in Great Britain
by Amazon